Murder at Giuseppe's

An Occasionally True Tale

Rodger B. Baird

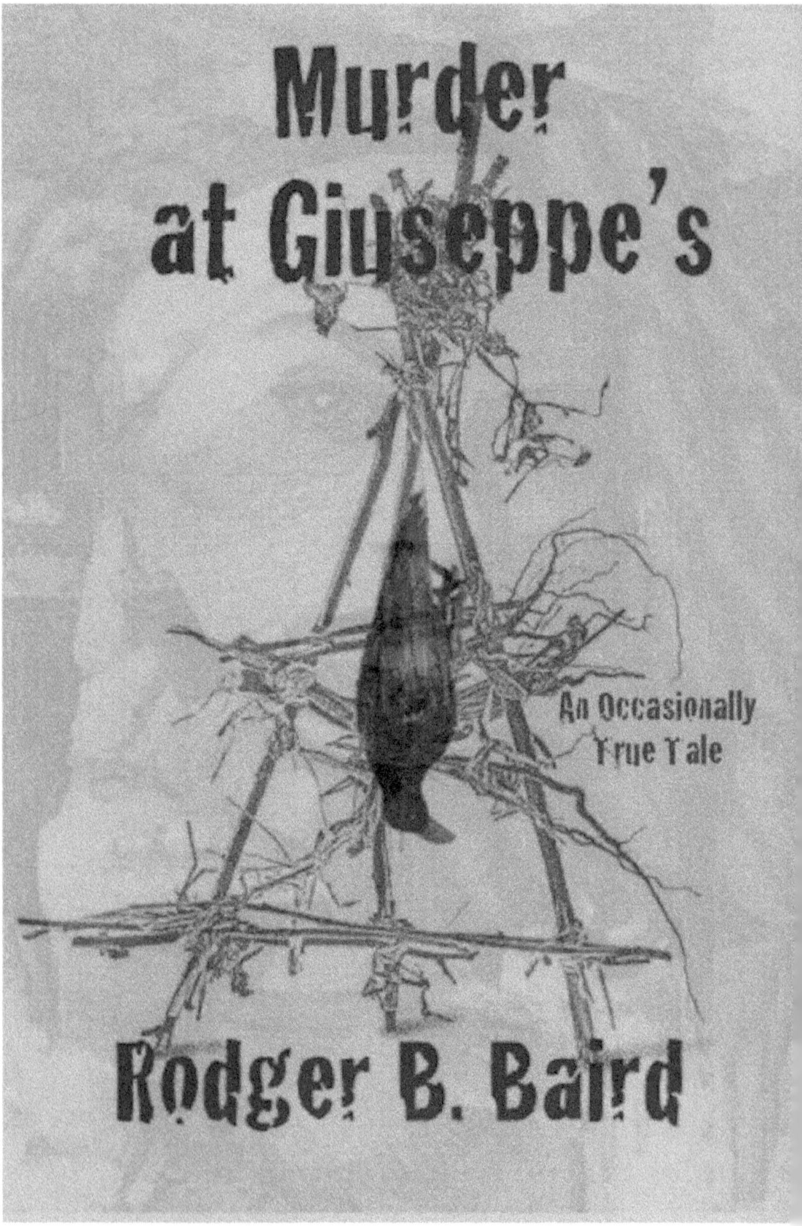
Murder
at Giuseppe's
An Occasionally
True Tale
Rodger B. Baird

MURDER AT GIUSEPPE'S

First edition. June 1, 2023.

ISBN: 979-8223086536

Written by Rodger B. Baird.

FOR DEAR JEAN
I HOPE YOU ENJOY
MY MYSTERY
LOVE
Bridget

Thank You

Rob for the Trip

And

Captain Rob for the Help and Laughs

And

Patterson for the Tour and Local Lore

And

Dave T for the Stories

Cast of Characters

Stevenson Simms—Homicide Detective, Treasure Coast PD

Gino Macina—Homicide Detective, Treasure Coast PD

Albert Whitehead—Captain, Chief of Police, Treasure Coast PD

Ike Harris—County Deputy Sheriff

Rodney—The 'Tibetan Monk', a hobo

Davo—Orphan Haitian street kid

Baxter Silverman—Simms' best friend, fishing guide in Key West, ex-cop

Joe Di Rossi—Giuseppe the younger, restaurant owner and entrepreneur

Maria Di Rossi—Joes' wife

Minerva Rossini—Joe's (Giuseppe's) aunt

Ricardo Avila—Chef at Giuseppe's Restaurant

Valeria LaCroix—Waitress at Giuseppe's Restaurant, Joe's mistress

Trinity LaCroix—Valeria's Sister

Madame LaCroix—Santeria priestess/ (*Santera*);Aunt Sonia to Val and Trinity

Scarlett—Valeria's housemate

Jimmy Daniels—Band leader, 'Danny and the Dirtfish'

Dusty Daniels —Jimmy's brother, guitar player

Dr. Chen—MD, Forensic anthropologist, Florida Department of Historical Resources

Aretha Cooper—PhD Sociologist, technician for Dr. Chen, expert in Vodoun practices

Zevon Harmon—South African fixer, Joe's agent

Words and Phrases

***Manatee** —aka* 'Sea Cow', any of three species of large, slow, voracious aquatic herbivorous mammals. Protected by Florida Law since 1893, and placed on the Federal endangered species list in 1967. Listing was reaffirmed in several updates of the Federal Act, then the Manatee was inexplicably removed from the endangered list in 2017.

Dago—Derogatory term for Italian immigrants; Also, see *Ginzo, Whop, etc.*

Vodoun—Often called *Conjure, Voodoo* or *Hoodoo* in different settings. Syncretic spiritual practices typically melding African religious traditions with Catholic or other Christian rituals and beliefs. Vodoun practices typically vary by region and ethnic roots. In popular culture, Voodoo may be conflated with dark arts, magic, and witchcraft, a viewpoint refuted by many true believers.

Santeria —A syncretic spiritual practice found primarily in Cuba or Cuban diaspora, a mix of West African (Yoruba people of Benin and southwestern Nigeria), Caribbean and Roman Catholic traditions that originated and evolved amongst African slaves in Cuba. Often considered by some to be Vodoun in nature. As in Vodoun, animal sacrifice is practiced, although primarily as offerings of sustenance to specific spirits. Spells are entreated from the spirits, and if just, carried out via associative magic.

Obeah —Black and white magic as practiced in the Bahamas, not necessarily to be confused with *Vodoun* spiritual beliefs practiced elsewhere in the Caribbean or States.

Stregoneria —From the Italian, meaning witchcraft, rooted in (*quasi-*) Roman Catholic sorcery found in old Italian folk magic. Superstitious practices involving saints' magic and blessings, and precautions against the "evil eye" are examples. Common household articles such as scissors, needles, red thread, salt, and many other items are used in accepted *Stregoneria* witchcraft.

Stregheria —Pagan oriented religious system with a magical structure for rituals and spells; practitioners differentiate Stregheria from the Christian-rooted *Stregoneria.* Practices in *Stregoneria* may be aimed at causing harm or healing through spells and associative magic, i.e. through objects related to the recipient. Strega, or practitioners of *Stregheria* identify and embrace with old world Italian and Egyptian religious traditions, where their bloodline is supreme and word-of-mouth traditions passed down are sacred foundations of the practice

Il Malocchio —The "evil eye"

Aficionado —Amateur practitioners of Vodoun; generally a disdainful term amongst the highest level practitioners

Bingo-Bongo —Italian slang for Black people; other derogatory Italian slang terms for dark skinned people used in this book include *Rasta Fazoul* and *Melanzana (*or '*Moolie')*

Cracker —Black slang for a white person; also *Honkey.* (Other slang words for whites not necessarily in this book: *Gringo* (typically Latin American), *Medigan* (Italian-American), *Jojoto, Blanc, Jincho, Blanquito,* etc.)

Iyabó —Initiate in the practice of Santeria, requiring a 7-day ritual and a year of isolation, following strict practices set by a Santera

Tía —Spanish for aunt

Cómo andamo'*?*—Cuban contraction (Spanish) for 'how are we?"

Bienvenidos —'Welcome' in Spanish

Fattone —Italian for pothead or stoner

Ganja —Jamaican/West Indies slang for marijuana; also *Erba* in Italian

EF —Enhanced Fujita scale for measuring strength of tornados.

Jaega —Band of indigenous Florida native people, once prominent near Jupiter Inlet, now extinct

Ais - -Another extinct band of Floridians, most prominent along the Indian River from Canaveral to the St. Lucie inlet

Past is Prologue

Dago Bay and the Seeds of Eden

It's doubtful that a West Indian manatee has ever seen Manatee Wells and, certainly, it is a place nobody would look for a murder plot. In fact, if asked, any local resident would scoff resentfully at the notion, or recoil suspiciously from the implication that the town could harbor a conspiracy. At least that's what aging Treasure Coast police commander Albie Whitehead told his lead homicide investigator, Stevenson Simms. "Look, Simms," the squat, red-faced chief reasoned petulantly, "it's not a famous place, and the people there are quiet, old-country families. See what I'm sayin' here? Even the County Sheriff says the crime rate is non-existent."

The taller, more imposing Simms would lean in and nod patiently when the chief blustered in condescension like this. It was a skill he had developed to control his own combative nature, rooted as it was in countless generations of Kenyan warriors. And in this case, Whitehead was not only the boss, but Simms reckoned in the moment that the old man could have been correct in his admonition. As Simms reflected a few minutes later, however, he silently questioned the chief's assertions. Even though the place was never destined to be a holiday getaway, did that detail make the village any less likely to incubate a murder mystery? Just because the crime rate was nil meant little, for Simms knew that small isolated communities often self-regulated within their own boundaries rather than risk outside scrutiny.

Detective Simms knew he should at least look into a list of people of interest in Manatee Wells, but when he tried this tack with Whitehead, the old man said he didn't want Simms stirring up trouble in the village. Maybe the old chief was right on this point too. Sure, the world and Walt Disney had largely passed it by for a century, and even the mafia types let it be—except for bootlegging liquor—and that was three, maybe four generations ago. Oh, certainly, there was that one moment of notoriety, but otherwise, it'd been a cloistered place where immigrant settlers and their descendants made fishing and farming a more-or-less honest way of life. In the early days, the main squabble amongst the town folk was whether to call it Port Palermo or Little Napoli. The crux of the matter depended upon the region of Italy from which the bickering factions had emigrated. In neighboring towns along Florida's treasure coast, though, it was derogatorily just called Dago Bay.

In any case, few residents knew why the place was designated as Manatee Wells on the map. And since nobody ever suggested it might have been a pirate hideaway or suspected that there could be buried loot awaiting discovery, covetous treasure hunters had not infiltrated the town either.

So, no. Nobody would look here in this quiet working folks' community for a nest of murderers, although that's not to say that they were all law-abiding citizens. Early immigrants either worked in the pineapple fields alongside the abject Black field hands, or on fishing boats, or they were merchants. However, before the Great War, a pineapple plague, winter freezes, and Cuban competition all but exterminated the local pineapple business, leaving fishing and mercantile enterprises as the economic fabric of Manatee Wells and, in the process, opening the door for a little entrepreneurial crime.

All they needed was the entrepreneur: enter the younger Giuseppe's grandfather, Giuseppe.

Grandfather Giuseppe liked to be called Papa Joe because it sounded more American, and he was determined that his family would stick it out in America rather than return to the old country. Papa Joe's livelihood revolved around the waterfront, where he tended to the hardware needs of the fishermen and helped broker and barter the fish and shellfish harvests in the community. Plus, old Joe had an eye toward expanding commerce into the outlying communities when automobile travel was enhanced by new road construction. He'd also had the foresight to bring what he called 'seeds of Eden' from the old country, enabling him to plant herbs and vegetables aplenty, and then generously spread the bounty.

Papa Joe was a serious man, and an opportunist. So when the stock market crashed and the Great Depression took hold in '29, he was steeled by the blood of ten generations of hard scrabble Sicilian ancestors to meet the challenges. Of course, he was already dabbling in the bootleg liquor industry of the Prohibition Era. After the Crash, he expanded the local bootlegging effort by organizing a larger group of fishermen to cooperate in distributing illicit Caribbean rum up and down the coast. Incidentally, one of his Garden of Eden herbs was the earliest strain of *ganja* in the region and, naturally, it ended up in the distribution chain too. The boatmen all knew by heart hundreds of waterways, inlets, and mangrove lagoons that could be utilized to cache and distribute the goods, and they shared the general American disdain for inconvenient laws. Their enterprises, then, helped realize Joe's aspirations of reaching even more new customers for the local fish and produce. So, almost everybody was as happy as was possible for the times.

Almost. Not everyone in their community was fortunate or adventurous enough to survive the Depression on their own, and many would have faded away. But Papa Joe found a solution for them too: a pizza kitchen. To be fair, it was *Mama Joe's Cucina*, but Papa Joe was the mover and shaker. Soon, the kitchen was turning out hundreds of pizzas each week to be sold, bartered, or donated to the hungry. And this is when the old feud between the Napolis and the Sicilians quietly died away in Manatee Wells, because Mama made Neapolitan pies, Sicilian pies, and anything and everything in between. And when wartime rationing made cheese, especially authentic mozzarella, nearly impossible to find elsewhere, Mama still made her own version from local milk using hand-me-down family secrets. Sometimes, when other ingredients were in short supply, she just made vegetarian pies with lots of tomatoes and onions, pure and simple. The point is, old Joe was everyone's Papa and he made sure nobody went hungry.

Prohibition ended long before the Great Depression was finished with the people of Manatee Wells and, while unfortunate for some, it presented Joe with opportunity. Although bootlegging was still a way to avoid taxes and keep spirits high, in many places, ganja was even more popular. Joe's bunch of boatmen was able to keep up a barter and trade business that kept most people out of the poor house and, in the process, eased a lot of pain.

However, the next World War changed the town's trajectory forever. The younger men flocked to the Army recruiting centers while, to the dismay of the elders, many of the young women took trains and buses north and west to the cities for wartime jobs. Navy ships and military planes patrolled the coastal waters looking for Nazi submarines, in effect shutting off the vestiges of the smuggling enterprise. Fuel was rationed too, debilitating the fishermen's trade and making clandestine marketing even less practical. The last straw was discrimination: Italian immigrants were viewed with suspicion—as Mussolini's fascist spies—by an angry and fearful country, and thousands were threatened with confinement in concentration camps far from the coast. Dago Bay shriveled, and *Mama Joe's Cucina* closed.

It could have ended then and there for Papa Joe and his extended family of friends and neighbors in Manatee Wells, had not a few old fishermen contributed to the boom in shark livers. Army sharpshooters and fighter pilots needed Vitamin A to promote acute night vision, or so it was supposed, and a new wartime industry sprang up on the Treasure Coast. Sure, the shark liver processing plants had a staggering odor downwind, but it wasn't as bad as the stench of starvation.

The Outsiders

The end of the War brought even more changes. Chemists figured out how to make Vitamin A in laboratories, thus pulling the rug out from under the small shark fishing conglomerate in Manatee Wells and, in the process, leaving an abandoned shark liver processing factory to decay on the waterfront. Nobody ever thought that the property had any real value, and so it sat on the edge of a muddy bay, where the encroaching mangroves preserved it as a sad but constant reminder of the fragility of good fortune.

The post-war era in Florida countered with a boom in other parts of the economy, though, as roads and bridges were built, canals were dug, and coastal waterways were finished or rehabilitated. More immigrants came to America, especially to Florida, and peacetime jobs seemed to return.

Some of these changes were good for Manatee Wells, and some were not. For one thing, not everybody in Manatee Wells was prepared for the next decade. The old people were... well, they were old and set in their ways, and few of the younger men and women returned to breathe life into the dwindling village after the war. Instead, there was an influx of 'outsiders', and the place could no longer be thought of as 'Dago Bay'.

Years on, the locals would blame the outsiders for the isolation and decline of their beloved 'Napoli Bay' and, to some extent, this could have been true. More likely, though, it began when Papa Joe was surprised by a heart attack one day. Once his entrepreneurial spirit and leadership were abruptly lost, the town again spiraled downward for a time. In fairness, though, Papa and Mama had spawned a son who loved the kitchen and adored food in general, one who could pursue the legacy. This was the younger Giuseppe's father, Giuseppe, who was known as *Uncle* Joe.

Uncle Joe, unlike old Papa, had a sense of humor, a trait immediately reflected in his name: he was an uncle to no one in any genetic sense of the word. Nevertheless, seeing an opportunity for his own gain, Uncle Joe did his best to spur revitalization of the fishing fleet. He re-opened the marine hardware enterprise and successfully petitioned the county for sidewalks and street lights on Main Street. Then he expanded Mama's kitchen into a full-scale gourmet Italian restaurant, the *Cucina Italiana,* where they set about trying to feed America's new-found appetite for pizza. Yes, the returning soldiers had developed a taste for the Old-World staple, and new pizzerias popped up all over the country. New York and Chicago had nothing on the *Cucina Italiana* on the Treasure Coast of Florida.

Uncle Joe was a dynamo when it came to development. He advertised far and wide, paid for billboards along Route A1A, and put ads in the newspapers from Fort Pierce to Miami. He hired chefs to be trained by Mama, bought her a new rocking chair and a black and white TV, then built a new house for his wife and two children a block off Main Street. He subsidized a facelift of the downtown storefronts, purchased or otherwise *acquired* abandoned houses and renovated them to rent to the Haitians, Cubans, and Puerto Ricans who came to work the fields and docks. And he raised the rents on any Germans who moved in, just to make sure they wouldn't stay.

All of this, however, is where the town elders say Uncle Joe went wrong and where the town went awry. They blamed this new wave of outsiders—in particular, the dark-skinned islanders and their customs—for the town's problems, and fixed blame squarely on Uncle Joe for renting to the Creoles and others in the first place. This old, deep seated resentment was most likely why Captain Whitehead didn't want Detective Simms mucking about with the White folks in town now, and why he sent the bumbling Gino Macina instead, figuring a *Ginzo* in soft leather shoes would get along better with the old *Dagos*. Of course, the Captain wasn't stupid enough to say this stuff out loud.

The locals had been mistaken about the outsiders back then, of course (and so was old Whitehead now), because, back in the day, there was nobody else to work the fields, and the fishing industry just couldn't thrive solely in the hands of the old fishermen anymore. So, without the new labor force and consequent economic improvements provided by the outsiders, the town would assuredly have suffered the same fate as the old shark factory. Likely, then, it was simple jealousy and prejudice that made the floundering homebodies turn their resentful tongues against Uncle Joe and the outsiders, because everybody could see that his restaurant was always crowded with customers, and his coffers were overflowing with cash.

Legacy of the Sandwich Curse

More restaurants and bars opened in Manatee Wells over the course of nearly two decades, and more of the resident outsiders went to work in restaurants and shops than on the docks or in the fields. The town started thriving again and, gradually, a few more tourists came to the quaint little town to see what the fuss was all about. That's when Manatee Wells was 'discovered' for a brief bit of time, and also when the local grumbling faded away once more. It's also about the time that the West Indian Manatee found itself on the Federal Endangered Species List, and this is likely when Uncle Joe's sense of humor went askew and the town's fortunes began to slide again.

Listen, nobody ever claimed to have seen a West Indian Manatee in or near Manatee Wells, and those who bore witness to this factoid had half a century on their side. In fact, in the post-war years, the once clear waters of Dago Bay had turned as brown as dark tea from inland development and runoff: seeing *any* creature in that water would have been a miracle.

Notwithstanding these circumstances, the fishermen and their boats took the blame for the 'disappearance' of the venerable sea cow, devastating the fragile local fishing industry once more. Uncle Joe mounted what he called a 'comeback plan' that included public relations ads in the newspapers, new billboards, and propaganda in flyers he personally tacked up all over the county. The poison pill in his plan, though, besides maybe his own brand of corruption, was a little joke that he planted in the menu. It listed 'Grilled Manatee Sandwich' with a footnote that read '*in season, market prices*'. Soon, with Joe's blessing, other restaurants added the manatee sandwich to their menus as well.

Uncle Joe never claimed that manatee sandwiches were a popular customer request and, of course, neither he nor any other restaurateur ever served a manatee sandwich to anybody. If a customer asked for one, the waitresses were instructed to either say that they were out of manatee at the moment or that manatee filets were out of season. Then they were to giggle at their own joke. The residents of Manatee Wells considered this to be great humor, but the various manatee protection organizations, and perhaps a government agency or two, girded for combat.

Some say that Uncle Joe ate himself to death. After all, at 290 pounds, he was far too short of a man. But the bad manatee publicity, investigations, lawsuits, and ultimate failure of *Cucina Italiana* likely contributed to his demise. Still, the old Italians began whispering again, blaming the islanders for scaring away the fish and the tourists with their spells and black magic.

It took only a year or so after Uncle Joe's diabetic plunge and subsequent fatal heart attack for the town's Restaurant Row to become a very quiet and rundown version of its former stature. To this day, unless one gets invited to an Italian friend's house for a meal, it's impossible to find a decent pizza—or any passable Italian food for that matter—in town. Sure, a block off the waterfront boardwalk, squeezed between the used book shop and antique store, there is a tiny counter where rollerbladers, skateboarders and the occasional wayward tourist can buy pizza by the slice to stuff in their faces while on the move. But it's a poor excuse for genuine Old World pizza.

New World: Giuseppe the Younger

For years now, when asked, any resident of Manatee Wells would give directions for finding good Italian food, whether they were of Italian descent or not. Even the Haitians and Puerto Ricans know this: "Go back out to A1A, turn right, and drive for fifteen minutes until you see a big sign on the right-hand corner announcing '**Third United Baptist Church**'. Next to that sign is another sign and arrow that reads '**Giuseppe's**'. Turn there."

Giuseppe (the younger) favored pizza as much as his over-fed father, but he had the good sense to merely taste, and not gorge all day long. He also had the understanding that his Italian restaurant needed a much better location, one free of the stigma of manatee sandwiches and two generations of ethnic divisions. And, worthy of note, Giuseppe shared his father's sense of humor, although assuredly in a grander, more generous style. He also shared the knack for empire-building.

The new restaurant's location on Route A1A was perfect for attracting customers. Behind the Third United Baptist Church was an ample parking lot for the small congregation, one that also served the tenants of the irregularly shaped strip mall laid out in the rear of the property. To the left of Giuseppe's restaurant were two shops that, although somewhat ironically located, he did not operate: a tropical bird store and a veterinary hospital for cats. To the right side of the pizza joint, separated by a narrow alleyway, was a weight loss salon run by Giuseppe's wife, Maria, who did not understand the irony of locating a fat salon next to a pizza palace. Next to the salon were three vacant storefronts and a local better business bureau leasing office mismanaged by a cousin. Around the other end of the strip mall, and keeping with the Floridian theme of fun and redemption, was a massage parlor of sketchy repute, and a small addiction clinic specializing in alcoholic rehab—both situated adjacent to a large wine shop and liquor store. All of these enterprises were co-owned by the good Catholic, Giuseppe, and the fathers of the Third United Baptist Church. The Third United Baptist church also happened to be where the majority of the islander employees of the shops and restaurant split their religious affiliation when not involved with the more traditional home-grown practices of their respective vodoun cultures.

Giuseppe's was open six days and seven nights every week, and featured nightly restaurant specials to honor various segments of the local community. For example, Mondays were for war veterans from anywhere. Every Tuesday, though, a crowd from the local mobile home retirement park, including some of the vets, came to dine on their favorite Italian food and listen to an old gentleman in a white toupee lip-synch crooner hits of the '50s. Giuseppe thought it worked pretty well except when the singer tried to jazz it up and cover Ray Charles. Still, the retirement crowd seemed not to mind.

Each Thursday, Giuseppe opened the doors at five o'clock and reserved tables for the residents of the Hazy Days Care Home, where the guests often were heard to remark about the luxury of eating at a new restaurant every week. Giuseppe was quite diligent in making sure that the Tuesday night crowd never caught wind of the Thursday night special, for even his sense of irony had its limits.

On other days, the specials were more family oriented. On Sundays, the doors of the restaurant never opened until well after any church services in the area were over, giving churchgoers and employees the chance to gather for family time. Fridays featured meatless dish specials and fish for the really devout Catholics, while Wednesdays were all-you-can-eat spaghetti nights for kids 12 and under, with bottomless carafes of house chianti for the parents from five to seven o'clock.

As famous as Giuseppe's sense of humor was, Maria was just as notorious for having none whatsoever. Many considered this a condition of her birth, given that her family was *Del Benevento*, a place in the old country known for its witches. Almost weekly, she'd fire one of the kitchen or waitress staff for some perceived offense, and Giuseppe would hire the person back the next day, or within the week at most, depending on how spiteful Maria's mood seemed to be.

Maria saw nothing wrong with body-shaming a chubby client at the weight loss salon, and then scolding the same client on her next visit for not dining next door often enough. Regardless of their various cultural backgrounds, all the employees agreed that Maria "had a very sharp tongue." That Giuseppe and Maria were even married to one another was a matter of considerable, though usually harmless, gossip. But it was perhaps a little of this gossip, coupled with Giuseppe's renowned sense of irony and humor, and a seemingly weird twist of fate that caused the problems one evening.

It was a Friday night after Mass when the crowd grew larger outside the restaurant. Would-be patrons sat on the wrought iron tables and chairs on the dining patio, and the restless bunch soon milled about in a quiet mob, wondering why the doors were closed and the lights were out. An old man dressed in a white and wrinkled cloak, bent wretchedly low by the pack on his back, managed to worm his way through the crowd up to the front door. He leaned in, pressing his ear to the glass, then pulled away quickly and, while tugging at his beard, mumbled something only audible to a few nearby. Then he disappeared into the night. "What'd he say?" rose from the crowd. "Yeah, what did he say?" repeated others. Then the answer rang clear, "The Monk said there's been a murder inside."

Chapter 1
Murder at Giuseppe's

Little Davo's disappointment gave way to fear, but not right away, because curiosity had gotten the best of him first. He'd been hoping for a handout at the back door of the kitchen, perhaps a slice of pizza or a leftover meatball or two. The closed door on a dark muggy evening was the first sign that it might be a hungry night. The clamoring from the front of the restaurant was the bait that drew Davo around the corner and down the narrow corridor next to the ladies' weight loss salon. From behind a row of waste bins, he peered out into the rising commotion in the parking lot. Curiosity had a hold on him now, which is likely how he was startled when the hunch-back form of the man nearly flattened him. The creature he knew as 'the Monk' paused for a second, looked at Davo and said, "Go now, quickly."

Davo shook his head, 'no', and recoiled into the shadows of the dumpsters as the Monk hurriedly shuffled down the corridor and turned into the darkness of the rear service alley. Davo knew that was the fastest way back to the oak hammocks and the swamp they called home, and his path was clear if he needed to run. Now, though, the new noises from the lot and bright lights drew Davo back to his lookout point. From this angle he saw a white-haired fat man bellowing orders over a bullhorn, and then a bunch of cops began moving the crowd around. Suddenly, he saw a face he recognized from the kitchen, eyes focused on-—him? Could the man see him in the dark? Why else would the man be staring at the dumpsters? Was he recognized? In a frozen panic now, the boy thought he might close his eyes and wish it all away. Instead, when the staring face was distracted by a cop, Davo bolted down the corridor and turned right, disappearing into the darkness to follow the old Monk to safety.

"Stevenson! Over here... what took you so long?" The cops had arrived, and Captain Whitehead was being self-important.

"Sorry, Boss," answered Detective Simms, trying not to sound aggravated, "I was out to dinner with my lady when the call came. What've we got?"

"All right, no worries," grumbled Whitehead. "I already got the uniforms doing some interviews in the crowd. Somebody called in a murder inside the restaurant..."

"Who found the body?"

"That's just it, Stevenson, there ain't no corpse yet. The joint wasn't even open. One witness said a Tibetan Monk saw the murder, then disappeared. Of course, a bunch of others overheard that, so these witnesses are busy getting their story straight. It's a circus right now."

"Sooo? What? We have a nothin' burger?"

"Maybe, maybe not. The head chef finally showed up, and he's inside with the forensics team. C'mon, I'll introduce you to him, and maybe we can get to the bottom of this."

Stevenson followed Captain Whitehead past the remaining crowd and into the restaurant. "Chief, the sign says they're open every night—why wasn't it open?"

“Simms, I’m sure you’ll find that out for me... now, here we are. Ricardo, this is Homicide Detective Stevenson Simms. Detective, this is Ricardo, the head chef.”

Simms held out his hand, “Just Ricardo, then, like an artist or something?”

Ricardo grinned, “No, my family name is Avila... everybody just calls me Ricardo... but I like the way you think, Detective.”

Whitehead slipped away to watch the forensics team finish sweeping the vacant and immaculately ordered dining room, then continued on his way to the kitchen and offices in the rear. Simms, wishing rather to be with the forensics unit, settled into his interview of the chef as he was ordered. “Ricardo, I guess my first question is why was Giuseppe’s closed tonight?”

“Detective, I’m still trying to find out. I wasn’t due in tonight until after the fish crowd thinned out...”

“Fish crowd?”

“Yes, it’s fish night for the Catholics in the diocese-they come from all over—anchovy pizzas are half price this month too... anyway, the assistant cook called to tell me that the place was closed up tight when he got here for his dinner shift... that was about four o’clock... a little before. He then called some of the other help, but they’d all heard that the place was closed, so stayed away... so I don’t know who started *that* string of gossip, but it must have been around eleven this morning, before the lunch hour.”

“So, nobody came to work today, and nobody called you?”

Ricardo shrugged, “It looks that way...”

“Where are the owners? Don’t they come in... is Giuseppe even a real person?”

“Oh sure! You haven’t met Giuseppe before?”

“Nope, never been inside this joint... I’m not a big pizza fan...”

"Oh, but we have lots of great dishes on the menu... you must come soon... let me show you that a Cubano can cook more than red beans and rice..."

Simms laughed and held up his hand, "I'm sure that the food is fabulous, but maybe tonight isn't the right time. We've been told that there's been a murder inside the kitchen..."

Ricardo took a deep breath, "Yes, so I understand. But there wasn't a body when I came in with the investigators... so who?"

"Right, my question exactly. Well it looks like the crime scene unit is being quite thorough at the moment... so back to my first question... the owners?"

"Oh, yes. Well, Giuseppe—Joe—went out of town yesterday to care for a sister in Miami, I think he said."

"And the missus? Other family?"

"Maria—the wife, and a couple of children... the son ran off to join the Navy, and the daughter moved to California to live with an aunt for a while. A few cousins and other family are over in Manatee Wells where they all live. Maria, she is usually here or next door at the fat ladies' salon... did somebody look for her there? I personally haven't seen her in a few days. Nobody misses her when she doesn't show up."

"Why is that, Ricardo?"

"Well, I can't say bad things about the boss' wife, you know, but she is rough on the help around here. So, nobody likes to see her coming around."

"Rough? Like...?"

"Very critical, Maria has a very sharp tongue... she fires one or two people a week, it seems..."

"How can you keep a staff if they get fired that often?"

Ricardo laughed, "Giuseppe... er, Joe, he always hires them back after Maria cools off. It's almost funny."

Simms smiled, "Yeah, I get the picture. So, who was fired this week? Or, rather, who hasn't been around or hired back recently?"

Ricardo nodded, "Well... I don't want to get anybody in trouble..." Simms stared at him expectantly, silently. Ricardo sighed, "Valeria LaCroix was fired last week... Saturday—or Sunday, maybe... I wasn't here at the time. But she has not returned. Nobody has heard from her."

"Valeria... unusual name. What can you tell me about Valeria, Ricardo? Is she Cubano, Puerto Rican...?

"Maybe both, maybe a little Jamaican... who knows anymore? She's strong-willed, so I don't pry... she's the prettiest woman in the place, too. And, of course, she knows it. Maybe that's why she gets canned so often"

"So which of these two traits do you think gets her fired?"

Ricardo chuckled, "Detective, please... you see my predicament, no? And why does there have to be a choice between the two?"

Simms laughed, "Okay, Ricardo, here's my card. And I'll be back to see you later—or someone will—we'll need a list of employees and their contact info. I'll really want Valeria's address. For now, you seem to be in charge of Giuseppe's. They'll probably finish up the forensics by tomorrow sometime, and you should be able to reopen soon unless they actually find a body stashed somewhere. Oh, and one last thing... there wouldn't by chance be one of those CCTV security cameras on the premises?"

"Not inside, Detective, but there's a couple of cameras on the church that view the parking lot—if they actually work."

Simms made a mental note to check on the cameras later, then went into the kitchen to view the scene. His first look stamped a picture in his brain that he knew would take a long time to erase. A bloody pentagram defiled the far wall like some medieval mural, and the stench of some concoction flooded his senses at the same time. There were blood splatters, bits of flesh, broken glass, and bird feathers strewn about the rest of the room. Whitehead was at the rear, speaking with a forensics technician, while another took photos, and a couple of others bagged bits and pieces of evidence. *"It's gonna be a long fuckin' night,"* he told himself.

"So... where are we, Stevenson?" demanded Whitehead, before Simms had a chance to take a first sip of coffee the next morning.

"Ricardo Avila came through with an employee list after you left the scene last night, Chief. The forensics team was still working when I left, but seemed to be about finished getting fingerprints in the kitchen. Oddly, there were no prints around that red diagram painted on the kitchen wall... they called it a pentagram of some sort. But, there was no corpse, and we're speculating that it's some kind of hoax. So I think this is gonna wrap up today."

"No, it won't. Forensics stayed way late last night, just like you said, but I looked at the preliminary report this morning—besides the blood spatters and smears, they found a human tongue in the kitchen, along with a few other things..."

"A tongue? You're bullshitting me..."

"Not in the least. It was in the garbage disposal, but it hadn't been run on through the grinder yet."

"The whole tongue?"

"Well, Stevenson, I didn't go look at the fuckin' thing—they told me it was a tongue."

"What can we do with that? Find a witness who doesn't wanna talk?"

Whitehead shook his head in amusement, "Forensics—they're gonna send the tongue and blood samples to California—some newfangled DNA testing or some sci-fi thing they dreamed up in

Hollywood... supposedly helped nail that football player who murdered his wife..."

"He got off..." said Simms, his voice trailing away.

"Oh yeah... So, what are your plans today, then?"

"I'm gonna try to get the security cam tapes from the church this morning... I want to see who was there during the day yesterday, and try to get a lead on this Tibetan Monk character. Then, I'll head over to Manatee Wells and start talking to family over there, then the employees..."

"Right, well, that's a lot of legwork, Stevenson. I'm assigning Gino Macina to work with you on this case... let him go over to Manatee Wells, and you take the Creoles and Cubans..."

"Seriously? Macina? He has the charm of a brick, and is about as lazy..."

"Maybe, but he can break the ice with the Italians and you've got a better chance with the..." his voice trailed off.

"The coloreds? You know I'm from South Philly, and not a bit Creole, right?"

Whitehead put up his hands, "Right, but your parents are from—where—the Bahamas? Listen, Stevenson, I know you hate anything that smacks of profiling, and I don't blame you, but look here... you can't tell me that just 'cuz you grew up in South Philly that you were all kumbaya with the Italians down there in the patch... am I wrong?"

Simms shook his head, "Anybody but Macina, Boss..."

"I get it that you don't like him," said Whitehead, "but listen, the family over in the Wells is a dead end—from what I've heard, anyway. They're just a bunch of old folks who don't like strangers much. Macina will save you from wasting time over there. And I sure as hell don't want him dealing with any of the rest of these witnesses... you see my point?" Whitehead then went on in great detail about why they shouldn't bother investigating this murder by harassing a bunch of old folks way over in Manatee Wells.

Simms nodded, knowing exactly what Whitehead meant by all of this, and took his frustration out in one last shot at Macina before acceding to the chief. "Macina needs to be on a scooter in the traffic division... but, okay, Boss, that's why you get the big bucks. I'm off to see some Third United Baptist preachers... Oh, one last thing... are you gonna call the County Sheriff for Macina? The Wells is out of our jurisdiction... and some of these employees live outside of our area too."

"Yeah, no worries, Stevenson, I'll make sure the County boys know... they can decide if they wanna run interference for us."

Chapter 2
An Odd Couple

Simms was at his desk sorting through employee addresses and marking a map when Gino Macina tapped on the door. Simms looked up and tried to hide the displeasure he felt creeping upon his face, but motioned, "C'mon in Gino... have a seat," hoping his eyes didn't reveal his feelings.

Gino's resolve to be totally business-like caved away almost immediately after he stepped through the doorway, and he stayed on his feet to deliver his speech. "Stevenson, Whitehead said you've got the lead, but we're gonna be partners on this Giuseppe's case... I want to try to clear the air about some stuff..."

"Gino, you've already apologized to me... just drop it."

"That's just it... I can't drop it if you can't."

"Look, it happened. You were drunk... we've been through all of that. I can forgive you, but I doubt that I'll forget it... see the difference? And listen, I've got my own biases that I have to get over, so... let's move on."

"Well, I hope you can tolerate me, 'cuz Whitehead isn't gonna budge, and my ass is on the line."

"Tolerate?" said Simms with an edge in is voice. "In my world, 'tolerate' doesn't usually mean anything positive..."

Macina, less submissive now, answered, "True enough, Simms... but you're not the only one whose people take shit and put up with a false veil of tolerance..."

Stevenson was taken aback for a few seconds, then said, "It's not gonna be... Gino, it can't be like that between us. I don't want to tolerate you, or vice-versa. We need to respect each other. Up 'til now, I've not necessarily liked the way you do business in this department, but it's not my job to control you... you're a cop, I'm a cop... we have work to do, and I'll have your back if you have mine." He knew he was trying to convince himself more than Gino, and there was more he wanted to say to him just now, but his thoughts were inconveniently awash in ambivalence, allowing that Gino hadn't intended to offend by his sophomoric jokes in the past. In fact, Simms, at that moment, considered that Gino might not even be a witless bigot through and through, but just another middle-age man with a school-age sense of humor when drunk. And the man was certainly trying to clear the air now. So instead of belaboring the subject, Stevenson just pointed at the chair with no more speeches.

Gino exhaled and sat, "Okay, fair enough. Whitehead is already up my ass anyway, no room for more... so what've we got? Captain said something about me going over to Manatee Wells to interview...?"

"Yeah, we need to find out when the wife, Maria, was last seen and where. Here's her photo and the address that the head chef, Ricardo Avila, gave us. And the other names on the list are the family members that he could recall... a couple of cousins and some in-laws. Hopefully, the list will grow once you've started talking to these folks. Whitehead said he would let the Sheriff know what we're up to..."

"Yeah, he already did... he told me they don't want to get involved right now since we didn't have a body, and— get this— according to Whitehead, the Sheriff says that there hasn't been a call-out in the Wells for nearly two years... lowest crime area in the county." Gino laughed and added, "He told me to get my 'Italian' on..."

Simms shook his head, "Really? Whitehead said that? This shit will never end..."

Gino chuckled, "See, I'm not offended by it... I know exactly what he means... Manatee Wells... they got a reputation over there... very Old World and clannish... you know that, right?"

"Right, so then it doesn't need to be said, does it? What if you had been sensitive... you know, like...," Simms paused, searching for an end to his sentence.

"You?" blurted Macina.

Simms finally laughed, shook his head and said, "Yeah, I guess... so, now get the hell out of here and go to work. I'll get with you late this afternoon and see where we are."

Whitehead looked up from the newspaper, folded it and pushed it aside, "What's up boys?" Then he pointed to chairs for Simms and Macina. Gino looked at Stevenson, who nodded back.

Gino began, "Well, Captain, Maria Di Rossi has been... uuhh, nobody we've talked with so far has seen her since Giuseppe left on Thursday, a week ago... at least nobody I spoke with... the old aunt that lives with 'em... and two cousins on the same street... nobody at the fat ladies' salon has seen her since this past Wednesday—a week ago, according to Stevenson's info. But get this: Some of the help at the salon think the kitchen mess was some kind of a prank by the owner—goes by Joe, not Giuseppe—they say he's always doing stuff. Maria's just off somewhere, according to them. Although one of these ladies said she didn't think his pranks were funny... just mean. According to her, Joe and Maria did not ever get along, and she thought Joe did things just to irritate Maria."

Whitehead nodded, "Just gossip, eh? Didn't the wife tell anybody where she was going?"

Macina shook his head, "Apparently, nobody dares ask where she's going, unless they want to risk a tongue lashing. So, no, it's like a holiday when they don't see her."

"What about this Giuseppe? Does anybody know where he went."

"Oh, sure, Boss... he was off to Miami to help his sister... some kind of health issue... I've got an address and phone number down there."

Whitehead nodded, "So, did it cross any of you nitwits' minds that maybe the wife went with her husband to Miami? We don't really have three missing people?"

Gino laughed, "Boss, it's unanimous amongst the family that the sister and the wife would as soon kill each other if they could get five minutes alone."

Whitehead seemed amused and satisfied, "So, Simms, tell me you've got some good news..."

Stevenson said, "You can be the judge of that, Boss. So, first off, I got security tapes from the church. The assistant rector resets the recorder every day sometime after noon if there's been no 'curiosity', as he put it, no incident in the previous twenty-four. I don't know what passes for curiosity with these people, but we've got no tape before noon yesterday. So, from then on, a few people were seen driving or walking up to the restaurant, then leaving when they saw it was closed. Nothing interesting. The lab zeroed in on the crowd that gathered around suppertime... and they got me some blowups of the guy the witnesses said was a monk..."

Whitehead interrupted, "Forty-three witnesses swear they heard the Tibetan monk say he saw a murder inside..."

"Right, Boss, but the guy's no monk, and he's certainly not Tibetan. His name is Rodney. Silvio, the assistant chef, he said he knows him... says he's just a hobo who squats with that homeless camp in the hammocks over by the Indian Creek ditch, or sometimes, he hangs out at The Gates down at the sound. The clerk at the liquor store and the preacher say the same thing. Rodney is just a panhandler, part of the local color. He's famous for seeing and reporting murders in that parking lot... the latest count is thirteen—according to our records."

Whitehead held up his hand, "We haven't had thirteen murders in the last three years..."

"Right, Boss, and exactly zero murders in that parking lot, but we get about two over-dose deaths a month in that area, so maybe the hobo is delusional, or maybe he isn't too far out to lunch. But all of these eye witnesses we've talked to are full of shit."

Whitehead ran his fingers through his thinning gray hair, pondering his lead detective's message. The aging chief knew better than to doubt either Simms or his instincts, "So, what about the rest of the employees. Where are we with them?"

"That's up on Monday's agenda, Boss... looks like forensics is done with the place, so Ricardo is going to open the restaurant mid-day for lunch and he's agreed to let me interview the help at work—in fact, he suggested it. It'll save a lot of time. I can follow up with anybody interesting after that. Oh, and the lab said there were two kinds of blood splatter... one was human, the other was avian—some kind of bird. They think that the State lab can figure out what kind of bird... do you want to send it off too?"

"I guess... what do ya think—chicken?"

"It'd be my first guess if they were killing the chickens in the kitchen, but they get all the meat and poultry from a local butcher shop. Besides, they got a large black feather too, the only one that wasn't white."

"Oh for chrissake. Send it off, then."

"Right," said Simms, "we'll see to it. I've asked the lab about that weird smell that was in the kitchen that night too—like vinegar with a shit-ton of strange smelling herbs. The technician said it was vinegar and had been in a glass bottle—they've got the shards of that, too. It didn't smell like Italian seasoning—more like some nasty incense... anyway, they're gonna take another look. Now, though, we're gonna go over to Giuseppe's to interview the daytime help, then I'll see if I can locate this fired waitress, Valeria LaCroix. I think Gino should take a look at the security footage too... see if Forensics missed anything in the tapes."

On Monday, Ricardo greeted Simms and Macina at the front of the restaurant and escorted them to an office for interviews. "Detectives, if it's okay with you, I'll begin sending some of the staff in after we get the lunch crowd going—it could take a while, though. We're short-handed today. But meanwhile, please enjoy a lunch on the house..."

"Short-handed?" asked Simms.

"Yes, well, a half-dozen of the more superstitious employees called in sick this morning. It seems that they think some kind of voodoo curse was cast over the kitchen last Friday, and all of the cops poking around have 'em spooked. You know how it is?"

"What curse? We don't even have a body... what about the others?"

"Well, Detective, that's the problem. It seems that spirits have carried away the dead person, and that is an omen... of some evil, you see? As for the rest of the staff, they all think that either the boss killed his wife, or the wife killed the missing waitress."

"Like, they think it's haunted or something?" asked Macina, fixated on the spirits and missing body.

Ricardo nodded vacantly at the question, just as a white-aproned man wheeled in a cart laden with food, and it was too late for Simms to either protest about lunch or ask more questions about the missing staff. Ricardo, with a flair, presented veal parmigiana to Simms and a chicken marsala entrée to Macina, with all of the trimmings. "Gentlemen, typically, we would serve this meal in courses, but for a businessman's lunch—well, I assume you do not have two hours to dine. I took the liberty of choosing two of my specialties for you; please forgive my presumptuous..."

"No, no, Ricardo, no apologies, please! This is both fabulous and unnecessary!" exclaimed Gino, spreading a linen napkin across his lap. Both men ate silently for a few minutes after Ricardo retreated.

Stevenson realized that he'd not eaten a hot meal since Friday night's call from Whitehead, and forced himself to slow down. "Gino, I might have to change my mind about Italian food," he said, wiping his mouth with the linen.

Macina nodded and smiled, "Some's better than others, but this is pretty great, even in my book—and I'm some kinda food snob. But I'm not sure why we're getting this attention."

"Maybe cuz I told Ricardo I wasn't a pizza fan—he was determined to show me that there was more to the menu..."

Gino laughed, "I guess we don't have to treat him as a suspect now..."

"Maybe just the opposite," smirked Simms.

Stevenson parked his car a few doors down and across the street from the rundown stucco house. It was a sleepy afternoon, or maybe he was just sleepy after a full meal, but in any case, he had to leave his air-conditioned car and push through the oppressive humidity. He walked across the cracked pavement, warily absorbing the neighborhood as if every eye were on him. Some of the houses and yards were tidy, others less so, but Valeria's was clearly the poorest on the block. No neighborhood children were outside— but it *was* stifling hot, so that made sense. Somewhere, the laughter from a TV game show echoed amongst the single-story homes, and distant Latin music thumped out base notes from an invisible source as if providing a heartbeat for the entire block.

Simms surveyed the unkept St. Augustine grass growing up in the cracks of the sidewalk and traced the unruly stuff to where it entwined the chainlink fence with its coarse tendrils. He noticed that Valeria's was the only fenced yard in sight, and it dawned on him that the three-foot high enclosure was intended to keep any denizen gators in the adjoining storm ditch from wandering into the yard or inside to the bathtub. *"It wouldn't be the first time,"* he mused. The heavy spring-loaded gate clanked shut as soon as he let go of it, and he trudged up the steps to a covered front porch. The front door was open for ventilation and, through the screen door, he could see straight into the backyard where clothes danced from a rope in the humid breeze. He knocked, then knocked again. Finally, "Hold your horses, I'm coming," came a lilting female voice with just a faint hint of annoyance in the last syllable that revealed the insincerity of the greeting.

Simms tried to guess the young woman's heritage as she strolled toward the door. It was a mystery, but he was certain that the woman's pale face did not match the photograph he'd gotten from Ricardo Avila's personnel files. "Hello, I'm looking for Valeria LaCroix. Does she live at this address?"

The woman's green eyes studied him suspiciously, "Who are you?"

Realizing his mistake, Simms said, "Sorry, I'm Detective Simms of..."

"You don't look like a cop," she challenged.

Simms produced his badge and ID and held them up to the screen door apologetically for inspection. "My mistake... from the file, I wasn't expecting anybody else living here, and I should have identified myself right away. Are you a relative, or...?"

"Housemate... Scarlett—with two 'T's', no 'E,'" she interrupted, and watched him make the notation in his little book. "I'm a model," she added as nonchalantly as if she'd been asked.

Simms started to say that she looked like a certain kind of model, but bit his tongue, nodded, then asked, "Is Valeria here?"

"No, just me and my baby."

Simms realized that getting information from Scarlett was not going to be easy. "Do you know where I can find her?"

"Key West."

"I really need to find her and ask her some things—there's been some trouble where she works..."

"Yeah, it was on the news— but she doesn't work there anymore... You should already know that if you're any kind of cop. She said she was sick of getting fired all the time. She had a job lead in the Keys... said she'd stay with a sister until she found out.."

"Right, I did know about her being fired... but I was told that she was re-hired."

"Well, she didn't go back this time."

"That's why I'm here... the chef told me that she made a lot of money with tips and such—more than the other girls... so I thought there might have been another reason she didn't return—like maybe somebody harassing her or something."

"Yeah, well that shit goes on all the time. I can't see any reason why the cops would care unless she's a suspect or something..."

"No, not at all, but we're trying to talk to all of the employees, and she was missing. But right now, if you know she's okay, then... well, look, we're not even sure that anything happened there except a misunderstanding..."

"Yeah, the news said that there was no dead body found, so... what's the fuss?"

"Sorry, I can't say more about it right now. There's already too many rumors out there. So, can you tell me how to locate Valeria, or not?"

"Her sister works at a joint called 'The Drunken Chicken' in Key West... her name's Trinity—try there. And if you see Valeria, tell her the rent's due pretty soon."

With a touch of irony in his tone, Simms thanked Scarlett for her cooperation and thrust his card through the edge of the screen door, "If you think of anything else, or if Valeria returns..."

"Got it. Goodbye," she said, and slammed the door shut.

Abandoning his normal slogging late afternoon pace, Gino Macina fairly skipped into Stevenson's office near the end of the day and plopped some new photos onto the desk. Simms looked up, "Must be good Gino, you look like it's Christmas morning."

Gino grinned, "You were right, partner—Forensics didn't notice this... look! Just past noon—in these frames from the security camera, right near the upper corner. See—that white blob!"

"It moves from frame to frame, then disappears," said Simms. "Somebody came out the back of Giuseppe's..."

"Right," said Gino. "Now, look at these from the crowd that evening... see that white blob? That's the hobo—the so-called

'Tibetan Monk'. He turned down that narrow alley... So he was there at lunch time too... supposedly when nobody else was."

"Maybe he was just looking for a handout at the kitchen's back door," said Simms.

"Yeah, and maybe he saw something he shouldn't have..."

"I guess you'd better go find him, Gino."

"Me? Why me?"

"Cuz I've gotta go to Key West to find Valeria LaCroix."

"What? How's Whitehead gonna let you go? It's a hundred and fifty miles out of our jurisdiction..."

""Well, he's not happy about it... so I told him I was goin' fishing with a buddy down there, and it wouldn't cost the Department a cent. I've arranged my own transportation too, so if I cause any trouble, he's off the hook."

"And he went for that?"

"More or less. Don't worry, I've got it covered. Here's my buddy's number if you can't get me on my mobile—it's Baxter—remember him? Oh, and maybe you should take a uniform with you when you go over to the marsh looking for Rodney... somebody to watch your back. Then, why don't you try calling Giuseppe's sister down in Miami again? She never returned the calls."

Chapter 3
To Key West

Macina leaned to his right as if to encourage gravity to hold the junker on the pavement as he steered the steel blue Dodge Stratus around the offramp. Simms ignored the death rattle of the car and Macina's theatrics and, instead, said, "Thanks for the ride over here, Gino. How'd you know about this seaplane base?"

Gino, now on straight road again, replied, "Oh... well, I had a girlfriend who lived by Bonefish Cove... we could see the seaplanes take off from her place. I used to hang out a lot over here." He changed the subject then, "So, listen, I was serious earlier... if something goes haywire in the Keys, call me—not Whitehead. I'll drive down and get ya if necessary... it'll save a lot of grief with Whitehead, trust me."

"Thanks, Gino... let's stay in touch every day or two. I'll be curious to hear what else comes out of our favorite Tibetan Monk. Oh, and also, don't forget to ask Ricardo if he's thought of anything else... that older Baptist preacher said he's sure some of the kitchen staff live over in Manatee Wells. But, that's different from what Ricardo's been saying... and what Whitehead has been parroting. I'm thinking that our Cuban friend may not've given us all of the personnel files."

"Yeah, I'll do that... also, maybe there are *former* employees who live over in the Wells... we didn't ask about them... and we never found out who told the employees the joint was closed that day. Hey—So, here we are... is that the guy you're supposed to meet?"

Without any thought of his previous gripes with Macina, Simms held out his hand, "Yup, probably the guy—Dusty— Baxter told me that this Dusty is the brother of a character named Jimmy Daniels—whose plane we're meetin'. See ya later... and thanks again, partner. Talk to you soon."

From a distance, Stevenson's contact looked more like an old man bird sitting hunched on the dock piling. But as Simms closed the distance between them, the bearded heron rose and hailed him, "Hello! Hey, are you Stevenson?"

Simms could see the fancy guitar case when the man stood up and stretched his awkward frame. "Yup. You must be Dusty."

"Yeah, I am that very soul. Jimmy said you'd make it... but he didn't say why you were goin' with us. Are you our drummer for this weekend's gig? Or the Marimba Man?"

Simms laughed out loud, "No, man, I couldn't get away with the castanets if anybody was watching me."

"So, you play *something*, then."

Simms laughed again, "I pick at my guitar when nobody is looking... takes my mind off other things for a time."

"That's cool, man. So, have you flown on a seaplane before?"

"Yeah, they're handy sometimes..." Simms deflected nonchalantly.

"So, wait 'til you see Jimmy's new bird... it's an old War surplus thing, and noisy as a vacuum cleaner inside."

"Well, I don't really know Jimmy... he's a friend of a friend... I'm guessing you guys are a band, then."

Dusty laughed, "We're just ragamuffins right now, trying out new stuff in small venues. We go by 'Danny and the Dirtfish' when we play this small venue shit. Jimmy's my brother—he's been around for a long time, though; people know him—Jimmy Daniels?" Dusty was searching for some inkling of recognition from Simms, but got nothing.

"So, who's Danny?"

Dusty laughed again, "We're all 'Danny'..."

Simms caught on, "So, everybody stays anonymous and has a good time?"

"You got it. You gotta come watch one of the shows—they're a hoot. I'm sure your friend will know where we play... so here comes our ride—see, up the river?"

Simms followed Dusty's pointed finger and watched the Grumman Albatross gracefully settle onto the glassy water, and then taxi toward the pier amidst a noisy cloud of spray. "Let's go," said Dusty, "he ain't gonna shut it down." Without another word, Simms hurried along the ell-shaped pier, turned left into the misty breeze of the idling props, and hopped through the open aft door of the plane just behind the guitar man.

Simms didn't know exactly what he was expecting, but he was still surprised by what he saw. The inside of the plane looked like somebody's idea of a man cave. There was a settee bolted to the floor on the far side, a built-in dinette on the near side with a booze rack in the middle, a surfboard strapped down along the fuselage, and a folded hammock hanging against the forward bulkhead. Through the bulkhead gangway, Simms could see two occupied seats and, forward of them, sat the pilot and copilot. Dusty pointed to an empty seat aft of the door, took the one opposite, and hurriedly buckled-in. One of the pilots peered toward the rear, gave a thumbs up, then wasted no time getting the plane turned into position for a takeoff. As they gained speed across the water, caught air, and finally cleared the sound, Simms fought to keep his breakfast down. It was his first flight in a seaplane.

Stevenson kept expecting the beast to gain enough altitude to provide a horizon that would allow him to stabilize his equilibrium. Instead, they seemed to be skimming the tops of the wind waves as the south Florida coastline streaked by, threatening to expose his little lie in a wretched way. Dusty had been right—there couldn't be a lot of casual conversation above the din of the motors just then. However, once the plane finally rose and settled into a level flight, the din subsided significantly. Simms looked around the cabin and realized that it was not a bare-bones surplus military plane, but rather, it was actually quite customized.

Dusty got up and poured a shot of tequila, offering it to Simms. Stevenson laughed and shook his head. "Too early for me," he declared. Dusty smiled, opened up a blue ice chest, and offered a beer instead. Simms, already regretting his decision on the tequila, gratefully accepted the beer.

"A hundred and twenty knots! Pretty good, huh?" Dusty exclaimed. "We'll be in Key West in about an hour and a half! Beats driving through Miami, yeah?"

"Absolutely!" grinned Simms, watching Dusty pour another shot and toss it down. Dusty opened an old guitar case wedged in the corner, handed it to Simms, pulled out his own instrument, and lightly strummed it. In the close confines of the cabin, though, the familiar chords were quite audible, even with the engine noise.

"What do ya pick at Stevenson? Show me," commanded Dusty. Simms looked flustered, then plucked out a few chords he'd been working on, then repeated the exercise. Dusty watched and listened, picked it up and followed for a minute or two until he said, "Try this—watch—yeah that's it—add some flare. Can you do this...?"

Dusty's little guitar lesson lasted all the way to Key West, with the noise of the motors dampening Stevenson's mistakes on the strings. When the props changed pitch to settle down for a water landing, they returned the instruments to the cases and settled back. Dusty announced their arrival, "Hurricane Hole Marina. That's where we play tonight, too... then we'll do a couple of sets at a joint called the Drunken Chicken tomorrow night... you should get your buddy to come on out!" Simms just smiled, nodded, and thought, "*Perfect.*"

"Hey! Stevenson—over here!" Simms saw his friend coming down the dock, with a big grin. "How was it?"

"Hey yourself, Baxter! How has your cracker ass been?"

Baxter laughed, "Still glows in the dark, brother—wanna see?"

"Hell no! Not now, not ever!"

Baxter said, "C'mon, I'll introduce you to your newest benefactor." They waited for the pilots to pop out of the cockpit hatch, then approached. "Hey, Jimmy! How's it goin'? This is your stowaway, Stevenson Simms. Thanks for giving him a lift—I owe you another fishing trip. Stevenson—meet Jimmy Daniels..."

Simms held out his hand and thanked Jimmy for the lift, just about the time Dusty ambled over. "So, Jimmy—you met Stevenson..." then turning, he held out his hand to Baxter, "You're

Baxter, right? Jimmy, I told Stevenson about our gigs—hope that's all okay."

"Hell yeah, the more the merrier, especially if the crowd turns ugly," Jimmy chuckled in a good-natured southern drawl. "Look, please do come out... but we gotta get busy right now... Baxter, you've got my number—let me know when the fishin' is wide open, okay? See ya at the show."

The other band members straggled up the gangway with Jimmy and Dusty, and meandered out of sight. When they were gone, and Simms and Baxter were finished inspecting the Albatross, Baxter said, "Let's go have a beer and a burger up at the marina bar, and you can explain just what your sneaky ass is up to in Key West."

A tall redheaded waitress came to take their order, and Baxter immediately began flirting, "Sorina, how is my Romanian girlfriend these days?"

Sorina smiled and answered with a strong accent, "Which one, Bax?"

"Why darlin', you're my only Romanian sweetheart... have you met my good friend Stevenson?"

Simms was busy trying not to stare at the bronze-haired woman, but her blush revealed that he was failing, and he simply shook his head and said something inane about her resemblance to a famous model. The girl chuckled courteously, and disappeared to fetch the beers.

"So, Stevenson," said Baxter, interrupting Simms' lingering spell, "have there been any really good murders up your way lately?"

Simms looked at Baxter with a blank expression, still mesmerized by the departing waitress, then looked past him to take in the view of the fishing boats lined up in the marina. He waited a few more uncomfortable seconds, then asked vaguely, "What makes you think there's been *any* murders in my town, let alone any good ones?"

"So, it's your town, now is it? Well, Mister Mayor, last I heard, you *were* a homicide detective... so I assumed... but if ya wanna be coy..."

Simms laughed, "Nah, I'm screwin' with ya, Brother. But can't a guy go fishin' with his best friend?"

"And who might that be? Oh, you mean the guy you called in the middle of the night and told that you just had to go fishing on a moment's notice? That best friend? You're up to something...wait... let me guess... you conned dumbass Whitehead into letting you come down here to work a lead—am I right?"

Simms flashed his white teeth, "You still got a hard-on for the Captain, then?"

"He's still a donkey dick, and always will be... but don't change the subject. Whaddya need me for. Don't you have a new partner yet?"

"Yeah. No. Whitehead put Macina back with me," said Simms resignedly.

"Macina? The only reason that guy got out of uniforms is he couldn't keep his shoes shined. Is he behavin' at last?

"He's trying... I've got no choice but to give him a shot... otherwise I'll sink with him like he was a millstone around my neck," lamented Simms. He paused for a few seconds to decide how to explain it, then finally said, "So, you're right, Baxter—I'm chasin' a lead on a murder case with no corpse, at least four missing people—and one is a crazy hobo who claims to be a Tibetan Monk who says he saw a murder. Or, at least forty-three people say he's a Tibetan Monk, and they all say he said he saw a murder..."

Baxter started to laugh, "Yeah, I would've gone fishing too—oh, wait, I did... and never came back."

When Sorina returned with the first round of beers, Simms saw his chance to change the subject, "So how *is* business these days, Brother?"

Baxter took a long draught from his mug and smiled. "Great! I just got my third boat—see that big center console down toward the end of this dock? I keep it here in this marina—can't fit it in my little cove with the other two... Plus, I still have the original flats boats and a half-dozen kayaks. And we're booked heavy enough for me to keep two full-time guides workin'."

"So, you said you had one of your cabins for me... but if it's full, I can stay..."

"Nope, you're staying with me at the house. Don't argue."

"But, what about your new bride?"

"She's fine—but not here... I smuggled her back to see her sick mother..."

"Cuba? You ran her to Havana?"

"No, hell no, that would be stupid. It's a little smuggling village called Puerto Escondido... no military base—only friendly fishermen... we go back and forth, you know-—they need stuff for their old outboards-—spark plugs, motor oil, propellers—shit like that. They gladly take her wherever she needs to go..."

About that time, Sorina brought their meals and more beer, and it gave Baxter his chance to change the subject. "So, your pilot, Jimmy..."

"Yeah, that was pretty cool of him..." said Simms. "He's a client?"

"To the max—the man's a fishing addict, and he sends me dozens more clients on a regular basis... good guy to know... we actually met up in Key Largo in a tournament, and I invited him and his lady out for a trip when they came to Key West. He's got his fingers in all kinds of businesses—music, recording studio, hotels, resorts—you name it. So, we should go see them play tonight—they're gonna be right here in Hurricane Hole under those awnings over there... small venues are the best..."

"That'd be fun, but I really want to go see them play tomorrow night at the Drunken Chicken—Dusty said they were playing there."

"Okay, then, we'll go both nights. But let's finish our beers and go over to the lodge and get you settled in..."

Chapter 4
Chickens and Such

Trinity plotted her strategic entrance from the right side of the makeshift stage, hiding amongst the props and potted palms. Filled with a schizophrenic mix of confidence and self-doubt, she waited and watched as the band leader pull the mic in close, heard his introduction, "Now, our very own Key West lady of the hour, Miss Danni..."

Trinity glowed and giggled inwardly at the stage name so recently bestowed for her latest appearance with 'Danny and the Dirtfish', then she exhaled and began her strut from behind the palms, moving her body in just the right places as if to encourage every man's eyes to fondle her and every woman's heart to beat in jealousy. She held the mic intimately, waiting for the drummer to *tap tap tap* with his sticks, anticipating the first guitar chords like the birth of a kitten. Nothing. Not a sound. She glance sideways to see the skinny guitar man strapping on a different guitar, leaving her to look into the crowd for somebody to sing to, somebody who had eyes only for her. Jimmy's encouragement came to mind, "*Always perform as if somebody important is watching.*" There! In the front row: he was a ringer for a young Belafonte, and the white dude looked familiar too, "*important people*," she registered silently. The drummer tapped, she took a deep breath, her chest perilously filling the cotton pirate bodice that accented her form just-so, then her voice rang-in right on time. She sang to the white 'music producer' with sincerity, and to young 'Belafonte' with passion, her brain racing through the song ahead of her voice, critiquing in self-awareness as she went. "*Not horrible... only missed a couple of notes, but the band covered it,*" she concluded at the end. She didn't know she'd been off key the entire way. The audience clapped anyway as 'Miss Danni' exited stage left.

Baxter shook his head when the singer was out of sight and watched as the band took a break. "That was pretty..."

"Awful?" offered Simms.

"Be kind, Brother... local color and all... you're getting' what you paid for tonight."

"She did look good—looked familiar, too..."

"Not likely you would've seen her before—she's a waitress at a joint down off Duval Street—it's where you said we're goin' tomorrow night—The Drunken Chicken... if you're game, that is... I don't wanna keep you up past your bedtime."

"Very funny—you're the old man around here... and I wouldn't miss this show for anything."

Before long, Jimmy and Dusty sat down at the table with them, plunking down fresh drinks, and taking over the conversation. "So, Baxter," said Jimmy, "How's the new bride?"

Baxter might have blushed a bit, but it was too dark to notice. "She's good—except I had to take her to see her sick mama—otherwise, I wouldn't be out with you hooligans."

Jimmy responded with a few platitudes about the mother-in-law, then probed, "So how did you meet her, Baxter? And so soon after the divorce? You were always kinda mum about that-—of course, I guess you never would've said anything in front of your new bride, I get it."

Baxter waved off the feigned concern, knowing that Jimmy was trying to get him to open up in front of Dusty. He glanced at

Stevenson, who was hiding his face behind his glass, then looked at Dusty and said, "Yeah, well, take my advice and never marry a pole dancer from Puerto Rico... they got enough savvy to take you to the cleaners."

Dusty, intrigued now, but somewhat embarrassed for Baxter, said, "Geez, it's none of my business..." Then he thought about it some more. "A pole dancer? How does one go about that?"

"Live close to a bar called Dirty Blondes... lotsa dollar bills... tequila shots... repeat as necessary for months. Need a better picture?" Said Baxter, with mock annoyance.

Simms chimed in, "Don't let him fool ya... he was proud of that girl—until he wasn't... what was her stage name? Banana Split?"

Baxter cradled his lowered head in his hands, then laughed a low—almost growl— animal sound, "Yup, that was her name—She was kinda sweet at first, but how could I know she was a con artist?."

Simms was of a mind to come to Baxter's aid, but Jimmy stole the moment, "But you jumped right back in the game, eh?"

Baxter tossed down a shot of tequila, and shook his head. "No, not really... I changed the rules of the game and took a different approach. Ya know, if you want a family, you need to find women from the right culture—one that's family oriented, right? You get that? I didn't, back before the first one. So, have you guys ever heard of internet dating? It's kind of a new thing—been around for a couple of years in Europe and a little while here in the States." His three companions looked at him without a shred of understanding. "No? Well, it's the greatest thing... you can interview lotsa girls from anywhere—I joined a dating service called 'Caribe Cupid'. You can go online—you know, from a computer, get on their web site—you guys have heard of this shit before, right? Look, you sort through photos of young women from different countries and heritages, find ones that have the looks you want, the ones who have the same thing in mind—not just one-night stands...right? You guys following this?

"What do you mean, 'interview'?" Jimmy challenged with a smirk.

"Sounds a little creepy," interjected Dusty.

Baxter held up his hand, and ignoring Jimmy's probe, said to Dusty, "Yeah, but it doesn't have to be. In fact, the point is to not be creepy. You gotta be stable... gotta have enough money to travel to their islands to meet, be chaperoned... it also helps if you speak the same language..."

By now, Jimmy couldn't control his mirth, and Simms was in need of a bathroom break. But Dusty was intrigued and Baxter was set free; he downed another shot and just kept on rolling about the virtues of Caribbean women, wading through the chuckles, wisecracks, and rolled eyeballs of his companions. Simms returned from the head followed by a waitress carrying a tray full of shots to add fuel to the fire. It all broke apart in laughter when Baxter admitted that he'd had his new bride's teeth fixed to the tune of four grand, and that she was scheduled for a boob job when she returned from Cuba. Finally, when he broke out the photos in his wallet, and everybody agreed that wife number two was a real beauty, especially now that her teeth were fixed, the table calmed down.

Jimmy said, "We're gonna go do another set in a few minutes—but, Stevenson, Dusty tells me that you pick a little... and he thinks you'd be good for a couple of numbers in our local artist segment tomorrow night...whaddya think?"

Now it was Simms' turn to hear Baxter's laugh when he shook his head. "No, man—look what happened to that poor girl tonight. I'd be worse."

"Nonsense," said Jimmy. "We covered her goofs, she was fine... it's all part of the local color..."

"Well, I'm not a local..."

"Treasure Coast, no? That's local enough for our gig, and it sounds good... 'fresh from the Treasure Coast...' Look, think about it. We'll rehearse in the club room here at the marina tomorrow afternoon... Dusty's got a guitar you can use... we'll work you into the act—no solos or anything to put you on the spot. Just come act like you're having a good time and enjoying the moment. And I guarantee you that the babes at the 'Chicken' will love ya."

Dusty added, "You can do this, man. At least come to rehearsal, yeah?"

As the two musicians headed back to the little platform stage, Stevenson sat quietly, stunned, searching for some shred of confidence or some thread of irrational brashness that would make this proposal seem okay to his reclusive brain. Baxter rescued him from his own self-doubt, "You should give it a try—after all, he did give you a free plane ride down here. Listen. You put on this persona when you go to interview a witness or a suspect, right? You cinch up that imaginary duty belt, grab the handle, feel that badge pinned to your manly chest, and become an authority figure. This is the same shit. Besides, you're on vacation, and nobody knows you. Hand me that last shooter, would ya—if you're not gonna use it."

"Stevenson! Dude! Time to get up!" Simms heard the voice, and the drone of a machine—or—what? He couldn't identify either. Baxter tried again, raising his voice above the noise of the air conditioner.

Simms rose up suddenly, confused by the sunlight streaming through the window. "Whoa! what time is it?"

"It's late... I'm back from my morning charter already! Good bite this morning... I coulda used your help with the clients... a father trying to teach his kid to fly-fish the flats... Coulda been worse, coulda been better."

"Sorry, Baxter, but why didn't you roust me?"

"You were out like a light, and we didn't talk about it last night... anyway, one of my guys has the flu—so it was a last minute thing. So get up and shower. We're going into town for lunch."

Baxter parked the Jeep on a side street and pointed toward the corner, "Captain Tony's Saloon is right down that way... we can walk it. How's that sound?"

"All's good," said Stevenson as they headed off. He tried to match Baxter's stride, but ancient tree roots buckled the concrete every 20 feet, and bird droppings were splattered like a crime scene. Baxter seemed to anticipate every obstacle as he zig-zagged the path, forcing Simms to sidestep every few paces. Suddenly, Baxter darted down what appeared to be not much more than an alley.

"Short-cut this way."

Scattering feral chickens in their path, they passed a couple of broken-down rust-bucket cars that poked bare skeleton tops above a rickety wood-plank fence. More chickens, unkept grassy patches that were once yards, and overgrown trees dotted the scene. In the middle of the block, they passed a small antebellum house set back from the pavement, protected by a once white-washed picket fence, fronted by a small hand-crafted sign that read

Madame LaCroix
Spirit Counselor

Stevenson pointed at the house, "Local fortune teller?"

Baxter said, "Voodoo Priestess, I'd guess. There's a lot of that sort of thing in town. See all the wild chickens running around? That's a tip off."

Simms laughed a little at his friend's attempt at exposing him to the local color, and continued hurrying to keep up. They rounded the corner, and across the street was a big signboard with a cartoon of an obviously inebriated bird holding a beer mug that read

The Drunken Chicken

Simms pointed, and Baxter said, "Yup, that's where we're going tonight. But first, we have to have a sandwich, then I've gotta get you to rehearsal." Simms groaned out loud. He'd hoped his commitment to the Dirtfish band leader was forgotten, but obviously, it was too late to back out now. Baxter just grinned as they continued their trek to Captain Tony's. "Here... go here first!" he suddenly commanded. Simms looked at the sign advertising conch sandwiches, then back at his friend with a confused look. Baxter laughed, "Nothing worth eatin' at Tony's... you grab a couple of sandwiches to take in—I'll get the first round of beers at the saloon."

Stevenson and Baxter chatted while waiting for the first round of amber lagers. While listening to Baxter's running narrative, Simms scanned the memorabilia and dollar bills plastered on the walls and ceiling like it had all been arranged there by an explosion. The scene made him laugh, and he laughed even more as Baxter reminisced about the old days together on the police force. But Baxter had an agenda that he finally got around to, and it dampened Simms mood. "How much longer are you gonna keep puttin' up with Whitehead's bullshit, Brother? You and I both know that he has no inkling of proper police procedures—or if he does, he's not making anybody follow protocols..."

"I know, but he'll probably retire soon, and maybe we'll get a real cop to take over..."

"Where are ya gonna find one of those? You're the only logical choice if they promote from within the department, and you have seniority. More than likely, Whitehead's gonna screw up before he retires and bring the world down around your ears— all of you. Look, letting you come down here is just one example..."

"Yeah, I know, Bax, but look, there was really no choice. He doesn't have any sort of positive relationship with other agencies—they just blow him off. So, he has to take chances like this, because nobody will cooperate in any investigations. Listen, I hear what you're sayin'... this current case is the latest example and it frustrates the crap out of me. He didn't secure the crime scene at this restaurant before I got there, and he just started handing out orders to the uniforms 'cuz he's the chief honcho. Witnesses weren't separated, nobody had a plan in the interviews, and we didn't get names and numbers from all of them. So, the statements are tainted, and we can't find a lot of 'em... we're just lucky that the forensics guys did their job right—at least I hope they did. Whitehead told me they were collecting fingerprints, but hell, he didn't even have all the kitchen staff printed when they came back to work. In fact, quite a few didn't show up for work—supposedly spooked by voodoo magic or some shit... so we don't have their prints either."

"Well, how on earth did that old fat-ass beat you to the scene?"

"The call came while I was at dinner, busy breaking up with my girlfriend—I thought I could make her see reason, talk her out of it... you know how that goes. If I'd left right when the call came in, she would have just said, 'See what I mean?' Anyway, it was all a waste of time, 'cuz it's been coming for a long time. I should've just left."

"Shit, Stevenson, I'm sorry to hear this news. I thought she might be the one for you. So, look, I've got the number for Caribe Cupid if you want," he suggested ironically.

"Oh, hell no! That'd be out of the fryin' pan, into the fire." Both men laughed, then finished their drinks with nothing serious to talk about except the tourists wandering by. As they wandered back to Baxter's Jeep, they once again passed the house of Madame LaCroix, Spirit Counselor, and this time, the name LaCroix registered in his brain.

"Hey, Bax, did you ever go see one of these Voodoo ladies... fortune tellers... whatever?"

"Just once," answered Baxter. "I knocked at her door, and she said, 'Who's there?' So I left." It took Simms a few seconds to register Baxter's malarkey, and then he just chuckled and shook his head. He'd have to find another way to see Madame LaCroix.

Chapter 5
Davo's Discovery

Gino Macina stood at the edge of the sandy knoll under the dripping canopy of oaks, and stared at the still muddy path wending into the thick brush near the mangroves that edged the salt marsh. Then he glanced down at his handmade brown Pradas and cussed at the early morning rain. The uniformed officer next to him hid his smirk when Macina cast a menacing glance his way, coughed, and said, "I'll go this way, Detective, if you want."

"No Stan, I'll go... you head around this thicket—that way," he said pointing at the stand of saw palmettos, "and I'll meet up with you. That encampment is supposed to be in the middle of the hammocks somewhere, and I don't want anybody running away from us... I should've asked Whitehead for another man." Stan nodded, and began picking his way along the tangle of palmetto and hackberry, and soon disappeared from Macina's view. Gino took a deep breath, pushed the thought of gators and snakes out of his head, and tried to hurry along the slick trail. But stepping around and hopping over the larger puddles slowed his progress. There was no way to speed up the trek without slipping and falling in the mud, and he'd rather take his chances with imaginary reptiles than suffer the humiliation.

Once again immersed in the oak hammocks, there were few cues to guide him. He stopped every few steps to listen, but there was no sound except the squishing of his toes inside his water-logged shoes. The sun was rising nearly straight overhead, and the humidity was rising with it. On about his fifth pause, he heard a small voice, "Mistah... yo, Mistah." Startled, Macina looked for the source. "Ovah heah, Mistah."

Gino's wary eyes caught up with the source, but seeing an unkempt creature not much over four feet tall, he let his guard down and smiled, "Yes, I see you now... do you need help? Are you lost?"

"No, Suhr, we ain't lost. Aahr you?" Gino shook his head, and the boy continued, "Aahr you with that cop?" Gino nodded affirmatively. "Aahr you a cop?" asked the boy.

Gino said, "Do I look like a cop to you?"

The boy looked at Gino with annoyance, studied him a few seconds longer, then repeated insistently, "Mistah, aahr ya'all a cop?"

Gino scoffed and said, "I'm Detective Macina, and my friend and I are looking for somebody who may have witnessed a serious crime. Are your parents here somewhere? I'm hoping somebody can help us locate this witness."

The boy looked fidgety, but stood his ground, "No, Suhr, no parents around. No witnesses, neitha."

Gino laughed a little, then said, "This can't be a safe place to play if your parents aren't around. Will you tell me your name?"

"I's Davo, and we ain't playin' heahr. Davo's livin' heahr with them othas. We ain't got no place else, Mistah Detetive."

"Other kids?" exclaimed Gino.

"Some," said Davo, "and olda folks too. But they's all scattered this morning, and left Davo behind... we was takin' a crap, and they just all left."

Gino tried to show a compassionate face, but was on the verge of laughing, "Why'd they leave, Davo?

In response, the boy asked, "Will ya follow ovah heahr, Mistah Detetive? You needs... Davo's needs to show ya'all somethin'." Gino followed the boy about 20 yards on a side trail, into a clearing in the grove. Davo pointed, "Look in theah... Davo thinks he seen a ghost... old Monk saw a haint, and just froze his self. He does that hoodoo shit that scare everybody, now he scared his self solid."

One glance at the mound of dirty gray-white coat, glassy eyes, and white hair, told Gino that old Rodney was as dead as a rock. "Davo, you better stand over there, and maybe don't look at him." Not wanting to risk looking into the eyes of a zombie, the boy silently agreed. Gino, convinced that the boy wouldn't bolt, turned his attention to the seated corpse. The body was leaning straight-backed against a short cabbage palm, eyes wide open, with just a trickle of blood on the collar of his coat from a gash on the back of his head. Except for the blood, Rodney indeed looked frozen in time. Only the bloody drag marks in the white sand suggested to Macina that the body had been staged after the murder and after the rain.

"Davo, I need you to show me through to your camp, and I need to meet up with the other cop. Can you do that? We need to get some people down here where the Monk is to take care of him."

"He dead, ain't he?"

Gino nodded, "Yup. Looks like he hit his head on something... Listen, I can't leave you out here by yourself... do you want something to eat? I'd take you for a burger or a sandwich until your people return, or... well you decide... but I can't leave you here alone."

Davo smiled shyly, "A buhrga sound good..."

"Is that you, Stevenson? Thanks for calling me back."

"What's up, partner?"

"We got a body... old Rodney turned up dead over in the hammocks on Indian Creek. His head was bashed in with a rock."

"In the swamp where that homeless camp is, near Giuseppe's?"

"Yeah, I took Stan over there to look for him this morning after the rain."

"Well, shit. Somebody whacked our only witness?"

"Well, the only witness that we know of."

"Good point... any other leads, then?" asked Simms. "Who reported the body?"

"Nope, no leads, really. A little orphan kid names Davo something-or-other led me to him—homeless bugger. Says his parents were from Haiti, but he claims he was born in Miami. He was raving about Voodoo, or Hoodoo, and shit like that... refers to himself by his name-like a third person. Apparently everybody in the encampment ran off when word got out about the zombie sittin' in camp. I took the kid to that shelter... it's one the Baptists run... they'll get to the bottom of his situation and keep him for a while, or until he runs away again."

Simms mused, "Escape artist, eh? Good work with him, then, Gino. Okay, well, what're you gonna do next?"

"I gotta go back down to Manatee Wells, and keep lookin' for the missus. What's up at your end? Did you get a lead on Valeria?"

"Well, maybe—I got an inside track to meet Valeria's sister, without revealing my intentions... we'll see how it goes tonight. Thanks for the call, Gino... and, again, good work."

Chapter 6
Live Music and Slow Dancing

Stevenson fidgeted as 'Danny and the Dirtfish' finished their first set and stepped down from the makeshift stage. He knew that he was going to be called up during the next set, just as soon as their waitress finished her number. Simms cringed at the thought of the woman singing the entire song off-key again, and then began to worry about his own stage fright. He tried to distract himself by surveying the inside of the Drunken Chicken's eatery. The entrance led past an indoor bar adorned with claptrap—everything from old fishing nets and mounted gamefish, to voodoo skulls and other assorted weird mumbo jumbo. Once past the bar, the restaurant proved to be a hardpan dirt-floor patio with countless layers of palm fronds as a roof, and a bamboo fence hiding the chainlink on the street side. Tables were scattered about haphazardly, amongst which, gangs of chickens freely roamed in search of table scraps in the dim lighting.

Simms had decided to forego the house special—spicy Jamaican jerked chicken—and ordered stone crabs instead. Now, he watched Baxter, who had not been bashful about the Jamaican special, but was currently tossing bits of the fowl from his plate to the feathered cannibals roaming below. Simms was laughing, but Baxter defended his actions, "If I can't feed this to the live ones, then this stringy bitch died in vain..."

Simms laughed again, "You want me to order some more crabs?"

"Nah, that's okay, I'll get two slabs of Key Lime pie, and call it good."

"What? Are you twelve, or what?"

No, man, it goes good with dark rum—try it!"

The distractions worked, because the next thing Simms knew, Jimmy was announcing, "Now, our very own Key West lady of the hour, Miss Danni..."

Trinity had been flustered the entire night. The 'young Belafonte' and his friend the 'white record producer', whom she had dreamed up the night before, had been at one of her serving tables all evening. Giving into her own fantasies that they might actually be important people in the music industry, she'd grown mute out of shyness when they flirted with her. Spinning in her own little orbit, she nearly missed her cue to get up on the stage. But, by the time the skinny guitarist had changed instruments, she was ready. And, importantly, she was more relaxed than the previous night, so her voice, absent the strain, was on key for the entire number.

Simms and Baxter exchanged glances, nodded in surprise, and clapped as Trinity stepped from the stage and into the shadows of the bar. Stevenson almost forgot what was about to happen next, engrossed as he was by the woman.

Jimmy finished thanking 'Miss Danni', then went right on, "Now, joining us from the Treasure Coast club scene, Mister 'Danny Simms', who has graciously agreed to join us for a couple of numbers.

If you know the words, feel free to sing along. And if you don't know the words, please don't."

Amidst the scattered laughter, Simms took a deep breath, stepped up on stage, where Dusty handed him a guitar. For the next seven and a half minutes, Stevenson became 'Danny Simms', guitar picker for Danny and the Dirtfish. If he missed a note or two in either number, no one noticed, and if he felt like a stone statue, his body didn't show it. He moved right in rhythm.

At Jimmy's behest, Stevenson took a little bow, stepped from the stage and headed to his table amidst generous applause from the patrons. With relief and a little glow of satisfaction that he allowed himself, he dodged tables, chairs, and chickens in the low light and, in the process, failed to notice that their waitress was sitting with a smiling Baxter. The woman reached out her hand, "Hi, I'm Trini LaCroix." Simms smiled, shot a quick glance at Baxter, then sat down, wondering how much Baxter may have revealed about his real occupation. "That was really good—your friend Baxter says you've been playing for a long time..."

"Off and on since I was a kid, I guess," said Stevenson nonchalantly. "Both of my parents were musical and insisted..."

Where do you play, mostly?" she interrupted.

"Oh, nowhere, really..."

Then Baxter interrupted, "What he means is, no place you've heard of... he prefers small venues." Simms kept a poker face, but his eyes thanked Baxter for his quick wit.

Trinity accepted the explanation without question, and moved on, "Well, I should get back to work—those tables look thirsty. Shall I call you...?"

"Simms... that'd be fine," said Stevenson with a grin. "It's what my mother calls me."

Jimmy's band finished with a flourish with another half-dozen numbers before calling it a night. About 10 minutes after the set, the band leader slid into the empty chair at the table with Baxter and Simms. "Nice job, Stevenson! See, nothing to be nervous about, right? Ready for an encore tomorrow night?"

Simms shrugged, thinking, "*Why not, what could go wrong?*"

But it was a trap he'd not seen. "Good... because, tomorrow night, we play the Paradise Casino in Nassau! Trini is coming too. It's all set!" Stunned, Simms cast a furtive glance at Baxter, who shook his head.

"Don't look at me, Brother, I've got full boats of fishermen for the next few days. You're on your own."

A few patrons stayed late in the bar of the Drunken Chicken, long after the diners had left and the kitchen shut down. Stevenson had wanted to leave right after Jimmy's announcement, but it was Baxter who wanted to party. "C'mon, Bax," said Simms, "you've got clients and an early start tomorrow, and I need to get some rest."

"Nah, we're okay," he said, referring to himself in the plural. Then he waved at Trini, and she changed her course from an exit to a barstool. "So, Jimmy says you're going to join them in Nassau, is that right?" asked Baxter mischievously.

She blushed a little, "Yeah, I've got a few days off, and it sounded like fun."

"You know Simms is going, too, right?"

She looked a little surprised, but her smile clearly showed that she approved of the company. "That's great! Do you know the Paradise Resort and Casino, Simms? I mean, have you been to Nassau? Oh, you must have, that's a silly question... you must have performed there before."

Simms smiled, "I was born in the Bahamas, so, yeah, I've been to Nassau. You know that the original resort was built by some rich guy on what used to be called Hog Island, right? It was a swamp overrun with feral pigs, mosquitos, and pirates."

She wrinkled her nose at the thought of the stench, but laughed, "I heard it was a swamp, but never heard of the pirate thing... anyway, they say the renovations and new wing of the hotel are going to open soon... of course, I imagine we'll be in the old wing."

Simms said, "So, you seem to know something about the joint too... is it one of your hangouts?"

"Not really... my sister and I went over a couple of times on vacation, but it's too rich for our pocketbooks to go on a whim— but she's there right now with her boyfriend, so I'm excited to see them. He's got some business deal or something going on, and she's bored when he's off wheeling and dealing."

Simms absorbed the info, then asked, "So, do you have family here in the Keys, then? I saw the sign for Madame LaCroix around the block. Is she related?

"Yeah, she's my aunt, and except for my sister, Valeria, that's all the family I have left. But, if Valeria marries Joey, well, that'd make us a much larger family."

Stevenson looked at Baxter, and changed the pitch a little. "So, is your aunt into magic or voodoo or something like that?"

"Something like that... it's called *Santeria* in Cuba... Auntie knows all kinds of spells and potions and such crap like that."

"So, you don't believe in that stuff?" he asked.

She shook her head, "No, but my sister is deep into it—at least she thinks she is. But our Auntie says Valeria doesn't know her butt from a hot potato. She tries, though, and she says it got her Joey..."

Simms decided not to probe too much more at the moment, sent Trini on her way, and finally convinced Baxter that they needed to sleep.

"Hi... Gino... is that you?" Simms was sitting under a palm tree at water's edge, in front of Baxter's house, watching unseen predators drive baitfish out of the water on a never-ending pursuit. "Sorry, man, reception isn't very good right here..."

"Yeah, same here, Partner. What's up?"

"I called to see what you've found out... if anything..."

"Right, well the professor up at Jacksonville said the black feather from the kitchen was a crow or raven, definitely not a chicken... and he said they can't tell much more about the bird blood than what our lab said..."

"That's it? Nothin' from the crime lab in Los Angeles?"

"Not yet... they said it would be several weeks! But... get this: remember that vinegary smell and broken bottle?"

"Yeah, so...?"

"So, the lab analyzed the stuff... let's see, my notes.. yeah, here... do you know what horehound is? Or wormwood... rosemary- that one I've heard of, and garlic... how about, oh yeah, lavender and marjo—something, can't read my notes... all in wine vinegar."

"Some Italian dressing recipe, then?"

"Maybe, but one of the techs said her grandma used these things in something she called 'four thieves vinegar'."

"So, a salad dressing, then?" said Simms impatiently.

"Maybe, but it's an Old-World concoction used to keep away the black plague... she said that in *conjure*, it's good as a potion for banishing people, or driving them away, or for protection from enemies..."

"*Conjure*? Good for..? What are you talkin' about?"

"You know, Voodoo and shit like that."

"Oh good God! Seriously? You know this how, exactly?"

"I told you—the forensics tech told me about her old Jamaican grandma..."

Simms put his irritation aside and tried for a moment to let Macina's information sink in. "All right, Gino, maybe I can learn some more about that kind of stuff—I seem to be in Voodoo-ville down here anyway. What else? Any luck over in the Wells?"

"Nope... going back today. What about you?"

"I've got a lead... I think... on Valeria LaCroix and Giuseppe. I'm flying to Nassau with her sister and a rock band in an hour..."

"What!?"

Chapter 7
Hog Island

Trinity nearly missed the plane. By the time she scrambled into the amphibious bird, there was no place to sit except next to Stevenson, so she buckled herself in, cast a sheepish glance around the eccentric cabin, and braced for the take-off. As the plane rose from the bay like a water-logged coot, she looked at Simms for the first time and said, “I can’t swim... not very well, anyway.”

Simms laughed, “It’s okay, we’re gonna fly most of the way.” She looked at him in confusion, and so he added, “Just relax, the stewardess will be around with refreshments pretty quick... just as soon as we get above the wavetops.” She was even more confused until she saw the crinkle of a laugh building around his mouth. Within five minutes, he nodded to Dusty, who poured three shots of tequila and shared them with his new bandmates along with a smile. Trinity held her glass hesitantly, and Simms said, “Don’t look out the window until you’ve tossed that down... take my word for it.” Without further delay, she gulped down the clear liquid, made a face, and looked at Dusty, who stood up, refilled her glass, and then raised his own as if to toast.

“How long... tell me again...?” she hollered at Dusty. “Last night, I thought you said...”

“Two hours, or so... Jimmy says it all depends on the winds...”

She nodded, then leaned over as if to whisper in Stevenson's ear, "Have you been in a sea plane before?"

Simms could smell the faint essence of her perfume and the warmth of her breath, sweetened by the tequila. He fought through the slight confusion her nearness created, and answered, "Yeah, you get used to it pretty quickly... but I'd be careful of Dusty's white lightning, there."

She patted his arm, "I'll be okay, thanks, though... I mean you have a soothing tone, and it helped settle me down. It's been a crazy morning, and I almost missed the plane."

Simms smiled, "No worries, Jimmy said he'd give you another five minutes..."

She blushed, "Really?" To which he just shook his head. "I couldn't help it," her voice pleaded. "The girl that was supposed to fill in for me at The Chicken... she bagged on me, and I had to beg another girl at the last second... I can't afford to lose that job."

He nodded, "Well, you made it, so no worries now. Just try to enjoy yourself..."

Trinity patted him on the arm again, then lightly touched the back of his hand, "So what do you do when you're not playing your guitar somewhere? How do you get to run off to an island in the Bahamas at the drop of a hat?"

Simms had thought the question might come up, and had an answer planned. "I'm just a humble civil servant up in Treasure Coast... I do whatever my boss asks me to do... I'm one of his problem solvers..."

"Like what?"

Now he sensed he was on thin ice, "Well, sometimes there's a problem in the community—like health and safety stuff, and if we don't take care of it, then the mayor ends up in hot water in the public eye... it's usually stuff I can't talk about, though."

Trinity nodded as if his vague nonsense all made perfect, logical sense, "I get it... must be nice to have that kind of job security..."

In Simms' life, he'd never looked at his job in that light, but there was something about how Trinity's responded that gave him pause, and in a brief second of self-awareness, he could perceive the level of cynicism he'd risen to in recent months. "I never thought of it that way," he said, "but you're right, I guess—there are some benefits to that security. I lose sight of that sometimes..."

"Is it because you're looking for something better? I think I get that way at times. I always want more... but it usually gets me in trouble."

Simms smiled, "I can't imagine you get into too much trouble, Trini."

Trinity was quiet for a time, and let the drone of the engines fill the lull in conversation. She declined another shooter, watched Simms accept a beer from an ice chest, and studied Dusty as he fiddle with his guitar strings. At last, she leaned over close and asked Stevenson, "So, what's the story with Hog Island? You know, pirates and stuff?"

Simms took a breath and let his mind go back to the old tales he'd heard as a boy. "So you know, Nassau was a haven for runaway slaves in the seventeen and eighteen hundreds, right? And the British and French and Spanish were always fighting over the islands, and treasure, and such?"

She nodded, "Yeah, I guess, I mean Jamaica, Cuba, Haiti, too, right?"

"Right, same kind of deal. Well, pirates got a hold on the place for a long time, and somebody introduced pigs and other livestock on this little island across from Nassau town on New Providence... yeah? You've heard this all?"

"No, but, I get the picture...that was Hog Island?"

"Right. Well, about fifty years ago, some tycoon who'd bought the island, petitioned the government to rename Hog Island as Paradise Island, and he built a hotel and airstrip..."

"And a casino?" She said, thinking she knew the recent history.

"Yeah, well, a bigger conglomerate came into the picture and got a gambling license from the Bahamian government... then some Hollywood guy bought it, and after that, some South African bigshot bought it. And he's the guy building the expansion..."

"So, tell me again why you know so much about this... I know you said you were born in the Bahamas... but in Nassau?"

Simms was getting in too deep with this woman for his own personal comfort level, but he couldn't see a way out at that point. "No, I—my people came from Exuma and Cat Island... they were farming families... but we have family members who've worked at the resorts over the years, and some worked the docks and for the shipping concerns in the port there."

She nodded, satisfied with the answer, as far as it went. "Thanks, Simms, that sort of explains some things about my sister's boyfriend."

"Yeah, like what?"

"Well, I'm not sure I know anything exactly, but he's supposedly meeting with some South African people about land and building a casino somewhere. That's all Valeria has told me... and he'd probably kill her if he knew she'd told me that much."

Simms laughed, "Well, your secret is safe with me. So don't worry.

The Grumman dropped quickly, skimming the little wind waves and creating its own chaos on the water's surface. Through the porthole window, Simms could see the dense green of the island, contrasted against the turquoise of the shallow water, all passing by as if in a kaleidoscope. Soon, they were taxiing toward the seaplane pier at the east end of the island, where rich waterfront homes peeked at them from lush private grounds along the narrow beach. Stevenson hadn't been back to the islands in years, and never had he arrived by sea plane on old Hog Island. But the landmark coral-red towers of the hotel, familiar only from magazine photos, were as outlandish as he'd feared. Old resentment at the rich white men that had owned everything of value on the island flickered in his heart but, still, he knew that it was the price to pay for the economic boom the resorts brought to the islanders. He took a deep breath and tried to hide his stare behind aviator sunglasses, pulled the brim of a baseball cap down as if to shield his face from the monstrous hotel complex, and prepared for arrival. After all, he'd allowed Trini to think he was a 'regular' in Nassau, and it just wouldn't do for him to gawk like a tourist.

Simms followed Trini and the band up the ramp from the pier, a resort employee in the lead. A small group waited for them under the manicured palms, smiling and waving. "*These must be the local musicians that'll play with us,*" Simms mused to himself. It was obvious that they were locals, but just as obvious was the fact that they knew Jimmy Daniels and the boys in the band. There were brief introductions, then they hurried off with the hotel guide to settle into their rooms. Trini had been correct—they were housed in the old wing of the resort, away from the glamourous offerings of the casino. "*Fine by me,*" thought Simms.

"Practice in two hours," announced Jimmy as he handed out room keys, "In the old ballroom... just follow this walkway... oh, and order whatever you want from room service, but they say we'll have a buffet lunch in the ballroom too, so suit yourselves."

Simms found his room at a bend in the walkway, admired the waterfront view, and went inside. Looking around, he absorbed the aging motel room décor. It was accentuated by garish tropical wall coverings that seemed to match the scuffed hardwood floors, and there was a small fridge and kitchenette at one end. A short fabric sofa and a small television that got two channels sat opposite a queen-sized bed that he hoped had no vermin hiding in its depths. The bathroom was oversized with a pink tub that had been intended as a whirlpool or spa, but was now retrofitted with a shower head and cheap plastic curtains adorned with comical seahorses that made him laugh out loud. He checked the fridge and found four tiny bottles of rum. Intent on keeping his morning buzz going, he opened one, took a glass, and went outside to hunt for an ice machine of some sort. *"I'm gonna have to drink to sleep in that dump,"* he told himself.

Within five minutes, he was slouched in a deck chair in front of his room, cold drink in hand, watching the gulls fight over the remains of some dead creature on the beach. He thought for a minute that it'd be good if Baxter were there too, then realized that there'd be no peace if he were, and laughed at the thought.

"You're quite amused at something, Simms!" It was Trinity, and her voice startled him. "Want to share? I could use a laugh right now... my room is sandwiched between one that's just been painted, and one that's being remodeled. The fumes and noise are awful. They're going to find me another."

"Well, why not sit here and have a drink with me, and chill until it's all settled? You have your choice of rum with ice, or ice with rum..."

She laughed, "Perfect. Surprise me!" Right then, Simms' ambivalence about Baxter being on the trip returned, but there was no sense in fretting now. She was easy to be around, certainly pretty enough to look at, and would almost certainly prove to be an asset. But no sooner had those thoughts crossed his mind, than he felt a pang of guilt. *"Have I become that cynical?"* he wondered.

Down to the last of the mini bottles, Stevenson had forgotten about his guilt, and now worried about other things. "Hey, do you still have access to your old room?" he asked Trinity.

"Yeah, my stuff is in there... why?"

"We're gonna be out of rum in about five minutes..."

"Bummer... there wasn't anything in my room, not even a fridge."

"Well, let's go look for a bar. This so-called paradise must have at least one of those. We'll charge it to the Band."

"What about rehearsal?" she challenged. "I don't want to be snockered when we do this..."

Simms laughed, "You're right, of course. The rum would only make me *think* I was playing okay... but I guess that two drinks are enough for that." They sipped at the melting ice for a bit, then Simms asked, "So, does your sister know you're here?"

"Nope. I was gonna surprise her."

"Well, how will you find her? This joint is massively huge."

"I don't have a plan. I was hoping she'd come to the performance tonight, but I hear there's another band playing at the other end of the resort..."

"Same time as our gig?"

"Yeah, Jimmy said nine o'clock..."

We could leave a message at the desk... what's Joe's last name?"

"I don't have a clue."

In spite of his maneuvering, Simms still hadn't found out what he wanted to know. He ruminated on the lack of information for a minute or so, then said, "Well, we'll be here for a couple of days, so you'll figure something out. Let me know if I can help. For now, let's go see about your room change, and then we better head to rehearsal.

Chapter 8
Paradise Unfolded

The sun had dropped behind the looming hotel monolith by the time Danny and the Dirtfish and friends finished with rehearsal and, as they trickled out of the ballroom into the humid shadows, Simms realized that his fingers hurt and his rum buzz was gone. Still, there were a few hours of daylight left on the other side of the buildings, and several hours before their first performance. "Are you hungry... or thirsty?" he asked Trini. "I'm going to explore this playground a little bit."

"Thanks, but I'm tired, and I need to get moved into my room... Raincheck?"

"Sure, no worries. See ya around." Once free of any social commitments, and somewhat relieved to have time to himself, Stevenson set off at a brisk pace along the flagstone walkways. It was a path that quickly took him out of the construction and remodeling zone, and into the main part of the resort. Following the colorful signs on the palm trees that promised food and drink, he passed a maze of swimming pools and saltwater lagoons—all the while, gawking at the luxuries like a tourist. Finding an open-air bar with small tables and umbrellas, he sat at the only vacant spot on the edge of the patio. The small, round Bahamian waiter looked at Stevenson suspiciously until he saw the room key on the table, changed his attitude, and took Simms' order for two shrimp cocktails. The waiter asked what he wanted to drink, and Simms pointed at a tall umbrella drink he spied at a nearby table. Expecting that Simms was waiting for another person, the waiter asked, "And your friend...?"

Simms smiled, "She's sleeping... maybe later." The waiter flashed a toothy grin as if he understood, and hurried away. Now, out of habit, Stevenson's attention shifted to the clientele, and he surveyed the patrons one by one. He knew it would be a long shot if Valeria happened to be at this particular bar at that particular moment, but at least, he could process those who sat in front of him. He'd only seen one photo of her, and that image was now blurred by his time with her sister, Trinity, so he was looking for some imagined hybrid. And, of course, she would likely be with a companion that resembled the photo of Giuseppe that was tacked to a board in his office.

It didn't take long to realize that everybody in the bar was far too sunburned to have been either of his targets, and so he focused on the shrimp and rum drink placed in front of him by the now curious Bahamian waiter. Neither the waiter, nor the shrimp, nor the rum drink, lasted long in his presence, as he dismissed the waiter with an absent-minded nod and wasted little time with the rest of it.

Stevenson craved another rum, but the lure of more undiscovered attractions beckoned him deeper into the resort's labyrinth. Meandering along the walkways, he wondered if it was possible for a man to drink himself from one side of the resort to the other, and then find his way back home. The image of a sweet rum drink hangover and a foreign commode, though, pushed the juvenile notion from his brain. Once on the marina side of the resort, he found a pizza joint and thought, *"What the hell? I didn't think I liked Italian food until last week."* He ordered a soft drink and a pizza slice the size of a magazine, then found a bench under a palm tree, where he managed to eat the pizza without smearing it all over his face.

Feeling satiated, he leaned against the back of the bench and slurped at his soda, watching the tourists milling about, going to and from the casino. *"There must be thousands of people here,"* he muttered to himself. *"Why am I obsessing over seeing these two individuals? I know they're alive."* But he knew it was necessary—he had to have his own eyes on Valeria and Giuseppe. That's when he began to reason his way through the problem. Trini had said that "Joey" was wheeling and dealing with an important developer or something. That almost guaranteed that they wouldn't be wandering around the resort with the masses. No, they'd either be in a penthouse suite someplace, or maybe at a high-stakes table in the casino... or in the priciest restaurant for an evening meal. *"Wait, stupid. Trini said that Valeria would be trying to amuse herself while Joe was doing business..."* Dropping the soda cup in a waste bin, Stevenson headed off looking for spas and fancy shops, of which, he was sure, Paradise had many.

Most of the shops were devoid of clientele, a fact that didn't surprise Simms at all, given that it was nearing happy hour in every place on the island, and he was just as happy to not pop in and out of a dozen boutiques and gift shops. Rather, he was content to simply case the layout and stroll around window shopping like a tourist. That's when he bumped into the LaCroix sisters exiting a nail salon.

"Simms..." stammered Trini, "I... uh... oh, this is my sister, Val..." Simms held out his hand, but Valeria held back.

"Sorry, the polish isn't quite hard enough... Trini's told me about you... nice to meet you."

Simms smiled, "Likewise, Trini brags about you some..."

Trinity, having regained her composure, said, "Simms, I didn't mean to blow you off earlier... it's just that I wanted to see my sister this afternoon..."

Simms flashed a sparkling grin and chuckled, "No worries, Trini, you don't owe me any explanation. So... I should keep moving if I'm going to get back to my room before we have to be at the club... so, Ladies, if..."

"Come have a drink with us, Simms—just a quick one. Val says Joey might show up before his dinner meeting, so you can meet him too."

Stevenson cast a quick glance at Valeria, who quickly said, "Right—let's do it. If Joey doesn't show, well, piss on him... I'll come watch you guys perform all by myself..."

Joey didn't show, so Valeria ordered a second round of drinks. Then, as the liquor took hold, she ordered plates of tiny rock lobsters, lobster rolls, and champagne, happily putting everything on Joey's tab. "If he's gonna act like a high roller, then he's gonna act like a high roller," she laughed. Simms smiled, thanked her for Joey's generosity, and accepted a lobster tail from the tray. Now regretting the pizza, he merely nibbled at the delicacies while he bemusedly watched Trinity and Valeria interact. His first impression was that Val was the prettier of the two, but over that hour, he realized that she lacked the sweetness of her sister, and alcohol was not her friend. She had a haughtiness about her that some might find annoying, but a man might put up with it as the price of her beauty if the guy hadn't known better than to make that bargain.

Trinity had stopped at one flute of bubbly, and was now checking her watch every few minutes. Simms knew it was a signal that they should be excusing themselves soon. She broke the scene abruptly, "Excuse me for a sec—gotta find a ladies room— then, Simms, we probably ought to go meet up with Jimmy and the band, right?"

Stevenson nodded, "See you in a minute..."

As soon as her sister was out of earshot, Valeria said, "So, you haven't told her that you're a cop yet, have you?"

Simms looked her straight in the eye and asked, "Why would you ask me a thing like that?"

Valeria snickered, "Because my roommate Scarlett told me that a cop named Simms was poking around, and she described you to a tee. There can't be two guys like you floating about..."

"Well, I'll be damned... I thought that lady was too stoned to even remember that I was there..."

"No, she's sober... has been since the kid came along..."

Simms thought it odd the way she referred to the baby as if it had dropped in like a pigeon looking for sunflower seeds, but caught himself in time to conceal his random musings. "She said you owe her a rent check pretty soon," he quipped.

"So, that's a 'no' on telling Trini..."

Simms nodded, "I guess I'll have to now, though—no sense in trying to shield her."

"Well, that's up to you, Simms, I'm not gonna rat you out— she likes you, though, so unless you're just using her—uuhh, that is, if you get to know her and like her... well, don't fuck it up." Simms was stunned into silence, and Valeria continued, "I've only got a minute or so before she gets back here, but—Joey and me, we had nothing to do with whatever happened at the restaurant, no matter what you think. Scarlett told me about the supposed murder scene and all—listen, we were shacking up in Key West for several days before, and we have dozens of witnesses. Besides, what do you have? Scarlett says that the TV news reported there was no dead body."

Simms looked at Valeria with a poker face, "We have a body connected to the case, along with a lot of crime scene evidence, and we had three missing people connected to the restaurant. I've found one tonight, and if I see your friend Joe, then I'll have a second. But his wife is still missing."

Valeria's face dropped. "Maria? She's missing? Nobody's said anything about that, and Joe spoke with Ricardo yesterday." She took the last gulp from her drink, then said, "It's just like that asshole Ricardo—he was always hitting on me, but Maria wouldn't do anything about it when I complained to her..."

Simms asked, "So, you two weren't close?"

"Me and Maria? Oh hell no! We hated each other. She fired me about twice a month... but, Jesus, everybody despised the woman... except maybe Ricardo—never could tell what he was really thinking. I expected he'd look out for his fellow Cubanos, but, no..."

Simms could see Trinity making her way back to the table, and as he stood up, said, "Well, somebody needs to tell Joe about his wife—I'll do it if you want. Look, I have no jurisdiction down here, so all I can do is investigate and stir the pot a little. But if you two have an alibi, then great—I can only ask questions. Meanwhile, Trini and I have an engagement this evening... then I'll have a heart-to-heart chat with her."

Trinity reached the table in time to stop any retort from Valeria, offered her hand to Simms, and said, "Let's get going, Simms. Thanks for the drinks, Val... tell Joey we missed him."

As they exited the lounge, Trinity hooked her arm into Simms' and laid her other hand on top of his, as if they were marching off to prom night. She began chattering on almost immediately, mostly about 'Joey', scarcely giving Simms a chance to get a word in. Finally, he said, "You seem to think highly of your sister's boyfriend... you must have spent a lot of time with the two of them..."

"Yeah, you know, they were in Key West for more than a week before they came over here to the island, and so I got a chance to see them together a lot."

"When did they leave to come over here?"

"Oh, let's see... it was the day before you and the band got here... I was disappointed that they couldn't stay for my little performance with Jimmy and the boys... actually, it kind of pissed me off..."

"Because?"

"Well, they knew Jimmy was coming down to the Keys and I was supposed to sing a number with the band again... but, no, Joey had to get to Nassau..."

"Bummer... well, business is business, I guess. Was that the first time you'd been around the two of them for that long? I mean, you seem to think that they're pretty serious and all..."

"Yeah, I guess I do think that... well, he's a bit of a control freak, but not as bad as some guys... So, they came down to Key West a couple of months ago for a weekend, and seemed to get along pretty well. But he was more in charge this time... or something... I dunno... we went out every night and he was fun... but he always called the shots on where we went..."

Satisfied for the moment that Valeria's alibi seemed credible, Simms changed the subject. "Trini, I'm going to go get cleaned up before we have to meet up with Jimmy and company... can I meet you there about eight? Or come by your room and walk you over? We should make sure we can stake out a table..."

"Yeah, come by and get me, okay? Room eleven thirty-one. You're good for calming my nerves."

Simms and Trinity arrived at the venue and helped the Dirtfish set up the stage for both performances, then settled at a table to the far right of the stage before the clientele began to trickle into the bar. It was a small venue, and Jimmy wanted to make sure that the volume of their amps wasn't going to chase the drinking customers out of the place.

Jimmy opened the first set with a solo guitar ballad, then introduced the main band for the second number, and they were off and running. They'd rehearsed with Trinity and Simms being up in separate numbers, and then again, together for the final song, leaving the two amateurs to squirm in anticipation during the interim.

Trinity kept up a nervous line of chatter before the finale of the set, occasionally looking around for her sister and boyfriend and trying to hide her growing disappointment at their absence. Stevenson patted her arm, "You need to forget about who is and isn't here—right now. Sing to me when you're up there, sing to me like you mean it. Okay? Then you'll be great, no matter what. This is Paradise, Girl! Yeah?" Trinity blushed and let his voice persuade her to change focus from what was *not*, to what *was* happening. She gave Simms a little kiss on the cheek as she stood up with Jimmy's introduction, "Now, from Key West, our own Miss Danni..."

Trinity finished her numbers, and breathed in relief as she stepped from the stage amidst polite applause. Silently, she mouthed, "Thank you," to Simms as he walked past her to take the stage. Confident then that the rest of the set would go as smooth as silk, she scarcely acknowledged that Val and Joe had arrived along with another couple during her performance. Instead, she made sure that Simms could see her singing along with the band while he played his little part in the show. Nothing else mattered just then, and she was primed for the finale when the time came. "*Nerves be damned*," she told herself when it was time to step up to the mic again.

They had little more than a half hour before the second set, but Valeria wasted no time introducing Joe and Stevenson to each other, "Joey, this is Trini's friend, Simms..."

Joe held out his hand, looked Stevenson straight in the eyes, and said, "I've heard a lot about you already... I'm pleased to meet you."

Simms returned the greeting, "And I've heard quite a bit about you—I feel like I've known you for some time." Joe chuckled, and introduced the other couple as Zev Harmon and his wife, Anya. The six of them sat back down and Joe began ordering cocktails, but against all instincts to the contrary, Simms declined a drink, "Maybe after the next set... I need to keep my feeble wits about me before I go back up there." Trini had just taken a sip of wine, thought better of it after Stevenson's comment, and pushed the glass a little way out of convenient reach.

The Harmons made little effort at socializing; in fact, Zev kept checking his watch every few minutes. Simms noticed it right away, but couldn't figure out if it was a nervous tic, or if the man was in a hurry to go somewhere. He had his answer sooner than expected when Zev tossed down the remainder of his drink and made an excuse about an early meeting the next day, then all but pulled Anya up from her chair by her arm.

In the awkward few minutes after that, Joe seemed to lose his animated demeanor. Trinity broke the silence, "Well, they seemed nice..."

Joe laughed, "Anya is just shy... she doesn't speak English very well, and Zev said she's already had enough to drink... so it's probably best that they left. And we do have a business meeting tomorrow—early, like he said." That seemed to smooth things over for a bit, but Trinity was fidgety. After a few minutes, she excused herself for the ladies' room, knowing that she'd never make it through the next set otherwise, and Valeria followed her into the darkness.

Simms waited until the sisters were out of sight, then asked, "What has Val told you about me?"

"Just that you're a detective... and look, I already spoke with my head chef, Ricardo... so I know that there's not much of anything that really happened in my restaurant... right?"

Simms looked grim, "Joe, your wife is missing... or at least she was still missing when I last spoke with my partner—in fact, until today, we considered that you were missing as well..."

Joe looked at Simms with a blank expression, then stammered "Missing? Maria can't be missing... Ricardo would have said something."

"He didn't tell you?"

Joe only shook his head, but in a few moments, he said, "He only said that the investigation turned up nothing, and the entire thing was probably a hoax..."

"Well, I had that same idea fluttering in and out of my mind too—until our star witness turned up dead over in the hammocks—in that marsh by your restaurant. And I don't believe in coincidences in a homicide investigation... plus we do have quite a bit of evidence from the restaurant kitchen."

Joe started to say something, thought better of it, and then smiled thinly as the women came back to the table. They made small talk for a few minutes, but just about the time that the Dirtfish went back on stage, Joe made excuses about his next-day meeting with Zev Harmon and associates, and abruptly left with Valeria.

Trinity was speechless for a minute or two, vacillating somewhere between confusion and anger, then said, "That's pretty fucking rude."

"Trini, I think he has a lot on his mind, but you need to push the last few minutes out of your head and get ready for our numbers... you did a great job last time—and I love the way you can sing to a person in the audience and make them believe it's just for them... c'mon, then."

Trinity took two gulps of her wine, and mumbled, "Okay... here goes."

Trinity was all smiles after the finale, and Stevenson was amazed that she'd been on key the entire way. Maybe it was just more experience, but she seemed to have found a way to compartmentalize extraneous emotions and focus on the music. When they got back to the table, she said, "I can't wait for tomorrow night... I just want to keep on singing..."

Simms let her bask in the glow, as patrons came by the table to compliment her and chat about whatever favorite songs they had... "Can you sing...?" "Do you know...?" Trini took it all in, like Cinderella at the ball. Finally, when all the fans had moved on and surrounded The Dirtfish for autographs, their corner was quiet. Simms struggled with what he must do next.

"That was all pretty cool, Lady. You were very professional—keeping your composure and all... Do you remember when I said that Joe had a lot on his mind when he and Val left?"

Trinity's face changed complexion one more time, "Yeah... how bad could it be that he just gets up and leaves?"

"Well, his wife is missing."

Now her expression was one of sheer confusion, "Wife? What wife? Val said he was divorced a long time ago."

"No, he's not, and she knows it..."

"Wait! What are you saying...? And how do you know all of this? We only left the two of you alone for five minutes..."

"Trinity, I didn't tell you the entire truth about myself... about what I do. I'm a homicide detective from the Treasure Coast..."

"Bullshit! You're lying..."

"Nope, it's true... there's been a murder in Joe's restaurant, and..."

"And so you used me to get to him... to Val? That's messed up."

"No, I didn't... this was all... this music gig was all out of the blue... I..."

"Oh stop! Asshole..." and with that, she got up and left.

"Lovers quarrel?" Simms looked to his side to see Jimmy Daniels reaching for a chair.

"Not exactly, it never got that far, and never will..."

"Well, don't give up so easily, my new friend... passion like she has, well, it has two sides. And they are at war with each other at the moment. So, likely, whatever you did doesn't match her response..."

Simms laughed, "I'm not so sure... but she's kind of stuck until your plane takes her back to the Keys, so she can't get too far away tonight."

"Did all of that have anything to do with the two men at your table during the break?"

"Yeah, probably... you know them?"

"Well, I've seen the one guy with Trini's sister—that *is* Trini's sister, right? He's been around Key West a couple of times with her... Joe's his name. The other guy, I know *of* him—Zevon Harmon—he's a big wheel around here... in fact, he's a big wheel just about any place there's a casino."

"How...?"

"We play at a lot of casinos... Atlantic City, Connecticut, here in Nassau, San Juan... this guy Harmon gets around. Lots of stories around, too. He has ties to South Africa—you know, the owner of this place is South African, right? Got his tit in a wringer for graft and so forth with some African chieftain... well, Harmon is the one who helped him get out of that predicament, and he helped smooth things over with the Bahamians too... And Harmon is the guy who helped clean up the mob's image in Jersey for that real estate mogul from New York when he did Atlantic City..."

"So, Zev Harmon is a fixer... is he a crook?"

Jimmy laughed, "He hasn't been caught at it yet if he is. But if his wife catches him with that Russian model one more time, he'll wish the FBI had him instead..."

"So that—Anya—wasn't his wife?"

Jimmy laughed again, "Hell no! Anyway, that's fast company you're keeping."

Simms shook his head, "Nope, not me. A man has to know his own limitations... singing with Danny and the Dirtfish is about as far out of my lane as I want to get."

Chapter 9
Lunch with Davo and Minerva

"Hey, Gino... it's me, Simms..."

"Hi, Partner, tell me you've got something interesting going on—or at least tell me it's a good vacation..."

Stevenson chuckled into the receiver of the pay phone, "It's going well, I think, but I can't go into much detail over the phone... I should be back home in a few days, and I'll explain. But... I was wondering about a couple of things. First, do we have any updates from the family members over in Manatee Wells? I can say that two of our missing persons are no longer missing... I've spoken with both Giuseppe and the missing waitress, Valeria... but what about Giuseppe's wife? Any leads?"

"Well, maybe... I'm taking Giuseppe's elderly auntie Minerva to lunch day after tomorrow, so I'm getting a little closer. These old clannish people don't trust anybody who they haven't sat down to have a meal with. But, there's definitely something not quite right in that town, and I hope to get a lead of some kind. What else do you have, then?"

"So, look," answered Simms, "first thing is that Giuseppe and Valeria have solid alibis and witnesses who say they've been in Key West during this entire case... so, if Maria is missing, well, something else is going on. Second thing... I was thinking about old Rodney... is that investigation still a dead end?"

"Yeah, so... the itinerants never returned to their camp down in the hammocks, so that's a bust—for now, anyway. I mean, there's a lot of vagrants scattered along the coast, but who's gonna admit they were at a murder scene if we just start randomly questioning them?"

"What about that homeless kid?"

"Davo? I don't know... I expect he's run away from the shelter by now."

"Where would he go?"

"I see your point. I'll try to track him down, and buy him a hamburger again. Maybe he'll have some insight. He didn't have much to say the last time I spoke to him."

To Macina's surprise, Davo was still at the Third United Baptist Church Wayfarer Shelter, and the boy thought that another burger sounded just great. Instinctively, Gino knew it would be tricky getting any more information from a street-smart kid. However, the fact that the boy hadn't run away from the shelter suggested that perhaps he'd be reasonable over lunch, even if it was in the presence of a cop. It wasn't until a brief negotiation over a second milkshake that Gino encountered the challenge.

"How about another milkshake, Davo?"

Davo looked up from the disappointment resting at the bottom of his empty shake glass, smiled, and said, "Okay, Detetive, but maybe ask us what ya want from us fuhst. Maybe ya'll won't be happy if'n Davo don't wanna answer..."

Macina had already made up his mind on this account, and as he gestured to the waitress for another shake, he said, "No strings,

Davo... you get the shake either way. I'm just glad that you decided to stay at the shelter, and that you're safe... and I'm happy that you're getting regular meals. I was worried, though, that you might've run back over to the hammocks..."

Davo was stubbornly quiet for a few heartbeats, and slurped on the last dregs in the straw. Finally, he answered, "You said that already..."

"Yeah, I know," said Gino. "I just really want *you* to know that I'm trying to look out for you. I was thinking I might be able to help you find your people, and I was also hoping to talk to some of the folks from your camp about the Monk. But nobody's returned to the camp... I've been back over every day. Do you know where they might have gone?"

The boy looked confused, and went silent again, searching for some response. The waitress interrupted his thoughts with the second milkshake, and the distraction was enough to bring his guard down. He glanced at the frosty glass as tears welled up in his eyes, "Gone?" he squeaked.

"Well, they haven't come back to the camp, so they have to be somewhere... I mean, there's camps like that all over, but I can't know who was at your camp when old Rodney died. Is there somebody... a person you were close to... that I can look for. Or take a message to? Do you want to go look with me?"

The boy pushed the straw to one side and dipped a spoonful of the thick concoction from the glass, wiped away a tear, and shoved the ice cream into his mouth. Then he shook his head. "No, Suhr. They doesn't care for Davo anyway—they left us whilst we was takin' a crap." He took another spoonful, then pulled the straw from the depths and licked it, plunged it back to the bottom of the shake, and answered in a low voice. "Maybe," and he paused for effect, "maybe they went back to Dago Bay."

"What? Back... Dago Bay...? You mean the whole camp was over at Manatee Wells?"

Davo nodded, "Yeah, mostly. We all had the ol' factory to ourselves for a yeahr... ya know, where dem folks cut up sharks and such in the old days?"

"Yes, I know the place, but nobody ever goes out there anymore, though. It's a swamp."

"Yes, Suhr, some's say it haunted too, but Davo ain't never seen no haint over theah. Fishin' was pretty good, though, all around the mangroves. But dey made us leave."

"Who was 'they', Davo? Who made you leave?"

"Dunno... dey brung a bus and loaded us and all our crap on it, and dumped us down at the hammocks where ya found Davo... Said if we didn't go, the cops'd come an' take us. So we took da bus."

"That's it? What did your people say about all of this... this move, it must have been a big deal? Any rumors, or... anything."

"No, Detetive, 'ceptin' we heard they's gonna knock da place down and build somethin' else." Davo tried slurping through his straw again, and after a little success with the melting ice cream, he added, "Davo don't think dey really gone back to Dago Bay."

"Why? Because of the construction?"

"Nah. Theahr's a White Witch ovah theah. She's da one... she made us leave, wit all dat white voodoo shit of hers. And dat old man with her. Scared most of our folks nearly white."

After patiently waiting for Davo to finish his second dessert, Macina deposited young Davo back at the shelter, and got a business-like handshake from a grateful boy with a full tummy. Gino couldn't resist giving the kid a little squeeze on the shoulder to seal the handshake. It was almost a hug, but not quite, and when Gino promised to take him to lunch again in a few days—but only if he promised to stay at the shelter—Davo returned the gesture and agreed to the proposition. There was something about the kid that brought out a big brother instinct in Macina, and he briefly mulled it over on the way back to his car.

Macina's next task was a drive over to the oak hammocks to see if any of the camp dwellers had returned, but all he found was a quiet, buggy swamp. The yellow crime scene tape had all but blown away in tatters, and so he scavenged the remainder and left the site devoid of any ongoing police activity. *"Maybe this has been keeping them away,"* he told himself as he put the trash into the trunk of his Dodge. As he drove away, his thoughts turned to his next lunch date the following day, and his still vivid conversation with Davo about the mysterious 'White Witch' of Dago Bay. He anticipated an awkward date with old Aunt Minerva, and was pretty sure that a milkshake was not going to be the key to unlock her tongue.

Minerva had surprised him by accepting the lunch invitation in the first place, now nearly a week ago. And contrary to Macina's expectations, she wanted to go to a French café, Le Bistro, down A1A outside the city limits of Manatee Wells. During their first encounter, he'd made small talk with the old woman, but then, it was clear she wasn't going to volunteer any useful information right on the spot. In spite of her recalcitrance, Gino sensed that she had a story to tell, and now he knew he'd have to muster all the charm that he'd once needed to navigate life with his own Italian *nonna*.

On the drive to Manatee Wells, as he rehearsed his game plan with the aging aunt, Gino's avoidance instincts abruptly hijacked his focus. Inexplicably, he began to worry about the condition of his car, the rattletrap Dodge Stratus. He'd already cleaned out all of the fast-food wrappers before driving Simms to the seaplane base the previous week, but it was still a pathetic excuse for a detective's car. "*Could they at least have given me one of the Intrepids?*" he whined to himself at the time. No, he'd gotten the departmental lemon—the Stratus, and it was a laughingstock. Already the victim of two blown head gaskets, the puny engine could barely accelerate to 60 on the Interstate unless he drafted a speeding semi. Would old Aunt Minerva judge him based on this pitiful car, and shine him on? It was too late to worry about it now—he'd already taken it to the car wash and had the inside detailed too. That was that, he could do no more. He'd just have to be charming.

The old lady was sitting on her stoop in a rocking chair when Gino idled to a stop at her curb. She wore a flowered dress that came to her ankles when she stood up, and a floppy bonnet of some sort that threatened her vision as she navigated the steps. Gino ambled up the walkway as she negotiated the stairs, and noticed that her hair looked a little less gray than it had the week before. She'd applied a little more makeup too, making her look even more cadaverous. He offered his arm and a smile, "That's a pretty dress, Miss Minerva." Minerva smiled coyly and chattered amiably on the stroll to the car, knowing that the neighbors up and down the block were snooping from behind closed curtains.

Once underway, Minerva was not bashful about giving Gino directions to the café, "Turn here, then left at that boat shop... it's the fastest way out to A-1-A... watch out for the kids, they're like black ants in this neighborhood..." And on and on she went until they arrived at Le Bistro.

Once seated with menus in front of them, Gino said, "Thank you for agreeing to do this."

"You seemed like a nice boy," she said, her voice trailing off.

"You mean for a cop?" he asked wryly. Her mouth turned upwards just a tic as her eyes answered his question. He laughed, "But I have to say that I'm surprised that you picked a French café instead of an old country Italian restaurant. Won't that be a bit scandalous in the village? Won't people talk?"

Minerva sipped from her water glass, and then deflected his question, "I like the French onion soup, and I appreciate a slice of quiche once in a while. Is it okay of we have some wine, too? You won't get in trouble...?"

"That'd be just fine, Miss Minerva... you just choose the wine you like."

She smiled and looked at the wine list, then picked up the conversation again, "I don't get out very much anymore... and as for the gossip, well, there's already plenty of that going around because of the things you've been asking about."

"I'm sorry, I didn't mean to stir up trouble for you, and you know, I'm out of my jurisdiction, so you don't really have to answer for anything. As I've explained, the County Sheriff has no concerns about anything here, and they're just letting us ask questions around the village as a courtesy..."

"No, Detective, you misunderstand me. I'm not blaming you for the gossip. It has to do with Joey and Maria being missing. Everybody in the village knows about it, and I'm the only one in my family that can help clear things up—if they can be cleared up. You see? And I didn't want to have you parked in front of our home for a couple of hours while we talk."

Macina suddenly realized that this was a business lunch, part of a transactional relationship—one that must either have mutual benefits, or none at all. Aunt Minerva was not some doddering, shrinking violet, old world dowager, and he'd misread the situation entirely. His game plan and rehearsal were now essentially useless, except for that part which had motivated him to polish his manners.

He sipped the light wine she had selected, passed a bread basket to her side, and fussed with a slice he'd never eat. Finally, he worked out an angle. "You know," he began, "it's my chief— Captain Whitehead—he thinks that there's been foul play at Giuseppe's restaurant, and with both Giuseppe— Joe—and Maria missing, he's got me looking into their whereabouts."

Aunt Minerva sat, spoon poised in one hand and bread crust held delicately in the other, waiting for Macina to spin his web. She tasted another bite, then another. At last, she dipped the bread in her soup and said, "Detective, ask me again what you wanted to ask me. You know... you started to last week."

"Okay, when was the last time you saw your nephew Joe?"

She smiled, "Same answer as last week, except now, it's been two weeks ago."

Gino had a moment of doubt, *"maybe it is the goddamn car..."* But his good sense caught up with him. "Right, you know, I didn't take notes last time we spoke... do you mind if I do now, 'cuz my memory can get hazy later on." She nodded and gestured as if to tell him to carry on. "As I recall, what I didn't ask was where you saw him and what the circumstances were."

Minerva chuckled, "Now we're on the right track... can I call you Gino?"

Macina smiled and agreed, and so she continued. "Joe came by the house to get some of his stuff. He'd been spending a lot of nights out—you know, elsewhere—for a couple of weeks, and he only came to the house when he knew Maria wasn't home..."

"So... this... was it a separation... was it by mutual agreement between them?"

"No, he was shacking up with his Haitian whore."

Macina's face flushed red as he bent over his notepad, stalling for time to process the information. "Her name, you have a name for me?"

"I don't know, nor do I care."

"So, I'm guessing that this is partly at the root of the town gossip, then."

"It is. A big part, anyway..."

Macina was aware that Minerva was playing a game with him, and he silently cursed daytime TV reruns. "When was the last time you saw Maria, then? And where?"

"The Friday morning before you came knocking at my door, she left the house and was on her way to work at the salon."

"Do you know where either of them is now, or have you spoken to either one?"

Minerva smiled and sipped her wine. "Not specifically... Joe left word that he was visiting his sick sister on Miami—but we all know that's a bunch of bird poo. I personally think that Maria is in hiding somewhere, but to answer your last question, I've not spoken to either one since I last saw them."

"Have you heard rumors or gossip about any of this that might be revealing?"

Minerva's face wrinkled into a scowl, and Gino realized that it wasn't caked-on makeup that gave her the ghostly appearance... it was something with her skin, likely a chemical peel gone awry. He blocked the distraction and answered his own question, "That's the other part of the town gossip, then—the part that you think is all wrong and an embarrassment to the family?"

Minerva took a bite of quiche, propped herself on an elbow, and idly pointed the fork at Macina, "Now you get it, Gino. They've got the case solved, right—the town gossips and tree-stump lawyering? The husband runs off with his whore, murders his wife, has an alibi... the perfect crime."

"But you don't think so?"

"No! That's too simple. He wouldn't murder Maria, and he wouldn't just leave all his fortune behind, either. It's merely a story for the tabloids and the jury, you see. But it's stupid. Look, Joe is a dog... he *is* my blood, but he's a hound. You need to understand, though, that Maria is impossible... she's another kind of dog, if you understand my meaning here. But Italians don't get divorced, see? They just take lovers."

Macina interrupted, "Did Maria have a lover?"

Minerva didn't miss a beat, "Probably, but I can't imagine what kind of man could put up with a mistress with such a sharp tongue. But, that's not for me to judge. I'd bet she had a man, though... I'd even lay odds."

"And if we had a clue about that man...her lover, we might know where she was hiding out?"

"Exactly, Gino, and that's what you need to solve for me... infidelity would be a better basis for gossip than murder, don't you think?"

Gino couldn't disagree, but he also knew she'd led him right down the proverbial daisy path. Minerva's fairy tale was no better than the town's version, and he knew they had a murder scene at the restaurant—not to mention a dead witness—or alleged witness. And there was the problem of trying to find a reason for Maria to go into hiding unless her life was in danger. But he also knew that he'd get farther down the road with Minerva if he seemed to accept her story. "Miss Minerva, I don't suppose you've looked about the house to see if there were any clues as to who Maria might have been involved with... or where she might have gone to stay out of sight?"

Minerva stopped with a fork full of quiche half way to her mouth, and blushed just a little, then stuttered, "I... I haven't found anything... yet. Do you want me to keep looking?"

Macina thought about it for a split second, then answered, "Well, only discreetly, Miss Minerva. I mean, first of all, if by some miracle Joe and Maria reunite, you don't want it to be an issue that you violated their privacy—no matter how noble your intentions.

Right?" She nodded in appreciation for the delicate position he'd found her in. Gino added, "Second of all, it'd be best if nobody else knows that we're working on an alternate theory, you and me... yeah? Do you agree?"

Minerva said, "Exactly," and poured more wine.

"Good," said Gino. "How about we try lunch again in a week, and I'll fill you in on what I've learned. Meanwhile, if you find a lead, please call me right away—don't wait for our luncheon date."

Minerva raised her glass as if in a toast to their partnership, and Macina clinked her glass gently. He put his notebook back in his jacket pocket and sipped at his wine while she chattered about the food. After the waiter disappeared with his credit card, Gino asked, "By the way, what do you know about the homeless camp over at that old shark factory on the bay? We have a case with a dead hobo that somebody said used to hang out over there. We're looking to see if he might have had any family somewhere."

Minerva thought a moment, then said, "No, I think they cleaned that place out many months ago. From what I've heard, there's nobody left over there."

"Somebody...? What do you mean, 'cleaned them out'?"

"Oh, I don't know who... brought in a bus and moved them all down the coast. People here were afraid... rumors of a graveyard, that there was a bunch of voodoo spells and other mumbo jumbo causing problems in the village."

Macina laughed, "There must be a lot of that going around—superstition, suspicion... what not. So everybody feels safer around here now?"

"Well, we hope the Haitians don't feel *too* comfortable, Gino. You do see the problems, right?"

Gino wasn't sure that he did see what her point was, so he acted obtuse, "Well, these folks do complain of the 'White Witch' or some nonsense... but we can't say that such a story has anything to do with our dead hobo case..."

Minerva finished her wine, and said, "Oh, they *should* be concerned, Gino. Very concerned, especially if they think their voodoo spells can help them out. But don't worry... there's no real harm being done to anybody. Like you said, it's all superstition."

The wine had loosened Minerva's tongue quite a bit, and on the drive back to her house, confident that she had a partnership with Macina, she prattled on about random town gossip. Gino escorted her up the steps of the old house, and as he was saying goodbye, he asked offhandedly, "Miss Minerva, I was thinking about a place to begin looking for Joe and his... mistress... and I'm was curious about something. You said she was his Haitian whore... but if you don't know her name, what makes you say she's Haitian?"

Minerva waved her hand dismissively, "Oh, you know, Bingo-Bongo... Rasta Fazoul... Melanzana... you know, the coloreds... Haitian, Cuban, Jamaican... who knows what? She went on at some length about the 'coloreds', finishing off with, "You'll figure it out, Gino."

Gino worked on trying to figure out the new puzzle that was old Aunt Minerva, all the way back to the station, but all he could be sure of was that it was a good thing Whitehead had sent him to Manatee Wells instead of Stevenson Simms. He knew from experience that his own family elders and their friends were hidebound in their beliefs, but he'd never heard from them anything approaching the level of malevolent bigotry so casually uttered by Minerva as if he himself were on the same wavelength as she.

Chapter 10
Old Kill Devil

After Simms finished talking with Macina, he went in search of an early morning breakfast in paradise. Finding a poolside table, a willing waiter, and a perfectly quiet place to sort through the previous 24 hours, he settled in. There were hundreds of details, dozens of threads—they all swam in a soup and Trinity seemed to be stirring the pot. He hadn't used her. Or had he? No, he'd only tried being a friend, and consciously went out of his way to avoid appearing like a predator—even when she seemed to be flirting a little. He was comfortable with that. Now she was angry. "*Rightfully?*" he wondered. "*Probably. Be that as it may, Simms, you've made contact with Valeria and Giuseppe himself, and Trini corroborated their alibi for the night of the murder without even knowing it. So, unwittingly, she's helped her sister's cause— at least in terms of the murder investigation, so it's gotta be an even trade, Simms. If you'd come clean with Trini any earlier, her story couldn't be trusted.*" And so, he kept arguing with himself.

The waiter came with more coffee and a plate of eggs and fried lobster, which, for the moment, saved Simms from more turmoil. Distracted, he pushed the red beans away from his eggs, and methodically cut one bite at a time of lobster and egg with his fork. The food diversion didn't last longer than a few bites. "*Then there's*

Joey, Giuseppe himself, so confident that all is running smoothly back home. But Chef Ricardo hadn't told him that his wife was missing... or was Joe pretending? Or outright lying? if so, it was a good act," Simms mused. He finished one egg and half of the lobster chunks, then lined up a few beans on his plate, side by side. Absent mindedly, he mixed the line of sorted beans with some of the egg, and began to reason some more, *"Maybe Ricardo wasn't aware that the cops considered Maria a missing person. Otherwise, why not tell Joe? Maybe Ricardo figured his boss didn't give a shit... or? Or what? Put that wild ass speculation in the file reserved for such stuff. Maybe Macina will turn up some clues in a couple of days... Rodney the old hobo held a clue, but he's dead too... Too? You writing off the wife, Simms?"* Simms knew if only they could grasp the thread Rodney held, it'd lead them to the answer.

The waiter returned with a fresh carafe of coffee, but Simms ordered a bloody Mary instead. Two little boys arrived at the pool and began creating a ruckus that made him laugh. *"Who brings their yard apes to a casino in the Bahamas... who's that stinkin' rich?"* he wondered. As he sipped his bloody Mary and the boys' antics became assimilated into the background noise, Stevenson started processing information again. Jimmy had kidded him about being out of his league last night—hob-knobbing with the likes of Zevon Harmon and his Russian model girlfriend. But from Simms' perspective, it was Joe who seemed out of his league, *"He's just a local bigshot in Manatee Wells... what connections could he possibly have that would bump him up to first class on this particular cruise? Taking Valeria as a mistress... well, that seems about par for a local entrepreneur... shag the help—if you can get away with it. But this? Running away to the islands and risking his little empire on the Treasure Coast for a fling in the Bahamas?"* Simms couldn't sort it—to him, it seemed unnecessarily risky. "*Unless... Maria holds the answer,"* he concluded. "*We need to get the lab work back from the crime scene evidence, and*

Macina needs to turn up something useful with the old aunt in Manatee Wells."

Trinity kicked at a seashell and looked at the swirl from the rip current created by the tidal refraction in the little bay. Farther down the beach, a lifeguard was setting up for a day of watching the tourists and preparing to shoo the adventurous ones away from the rips. Trinity could read the ocean, and she could read the lifeguard's intentions, but she couldn't read her own mind. Maddening. "*And where has Val gone? Valeria and Joe checked out quite early—at least according to the desk clerk—but the little twerp wouldn't say more.*" Then, there was Simms. "*You can really pick 'em, Lady,*" said a voice in her left ear. But in her right ear, all she heard was, "*He's okay—you just over-reacted— really— look, where's your sister gone, anyway... She's the one...*"

Trinity nodded at the lifeguard and laughed a little. It was obvious that he was hung over, and it was going to be a long day in the sun for him. The nagging voice again, "*A young Belafonte? That's a laugh. He's probably married with seven kids. You live in a fantasy world, Woman. What are you doing all the way out here in the islands, two-hundred miles from home and no way to get back? A singing career? That's a laugh.*" The noisy creature on her left shoulder was beginning to be annoying. Another few yards and another conversation started up, from the other side. "*Simms didn't coax you out here. He had nothing to do with it—like he said—it all happened out of the blue. There's no way he could have planned any of this... a ride on a sea plane out to Paradise doesn't come around very often... don't waste it, Girl.*"

Trinity made a left turn up away from the water, and headed for the shops in the interior of the resort, making straight for a gift shop she'd been in the day before. The doors were just opening, and she walked right in before the clerk could turn around. At the back, she found the shelf she was looking for, and began perusing the gift boxes of rum. Spying a brand she'd known since her Cuban grandfather was still able to drink smuggled rum, she pointed at a dark bottle of Kill Devil and said, "Wrap it up please... and these two glasses, as well."

Leaving the shop, she walked like she was going downhill, heading straight for Simms' room. She came fifty yards short, and changed direction to her own room. The left and right voices were battling again, and she didn't want to hear any more of the argument. She changed into a bikini, wrapped a new tropical sarong around her waist, and deliberately walked to the pool, leaving her squabbling alter egos behind.

She let her imagination wander. *What is Val up to with Joey, anyway? Is he in some sort of trouble? Val is no airhead, so what's her motive in lying to me about her boyfriend's marriage? And the wife is missing. That sounds like a lot of trouble.*" She picked up a magazine and thumbed through the photos of the casino, white beaches, the iconic lighthouse—all suggesting an exciting vacation or romantic getaway for lovers. *"Maybe it's just that simple,"* she told herself, and put the magazine down, closed her eyes, and tried to doze off.

It wasn't to be. *"Why should everybody else have all the fun?"* She sat up from the lounge, *"It's just up to me—as always."* She scooped up her belongings and headed for her room, grabbed the gift box, and headed out the door. Five minutes later, she knocked on Simms' door, and when he answered, she said, "Simms, you got any ice?" and held out the wrapped carton.

He looked at Trinity standing in front of him in her skimpy bikini, and tried to stifle his surprise. His bloody Mary buzz was fading, but his instincts weren't strong enough to resist the temptation that seemed to have appeared at his door. "No, but I can get some just around the corner of the building... make yourself comfortable." In the two minutes it took him to fill an ice bucket, she'd arranged chairs in the shade from the morning sun and unwrapped the rum bottle.

"My Grandfather Santiago drank this brand before leaving Havana, and always looked for it on the black market in Miami... until his accident," she said. Simms carefully poured exactly two fingers into each glass and let her put ice in her own drink. Realizing that it was up to him to keep the conversation going, he asked, "What happened?"

"They said he must have had a stroke running for the bus... he couldn't even walk after that, and he couldn't open a bottle or hold a glass very well. He was very unhappy from then on... he couldn't sing any more or play his guitar either. My old auntie tried all kinds of her *Santeria* spells and potions, but nothing worked."

Simms listened to more of the story, but decided against questions that might have bothered him under other circumstances, like, where were the doctors? Was anybody surprised that voodoo didn't work for a stroke victim? Why would anybody leave a rum bottle where the poor old guy could see it?" Instead, he said, "Well, this is pretty nice cane rum... your grandfather had good taste... and I guess you must, too, but drinking rum this early in the day is... well, I hope you're celebrating a special occasion and that this isn't normal..."

Trini laughed a little, "No, I've never had this before... But shit! It's kinda strong... Grandfather would only drink this dark rum from Cuba... he said the white rum was impure like gasoline... and he wouldn't touch Jamaican rum. His prejudices ran deep on many things, but it may have started with rum. And no, I don't drink before the sun goes down unless I'm on vacation... and I've decided that this *is* a vacation... I'm sorry about last night."

Stevenson shook his head, "No, not at all, I get it. What surprised me was that your sister wasn't pissed off at all, and you were... but, look, if what you told me is true, then they are in the clear as far as any suspicions go. I mean, I've got a lot of questions I'd like to ask them, but they're way outside my jurisdiction right now. They might talk to me before we leave the island... but I've still got to get through one more night with the Dirtfish..."

Trinity chuckled again, "Well, good luck on any questions you've got... the hotel said they checked out at dawn this morning..."

Simms interrupted a sip of rum and looked at her, "So, you didn't see them or know they were leaving?"

"Nope... I think I might have mentioned something about Joey being an asshole..."

Simms laughed, "I do recall that charge last night... but as I also recall, it wasn't a term of endearment reserved just for him."

Trinity blushed and held out her glass, "Just a splash, this shit is going straight to my brain... Well, I apologized... and brought this peace offering, okay?"

"Okay, apology accepted," and he clinked her glass in a toast.

"So, Simms, are you married?"

Stevenson looked a little surprised, "Do I act married?"

She surveyed him, "Well, most guys would have hit on me by now, so... well, I didn't think you acted like a cop, either, but you're being kind of evasive now... answering a question with a question, so... how many kids?"

Simms laughed, "It's a long story, but to answer your questions, none, and no. I'm told that I'm not fit to live with, not marry-able by any stretch."

"Is there a short version of the story you'd tell me?"

"I don't think we know each other well enough for me to dump my crap on you... let's just say that there's been a recent, rancorous breakup... but only the latest one in a series of ladies who found it impossible to put up with a cop's weird hours and cynical demeanor..."

Trinity nodded, sipped her drink, and said, "Fair enough, then. I suppose that'll have to satisfy my curiosity for now. I didn't really think you acted like a man with seven kids."

"What? Not haggard enough? Not enough gray hair?"

She looked at him closely, "I don't see any gray hair... ooh, wait." She got up from her chair and bent over him, looking intently at the top of his head. He could smell the tropical scent of her suntan lotion, and one bikinied breast was perilously close to his face. "Nope, just the light." Then she leaned in and kissed him. And kept on kissing until he kissed back. In a breathy voice, she asked, "Is that too forward, too slutty?"

Simms brushed her hair from her cheek, "No, it was nice... I've been wondering what that would be like, if it would even be..."

"But?" she queried.

"But... I might complicate your life in ways you will hate me for later, and... we have rehearsal in twenty minutes."

She kissed him again, then said, "I'll decide how complicated I want my life, thank you very much. But twenty minutes isn't enough for anything, one way or the other. See you at practice." She straightened up, patted his face, turned and walked off with a flair in her step intended to fix his attention on her backside until she was out of sight.

Chapter 11
Last Night's Wine

Trinity scarcely paid attention to Stevenson during rehearsal or, for that matter, even after it was over, but he decided not to take it personally. After all, he'd basically rejected her—at least he knew she saw it that way. For his own peace of mind, though, he felt it necessary to keep her at arm's length. Not only was her sister still a person of interest in his investigation, but he wasn't ready to jump into another woman's bed a week after breaking up with old what's-her-name. "*That felt better*," he thought, acting like he couldn't remember his exe's name. *"But Trini has something about her... something vulnerable but good... maybe down the road...? Don't do something you'll regret later, Simms."* For now, his conscience and common sense were in command, if only by a thin margin.

After rehearsal, he decided to put in a call to Whitehead, but the chief was out of the office, so he just left a message that he'd be back in a couple of days. If the old man wanted information, he could damn well ask Macina. Returning to his room, he glared at the bottle of Kill Devil, put it back in the gift box, and changed into beach attire. *"Might as well enjoy the rest of the afternoon... God knows when I'll get anything close to a vacation again..."*

He took a chair and a towel, then headed for the water. It'd been years since he swam in clear Bahamian waters, and he let the feeling soak into his memory. He sank down through the turquoise until he hit white bottom, and stayed weightless as long as he could hold his breath. Then he repeated it again and again, tumbling underwater like a little boy until up was down and down was up. Surfacing and catching his breath, he swam about fifty yards, only stopping because he was totally winded. Disappointed in himself, he waded ashore to dry off in the sun while contemplating the effects of age on his soul.

He thought he must have dozed off when we was startled by a voice, “Hey, man... you want a little company?” Simms looked up to see Dusty, still dressed like the hippy that he was, blocking out the falling sun.

“Oh, yeah, of course. What’s up, Dusty?”

“Nothin’ much... I scored a little weed off a local, but it’s strong shit, man... I had to walk it off as best I could before tonight...”

“Try goin’ for a swim...”

“No, man, there’s sharks and stuff here... and I ain’t just being paranoid.”

“Okay, well, sit a spell, you’ll be okay. What are the others up to?”

“Oh, probably the same as me... I dunno... Jimmy was meetin’ with the entertainment manager from the resort... somethin’ about playin’ a private party tonight instead of a second set...”

“How, uuhh, well... is that different for the band?”

“Well, other times, it’s been like a backstage event or some shit, and we have to mingle with the guests. But it gets pretty messed up if the partyers are wasted. So, Jimmy’s tryin’ to set some ground rules with management ahead of time.”

“Right, and I know he wants to get up and get back to the Keys early before you guys go down to Provo...”

“Yeah, he was sayin’ something about havin’ to get you and Trini back to Key West... but that it might also make sense for you two to fly commercial, and for us to go straight down from here... it’s like four hundred and some miles from Nassau, and six-somethin' from Key West... so he's sayin' it'll double our flight time."

"I totally get it... let's go find him, and I'll tell him that Trini and I will go back on a commercial flight..."

The party was subdued—by island standards, that is. The revelers were middle-aged couples from middle America on a Kansas church outing— and they all had more money than common sense, with no apparent tolerance for alcohol whatsoever. Sure, there were a couple of loud mouths that fancied themselves the light of creation, but their wives reeled them in before long. Trinity, on the other hand, was in the process of getting skunked.

It all started well enough in the early set. The two amateurs were on key and in tune, and Trini was friendly enough to Simms. The problem sprang from the long interval between the early set and the party. She managed to get through her numbers, even after a couple of extra drinks, but then settled into one glass of wine after another until she was nearly fried. That's when Stevenson decided to intervene discreetly and escort her back to her room. She left without much of a scene, and none of the Kansans noticed. Jimmy laughed and kidded Simms again about the fallout of their 'lovers quarrel', as he persisted in alluding to the previous evening's dustup. Simms laughed it off, thanked his host for a lovely cruise, and helped a wobbly Trini to her room. "Remember, we have an early flight home tomorrow, Trinity—we have to get a ride to the airport, so..."

"Yeah, yeah, I'll be okay..." she kept insisting, all the way to her room. Simms helped her inside, where she flopped on the bed like a rag doll, and he left quietly. Once back in his room, he packed his duffle for a quick morning departure, showered, and lay down in an attempt to sleep.

The effort was short lived. The interruption started with a tapping at his door, barely audible at first, but escalated to a persistent knocking. "Simms... are you still awake? Simms... it's me, Trinity."

Once Simms realized that he wasn't imagining things, he opened the door, and she all but fell into his arms. "I don't feel good, Simms... I think..."

"Come in here," he coaxed, "hit the tub... that-a-girl... one more... catch your breath... get it all out now..." When he thought she was finished barfing, he turned on the shower to wash it all down the drain, and tried to clean up her face with a wash cloth while she seemed to sleep. The cold wet cloth, however, abruptly revived her, and she climbed into the shower, clothes and all."

"Damn it, Simms, that's cold water..."

"I didn't tell you to get in, I thought you were asleep..."

But she didn't wait for an answer. Instead, she started peeling off her wet clothes. Quickly skinned down to her panties, she wobbled and said, "Don't let me fall down, Simms..." Then, in his arms, she muttered, "I'll be okay." He helped her sit down on the edge of the pink tub, wrapped a towel around her as best as he could, then started to dry her hair with another towel. "Do you have a tee shirt I can put on, Simms?"

A few minutes after tucking her in on one side of the king bed, he started thinking about the entire comedic scene. *"Nobody will ever believe any of this, not even Baxter. Where is that fool when I need him?"*

Morning arrived far too early for Trinity LaCroix. Her first realization that something wasn't as it should be was the taste in her mouth and the pounding in her head, both of which hit home simultaneously. She stifled a moan and sat up on the edge of the bed. *"Where the hell... oh shit, don't tell me,"* flashed across her frontal lobe, momentarily overriding the much wider ache in her skull. *"At least I'm dressed... or am I? My underwear, yeah... but certainly not my shirt... gotta pee... slowly now."* Behind her was a sleeping Simms—at least that's who she hoped it was when she first glanced at the rumpled figure on the far side of the bed. By the time she got to the bathroom, the scene was starting to come into focus, with her damp clothes draped over the shower rod and the vague smell of barf coming from the same general direction. She finished her business, donned her still wet clothes, and crept out of Simms' room.

Trinity had heard of the walk of shame before, but never experienced it first-hand. If she was to be spared the embarrassment, she'd have to make it to her room without being seen in the gray dawn light. She found that running was out of the question, but hurried along the flagstone as fast as her body would otherwise allow. Once in the safety of her own room, she hurried into the bathroom, puked one more time, brushed her teeth twice, took three ibuprofen and a very long shower. Now all she had to do was be ready to leave for the airport with Simms by 8AM, and that was going to require lots of hot coffee.

For his part in this comedy, Simms feigned sleep until he was sure that Trinity had left his room and, even then, he remained motionless for a quarter hour. Only the call of nature and an argument amongst a flock of tropical birds outside his window forced him from between the sheets. *"Today,"* he decided, *"will play out as if none of last night ever happened."* But he knew that 'today' would also require an endless supply of black coffee to replace the sleep he'd missed from the night that never was.

Simms and Trini spoke little on the shuttle to the airport, she out of embarrassment, he from common sense. They each stared out the window, taking in the panorama from the bridge connecting the two islands, and passing separate judgements on the town and neighborhoods that marked the route to the airport. He made one attempt to ask how she was feeling, and another to let her know that 'nothing' happened the night before. She simply replied, "Okay," in each case, and sank deeper behind her sunglasses. When they boarded the turboprop plane, it was clear that Jimmy's agent had booked their seats together—a natural thing. But when the flight proved to have only half of the forty seats filled, Trini moved across the aisle to the single-row seat, explaining, "I want to see out the window..." Then she fell asleep.

The take-off woke her a few minutes later, but she drifted off soon thereafter. Only her bladder woke her again, and she maneuvered down the narrow aisle to the restroom, silently swearing at herself all over again. The cramped, noisy restroom didn't invite long visits and, as she muttered, *"Wasn't designed by anybody who ever had a hangover."* When she returned, she sat down next to Simms, and patted him on the arm, "Thank you, Simms." She was quiet for a time, but as the turboprop began its descent, she said, "I haven't been that drunk since my divorce."

Simms absorbed the new information for a few seconds, then asked, "How old were you?"

"Eighteen... it was a short affair..."

"So, not too long ago, then..."

Trinity chuckled, "It seems like an entire lifetime ago, and even that doesn't seem long enough."

"Between hangovers, or marriages?"

Trinity just laughed, but didn't answer the question at first... then she said, "From what I do remember, there wasn't much difference..."

Simms laughed quietly, but let it go. As the plane made its final descent, he said, "I called my friend Baxter, and he'll meet the plane and take you to your place. He has room for me at his fishing lodge... and I have to go back home tomorrow. Duty calls. But, I was wondering..."

"What were you wondering?" she asked suspiciously.

"If you could arrange a meeting with your aunt—tomorrow morning? I'd like to meet her..."

Trinity tried to absorb the request and its possible implications, but she answered reflexively, flatly, "You want to meet Madame LaCroix?"

"Sure, is that okay? I mean, do I need to make an appointment, or can you arrange it, or can we meet for breakfast and then pop in? Or... whatever you think would be proper..."

Trinity, at this point, thought it seemed like a weird request, but it seemed to mean that Simms wasn't just blowing her off and returning home. "Yeah, I guess... I've got your mobile number, and you have mine... let's talk before the sun goes down." As the turboprop touched ground in Key West, her hangover suddenly seemed less important.

Baxter could barely contain himself until they dropped Trinity at her little apartment, and even afterwards, he wanted to know everything at once, so that he learned almost nothing with his shotgun questions. "So, how is the girl? She looked worn out... you must have been hard on her... What happened with the sister— and her boyfriend? Have you heard from Macina? Has he screwed up the case yet?" His questions came rapid-fire, and Simms, knowing Baxter's effusive nature, just let him roll until he ran out of breath.

"She's hung over... and no, I didn't take advantage... the sister and her boyfriend have alibis, and Gino has made more headway than I have... and I need to sleep before I can say any more."

"Okay, Brother, if you wake up in time, you can come into town with us tonight— I've got a group of fishermen who want to see the night life tonight... don't worry, we'll be back home early for the charter tomorrow—they want to fish offshore, so we'll be out early and back to the dock late. You can use the Jeep all day of you want..."

Simms skipped the night out on the town; in fact, he slept until dark, then called Trinity. They made a date for breakfast at a café off Duval Street, and then a 10AM audience with Madam Lacroix. it was obvious that Trinity was still nursing her headache so it was a short call. Afterwards, he made a sandwich from Baxter's well-stocked kitchen, opened a beer, and started on a list of things he wanted to ask Madame LaCroix about voodoo.

"First thing, Simms, if you know what's good for you, you'll do whatever my auntie asks of you," Trinity instructed him after breakfast. "See, you aren't clean—right off, she'll know that—so she'll need to ward off whatever bad spirits might be attached to you..." Simms started to protest, but she held up her hand and admonished him, "Don't... I know what you're about to say, but you can't see 'em." She took his arm, as they were now only a few steps away from Madame LaCroix's house, adding, "Then, she'll want to check you out, see if you're sociable—if she offers you a puff of her cigar, my advice is to take it..."

"Really? She smokes cigars?"

"Only Cubanos, but they're scarce and expensive, so it's a big deal if she shares a puff or two... she likes to keep one going for five or six days if she can... anyway, we'll go from there... she's gonna be suspicious of your intentions at first, so you'd better be able to look her in the eye."

Simms hadn't caught the meaning behind Trini's last warning because he was bracing himself for the interview—just like he did for all police interviews. He merely responded, "I get the picture, so... thanks for the warning... or, advice, rather," which elicited a quiet chuckle from his escort.

Simms followed Trinity up the steps of the little clapboard conch house, turned and looked down from the porch, curiously observing that it felt much larger once they were up just a few feet above flood level. He absent-mindedly scanned the neighborhood, waiting for Trini to knock, but she just opened the front door and walked in, pulling him in by the hand. He smelled the faint odor of something burning... not pleasant, not really unpleasant either. As his eyes adjusted to the light, he absorbed the modest surroundings of the entry. A makeshift foyer had been devised using a maze of folding screens, all adorned with lizards— or dragons— Simms couldn't discern. Trini saw him inspecting the lacquered paper artwork and said, "Auntie calls these her pingfeng geckos... she says they're from Cuba by way of China, but she really got 'em at Sears a hundred years ago..."

Before Simms could answer, he heard a hoarse voice from behind the last fold of the screen, "*Cómo andamo*'? Trini, are you here?"

Trinity answered, "We're fine, *Tía* Sonia, just us... come meet my friend Simms." She led Simms into the hazily-lit room, where he realized that the muted morning light was clouded by a layer of smog born from Madame's cigar, a few random candles, and sticks of pungent incense scattered about the room. There wasn't a lot of décor in the room, not that Simms knew what to expect—maybe a few skulls, or stuffed toads, or dried chicken parts—or something similar, but there was none of that. The most prominent feature was an altar or shrine of some sort that Simms easily envisioned hosting animal sacrifices—or worse. He was just beginning to doubt his own judgement in asking for this interview, when the old woman took his hands and stared intently at him. "*Bienvenidos,*" she said, then turned his hands and looked at his palms. "Please," she said, gesturing that he should keep his palms open. She then produced a bottle from somewhere amongst her layers of clothing, put her cigar on the edge of the table, and sprinkled what he thought surely smelled like rum into his hands. Taking a rag from another fold in her costume, she dried his hands, picked up her cigar, and offered it to him.

"Thank you, Madame LaCroix," came from his lips moments before he puffed three times and handed the stumpy tobacco log back to her. "Real Cubano, yes?" She nodded, handed it to Trinity, who complied with the old lady's ritual, and handed it back.

"Come," said Madame, leading them to a table near a side window of the main room. Without any small talk, the old lady demanded, "You like my Trini,?"

"Certainly, I... "

"Good," she interrupted. "Do you love her?"

This was a critical moment, and Simms knew it, but he couldn't let either of them see him sweat—so he smiled, "Not yet—I've only known her for four days, and..."

"Good. Honest man. Why you want to see me? Trini say it is *importante.*

Simms knew not to answer Madame's question with a question, but he was clueless what Trini had told the old woman about him, or about the case. "I'm not sure what Trini has said about me, but I am..."

"She say you are a police man... yes, yes... so you are here about police man business?" she asked, emphasizing 'policeman' as two words. "Not romance?"

Simms got a cold feeling, but the muted light in the room masked the shadow that came across his face. He glanced at Trinity, only now realizing his mistake as her eyes told it all. But there was no turning back... honesty had to be the best policy all the way now.

He looked Madame in the eye and answered, "One day, perhaps I will come back with a different purpose in my heart, but just today, this moment, I have important questions that are about my job. If I seem to have come here under the wrong pretense—if I've given the wrong idea, I am sorry... I can leave... rather than offend..."

"No, Señor Simms... we can speak of other things another time. What are your questions?" answered Madame, quite business-like.

"Well, they have to do with Voodoo—or as my relatives called it in the Bahamas, Obeah..."

"*Sí, pero*, we call it *Santeria*, we from Cuba... it is different, I think... not what people call Voodoo. Do you know of it?"

"Almost nothing... just memories of stories about Obeah from my childhood... but I have questions about certain objects that might have meaning in one form of worship, but not another... does that make a little sense?" Madame shrugged, and gestured for him to continue. "So what is the significance of a black crow feather?"

The old woman looked puzzled, "What other color might there be?"

"Sorry... would you use a crow feather for an incantation or a spell or something like that?"

Madame laughed and put her cigar on the edge of a glass ashtray. "No, Señor Simms, I would use a feather of a wise crow to send a message with the wind, so my words would fly where I wanted as quickly as possible. Only those in the north—where they practice hoodoo, you see—they might have evil intent with a crow... or they might be very afraid—as in an omen. See, these are different practices. They are quite savage sometimes, those northerners."

"What about chickens, then... black chicken or roosters? Do they have a special meaning?"

The old lady laughed and said something to Trini that was unintelligible to Simms, and Trini translated, "She says you are a black rooster— quite virile..."

Simms was now self-conscious, but he had to plow on with just a smile and a shake of his head. "But chickens— they are important, yes?"

"*Sí, gallinas, pero, no gallos*—they are for comida—food for our spirits... we must sacrifice the hens for to feed them to our chosen spirits, or they will pass away. Roosters, no. The chickens, they are not for evil or good—they are just... *necesito*... but we may keep the *garras... como se dice*? ... oh, *Sí,* the... claws—as talismans... you see?"

"What happens to the blood and feathers of the chicken after it is sacrificed?" asked Simms.

"Oh, police men say we must clean up... not healthy to leave laying around. So... we bury or burn or bag into trash can. Nobody like it much. But we have many chickens now, too many. New law says we can not sacrifice chickens anymore." She scoffed and shook her head, then reached for her cigar as if to take comfort in a last pleasure.

"Still, you must do what you must do to preserve the spirits, Madame. Just be discreet, yes?"

The old lady smiled at Simms, "Yes, you understand, then."

"I have a couple more things, if you don't mind..." Madame pulled the air between them with her hand as if to tell him to continue. "We are told that in certain dark practices associated with something called 'conjure', that vinegar mixed with special herbs is used for many things... is this true in Santeria?"

"*Sí, pero,* one must know certain spells or verses to say... or perhaps write on paper or wood, or stones—to go with the— we call it '*Siete*' or just '*vinagre*.'"

"*Siete?* That is seven, yes... so not four."

"*No, no es cuatro...* it is '*vinagre de los sietes ladrones*' – seven thieves, no four. Four is for *aficionadas*.." she said smugly."

Simms looked at Trini, who explained, "Amateurs... it's her little joke about the old-world Catholics who practice hoodoo in the north."

Madame chimed in, "*Sí, pero,* one must understand the correct herbs also... for we must... *es necesario*... to keep evil away... to do correctly."

"To keep evil people away, you mean?"

"No... well maybe sometimes... but bad luck, sickness, craziness... and other things that can make for bad life... these require the correct words, as I said."

Simms nodded and smiled. So, who would know the correct incantations—or how to use them correctly? Can anybody be taught?"

"No, Señor, no outsiders and no mere ... we say '*iyabó*'... you see, there are many fakers around."

Simms looked at Trini for help, and she said, "It means initiates..."

Simms nodded, "So, who would you teach? Could you teach me, or my friend Baxter, perhaps, if he had a curse from his Cuban wife?"

Madame scoffed, picked up her cigar again, puffed smoke in the air, and said adamantly, "No, never. You must be chosen... I have chosen but one *iyabó* in thirty years... but she disappointed me... did not finish the initiation."

"Oh. So, the vinegar... it is nothing more than salad dressing in the hands of common folk?" Both women chuckled at his humor, and Simms continued, "So, one last thing on my list of questions,

Madame LaCroix, if you please... in Santeria, would anybody cut off a person's tongue for, say, gossip or slander, or...?"

Madame looked at Trinity in disgust, and said a few expletives and some other things in Spanish that Simms couldn't make out. He turned to Trini, who said, "My Aunt Sonia was disgusted by the idea... she said only mafioso do things like that... not religious people."

Simms started to apologize, but Madame held up her hand, and told him it wasn't necessary, "Many people think such things, and so it was an honest question. In your country, Obeah does not follow such practices either, true?"

Simms' tension abated a little, "I've never heard of it being said, but I know so little of such things."

Madame stood up, walked to a cabinet, retrieved a bottle of rum and three small glasses, then returned to the table and asked, "Señor Simms, is that all, or is there more that you want to ask?"

As she poured out a dram, Simms said, "Well, if you were asked by a client to make an undesirable person disappear... or leave somebody alone, what would you do? I mean, what steps might you take to help?"

The old lady reached her glass out for a toast, "I would need... I must have something of the undesirable person—a personal object, and I would have to know what the offense was... infidelity, violence, drunkenness, unwanted suitor... you see, it is not that simple... there are many spells that may be attempted, and if the spirits consider the effort to be just, they perhaps might work. But I would counsel my client on their own lives too, for they must come to an understanding of what has brought this bad person into their lives."

Simms sipped his rum thoughtfully, then concluded, "So, that is what your sign says out in front... I understand more now. Thank you, Madame LaCroix."

Stevenson and Trinity visited with Madame LaCroix for part of another hour, until she shooed them out so she could see an actual client. Simms asked if he could pay for the counseling, but the old lady merely scoffed and showed them the door. They drove around Key West in Baxter's Jeep for a couple of hours, Trinity doing her best to prolong their time together. Finally, when Simms insisted that he had to return Baxter's Jeep and then get to the airport, she guided him to her place. Her goodbye kiss was wet and more of a promise than a farewell, and Simms heard himself say that he'd see her again soon. It was a pact that stayed on his mind.

Chapter 12
Davo's Lookout

It's not that Gino Macina was at a dead end. Rather, he had no compelling reason to follow any of the faint trails in front of him, and he simply wasn't motivated to leave Juliana's Café. He'd heard nothing from Simms in a few days, Whitehead seemed uninterested in the case, the lab was still waiting for test results, and there had been no luck tracking down any of the homeless camp vagabonds. He'd gone to see Ricardo Avila to ask a few random questions about Rodney, eaten a big lunch, complements of the chef, and left no wiser. The only other interesting people in the entire picture were Davo and Aunt Minerva. It took him the better part of a night and another day to map out the bits and pieces he'd gotten from both of them and, of the two, Davo was the least complicated to be with in person.

That random thought was all it took to move him. Well, he first dithered over the makings of a plan, but then just got in his car and started driving to the Third United Baptist Church Wayfarer Shelter, outlining his plan on the way. It was late in the morning, but not too late to drop in and invite the boy to lunch one more time, and he was sure the kid would take him up on an offer for another burger. On the way, Macina decided it would be best to negotiate with Davo rather than just corner him as a captive audience in his new plan.

Once the boy was strapped into the front seat of the Dodge, Macina said, "Davo, I have an errand to run over in Manatee Wells, and there's a good place to eat in the village—that okay with you?"

Davo nodded his head, "Don't mind, Detetive. Dago Bay is okay wit Davo."

"Thanks... you know, you might be able to help me... I want to check out the old shark factory, and I thought you might be able to show me around..."

Davo squirmed a little, "Davo don't mind, like we say, you being a cop and all, Davo can't get in no trouble..."

Macina laughed, and changed the subject a little, asking about the fishing in the mangroves and the condition of the old factory. The boy answered his questions without enthusiasm, and stared out the window as the world whizzed by. "Davo, can you read a map?"

The boy turned and said, "No, Davo can read words and knows numbers and such, and we been to grade three—but we ain't never seen no map up close..."

"That's okay," answered Gino, "I looked at one before we left, so I have a pretty good idea where to turn down those old roads. If you see something that looks familiar, you'll tell me, okay?"

"Okay, Detetive, but we only seen these roads once, and dat was on da way out— onna bus."

"Well, how'd you get there the first time?"

"Came wit some others... was a long walk through the mangroves and palmetto from out on dat highway... but dem folk know da way."

All Gino answered was, "Oh." They drove through the middle of the village, and then he pointed out, "That's where we'll come for lunch, after we've driven out to the factory." The boy nodded, and took in the scenery as if cataloging every sight and platting his own map. Macina turned away from the developed part of the bay, and headed north along a worn asphalt road that soon turned into a lacework of potholes connected by remnants of eroded macadam.

The Dodge groaned, creaked and rattled painfully, no matter the speed. Abruptly, they reached a chainlink fence and a gate secured by chain and lock, protected by a 'No Trespassing—Private Property' sign, with a smaller sign that suggested that a dog and armed guard might be on watch.

Gino got out of the car to inspect the lock and have a look at what was now only a damp dirt track that showed fresh signs of recent travel. He returned to the car and told Davo, "Well, I didn't expect this gate or fence..."

"No suhr, it ain't been heahr when we took dat bus out..."

"The bus came on this road?"

"Oh yes, Suhr, Davo wouldn't never forget dat ride on dis road."

Gino pondered his predicament for a few seconds, then asked, "So, Davo, do you remember the old way you came in with your people that first time?"

"Yes, Suhr. We knows dat path, and also where dis road come to da old buildin'. Davo's job sometimes was to be a lookout fo' trouble dat may come along da trails. If'n we go back to dat highway, Davo can find it... but you gonna need different shoes, Detetive."

Gino laughed, "I'm prepared this time, my friend... let's go do this so we can get to lunch pretty soon."

The ride back out to A1A seemed shorter than the trip in, and Davo was mapping everything he saw. Without warning, he ordered, "Stop. It ovah theah," and pointed off to the right. Macina obeyed, looking for a place to pull off the road and out of sight of any traffic flow. Davo scrambled out and impatiently waited for Gino to change shoes and grab his binoculars, then hurried down the path into the brush as fast as his short legs would go.

In the months since he'd first traveled through here, the undergrowth had begun to reclaim the trail, slowing Davo's pace after just a few minutes of progress. Macina estimated they'd come about a half mile or more, when the boy held his hand up and stopped. In a low voice, he said, "From dis place, we mus be quiet... if somebodies has a lookout...unnerstan? Dis is close to Davo's ol' lookout, where we can see da ol' factory, and da trail... you watch, you see, Detetive."

Abruptly, the trail seemed to end. A solitary earthen mound as big as a boulder blocked their way. Davo waved Gino to follow him around the thing, and then scrambled up the back side with the cop in his wake. There, standing above the palmettos and taller white mangrove trees, just as the boy had claimed, the top of the old buildings could be seen a few hundred yards distant. Davo pointed to a fork in the path, and whispered, "Da ol' graveyard is over theah on dat trail, and dey say it be da place to bury dem ol' pirates and robbers." Macina mouthed the word 'graveyard' and the boy nodded. Gino first scanned the trail to the graveyard with his binoculars, but it disappeared into the woods. Next, he focused on the old factory and surrounding area while Davo fidgeted around the rock, watching the cop and waiting for a report. Eventually, Gino handed him the binoculars, and the boy smiled as if he'd been given a pot of gold. After fiddling with the instrument for a few seconds, though, his smile faded until Gino helped him adjust the width and focus to fit his small head. Davo scoped out everything in sight, and once satisfied that he'd surveyed the scene to refresh his memory, he handed the glasses back and whispered, "Well, Detetive...?"

Gino answered, "Let's go back, we can talk in few minutes."

Arriving back at the car, Gino said, "So, I counted three pickup trucks and maybe twelve men going back and forth, Davo. What say you?"

"Only eleven, Detetive... but Davo thinks mo' inside... they's a carryin' somethin'."

Gino said, "Excellent... you'll be a good detective one day... but now, here's the deal... It didn't look to me like they were tearing the place down or building anything—but if I remember correctly, you said your people were told that something was gonna be built there."

"Yes, Suhr, you remembers correct... dat is what da old man and White Witch say to our bunch."

"Okay, well, I can't snoop around while there are so many guys in the place, so let's go back to the village for lunch, yeah?"

Macina turned off A1A onto a forked road that led into Manatee Wells, took the wrong fork, and ran a stop sign—all in a matter of seconds. Swearing under his breath, he made a right turn, intending to go around the block and try again, only to find that he was on a dead-end street. Muttering again, he turned around and drove back toward the heart of the town. All the while, Davo was cataloging the sights. Suddenly, he reached across and grabbed Macina's arm, "Detetive—Davo needs to tell ya'all somethin'... stop da car, okay?" Gino pulled to the curb and looked at the panicky boy.

"What?"

"Rememba when Davo says dis old white fella was wit da White Witch?"

"Yeah..."

"Davo jus' seen him again—back theah—"

"Show me?"

"Yeah, Davo not afraid wit you around... turn back to da last road... go dat way," he said, pointing to the left.

Macina said, "Okay, but maybe I'll stop where I can look first... see, a good detective doesn't just barrel on into a suspect... get it?

"Yes, Suhr, but hurry up... he was gettin' inna old blue car..."

Macina edged the Stratus into the intersection, and saw the dark blue Dodge pulling away from the curb in front of a delicatessen. "I see him... we'll follow from a distance... let's see where he goes."

After a couple of blocks and two more turns, Macina realized that he was in Minerva's neighborhood, and slowed down even more. Off in the distance, the blue car stopped in front of Minerva's house, and Gino fumbled for the binoculars. "Here, Davo, when the man goes up the steps, you see if you still think it's him, and tell me if you recognize anybody that answers the door."

"Yes, Suhr, das him and she's da White Witch herself."

Chapter 13
Loose Tongue

When the taxi driver dropped Stevenson Simms in front of his home, it was nearly dark. All Simms wanted to do was unplug his brain and sleep for a week. The first obstacle to sleep, though, was the pile of mail shoved through the slot in his front door. He couldn't abide the disarray and implicit chaos in his living room, and therefore, sleep would be impossible. He turned on the air conditioner, scooped the mail onto a table, and sorted the junk from the bills. Next, he pulled a bottle of beer from the fridge, took two swigs, and headed for a hot shower, beer in hand. He couldn't even count the days that he'd been gone, let alone assimilate all of the information, people, and events that connected those days together.

As the water sprayed down over his head and shoulders, he forced himself to blank out all the noise for thirty seconds, then thirty more. He tried to imagine what 'old what's her name' might be up to at that moment, and considered giving her a call, but when Trinity's smile rose from his memory to blot out his most recent ex-girlfriend's face, the temptation passed. Moving on through his collection of memories, he laughed at a scene he imagined would unfold when Baxter delivered a box of smuggled Cuban cigars to Madame LaCroix, and he knew Baxter would follow through on the promise just to verify the story he'd been handed about a cigar-puffing priestess of *Santeria*.

Still dripping and wrapped in a towel, Simms went looking for something to eat in his kitchen, but all he found was a jar of peanut butter and a box of saltines. He reflected on the over-stocked fridge at Baxter's fishing lodge, contrasted that with the nearly depleted beer supply in his own otherwise barren reefer, sighed, and opened another bottle. *"Time to sleep,"* he told himself. *"This should do it."* He sat down on the sofa, flipped on the television, mindlessly clicked through the local stations with the remote, turned it off, laid down and slept through the night.

Only a neighborhood dog barking woke him just before dawn. Startled and confused for a few seconds, he sat up trying to figure out where he was and why he was clutching a half full bottle of warm beer like a teddy bear. The realization that he'd spent the night on the sofa like some slob needled at him. "*Get your shit together, boy!*" he growled at himself, then headed for another shower while the coffeemaker worked its magic. *"Seven hours and a shower... it's like a miracle*," he thought afterwards. "*It never fails*". Now, with caffeine beginning to course through his system, he went to his closet and picked out a clean shirt. There were only four clean ones left on hangers, so he made a mental note to take the pile in his car trunk to the cleaners after work.

Once dressed, Simms opened his desk drawer where he kept his holstered Smith and Wesson, badge, wallet, and car keys. Except the spot where his wallet should have been was empty. "*Wallet? Where the hell, Stevenson? You paid the driver last night...*" After a few minutes of retracing his steps, he found it with his dirty clothes in the bathroom where he'd dropped everything the night before. Now he admonished himself once more, cleaned up his mess, and tried to slow the morning down to a manageable pace. He was impatient to get to the station and map out his findings on the big board in his office, but he knew it'd be no good if he didn't organize his apartment first... it would nag at him all day otherwise. He still had time—arriving at 6AM would give him plenty of time to sort through it all with nobody there to interrupt him. "*Vacation is over, Simms, get organized, get back on track.*" Then, with another cup of coffee and a clear head, he went to the station with a plan of action, one to be executed before anybody showed up to distract him.

It was a good idea in the making, except Macina was already there. Gino, knowing that Simms liked to work early when nobody else was around, had the good sense to let Simms settle into his office before invading his partner's solitude. In the few minutes that he could stand it, though, Macina re-organized his notes, added the latest information from the forensics lab, paced the long hallway to grab the coffee pot, and then gathered it all together to go see Simms.

Stevenson merely sighed when Gino tapped at his door, because, once he saw that his partner was already in the office, he'd prepared himself for a different kind of morning. "Hey, Partner," Gino began, "I didn't know if you'd be in early, but I took a chance..."

"You got my message yesterday, right?"

"Yeah, the watch desk gave it to me late, but it didn't say if you would be in..."

"Had to come in and get goin'... but what's up? Why are you here so early?"

"We've got a problem... a big problem," blurted an agitated Macina. Simms couldn't imagine what kind of 'big' trouble Macina could have gotten into, so he just waited with an expectant look that said, "*Well?*" "So, Stevenson, remember I said I was taking Giuseppe's Aunt Minerva to lunch?"

"Yeah..."

"Well, I did..."

"C'mon, Gino, I don't need the baby steps... did you kill her or something?"

Macina laughed, "No, it'd be easier if I had... well, maybe not... a couple of days later, I took that Haitian kid out again—we went over to the Wells for lunch, but first I wanted to see the old shark factory, so I had him take me out there, then..."

"Good Christ! Gino, you didn't kill the kid too?"

Macina stopped mid-sentence, "You want me to tell you frontwards or backwards, Simms? Geezus! Last week, the kid told me that a woman he called the 'White Witch' and an old man had come out to the old factory with some others and ran his people off a few months ago, and threatened to throw 'em in jail if they returned... well, the kid saw that old man over in the Wells... the guy got into a blue Dodge and we tailed him to—wait for it—Minerva's house."

"That's it, your big trouble is that the old lady is a witch and ran a bunch of homeless people off her family's property? With the help of some old man?"

"No, goddamn it, Simms, the old man in the blue car was Captain Whitehead!"

"Oh. No shit?" said Simms quietly, assimilating the information and trying to synthesize something that made any sense. "That could be a problem if... shit... well, Gino, what've ya formulated? You had a lot more time to grind on this than I have... was this yesterday?"

"No, day before... so, look, I went to the County Seat to see who owns the shark factory property and also who owns the house where Minerva's been living with Giuseppe and Maria..."

"And... it's not Minerva?"

"No, I did a lot of digging-—and it looks like Giuseppe's old man died and left everything to Giuseppe *aka* Joe Di Rossi... the old man even cut out his sister and his own daughter when it came to property... so Minerva's got dough, but none of the businesses are in her name... and everything would go to Maria and their kids if Joe kicks it, unless... well, unless he's got a will or a trust or something that I couldn't find."

"So, that's good and thorough, Gino, but I'm not makin' a connection with our case... what's the angle with Whitehead? Is he boinkin' the old woman? Or what?"

"Yeah, maybe, but she seems past the boinkin' stage, if you get my drift..."

Simms got a flash of a mental image that he was afraid would haunt him forever, shook it off and said, "Well, you had lunch with her... what was your take on her and the deal with Joe and Maria? Does she know I found him and his mistress?"

"No, she'd have no way of knowing you found them unless he has contacted her since then... So, you were right, then... he ran away with that waitress— Valeria LaCroix... well, Minerva knows about the affair... says the girlfriend is a Haitian whore... but..."

"Nope... she's a Cubano, which seems odd... but go on."

"Well, Minerva says Maria must have a lover too, and the old lady thinks Maria is hiding out somewhere. She wants me to track down Maria and help stop the town gossiping about a murder in the family... you get the idea."

"Yeah, right. So, do you think Minerva has something to gain by Maria's demise? Or, could she be hiding Maria somewhere? I mean, criminy, this family owns about half the real estate in the area—if the rumors are true... she could be anywhere."

"I can't think of any way the aunt benefits directly in either scenario... meaning if either Joe or Maria are dead... and we know he's not... and look, I can't figure out why Maria would be hiding out... so unless Minerva's shielding Joe and trying to misguide me..."

"Possibly... but it would be pretty gutsy of her to try to manipulate the cops face-to-face... what about the old shark factory? Could Maria be hiding out over there? What did you find when you went?"

"Well, that's just it, Simms, we couldn't get to the building because the property is fenced-off and there's a locked gate across the road now... so the kid—his name is Davo... he takes me in though the scrub and palmettos, on a trail he knows... and we go to his favorite lookout with my binoculars... turns out there's a lot of activity there... pickup trucks and about a dozen guys loading or unloading stuff."

"So, let's get a warrant and search for a body..."

"How are we gonna do that without the Captain?"

"Fuck me. We're back to the beginning of the circle. What the hell is Whitehead up to?"

"I dunno, but it seems to me that we have to be really careful about what we tell him from now on... let's sit on this for a little while, okay?"

Almost immediately, Macina had another idea, "Hey, so, I've got a contact in the County Sheriff's Department... remember Ike Harris? Look, we don't need to go through Whitehead for a search warrant—it's not our jurisdiction... Remember? Let me see if Harris can work through the Sheriff for a warrant... I think we've got reason to believe there's been a crime committed over there, or at least that we'll find clues that will lead us to one murder or the other."

"Cool, let's do that. Now, what else happened while I was gone? Tell me, and then I'll fill you in on Joe and Valeria..."

"Well, here's what I know so far. Forensics ran the fingerprints from the kitchen, but there's nothing in any data base anywhere to match up..."

"What about the help... the employees? Surely there must be employee fingerprints from the kitchen—at least there should be some matches there?"

"That's just it... Whitehead didn't follow through and so the forensics crew still didn't get 'em all fingerprinted yet."

"You've gotta be shittin' me. Now we have to figure out if it was deliberate or just sloppy on his part... you know he took over the scene himself that night, and ordered me to interview Ricardo instead..."

"Well, while your contemplating that, Partner, get a load of this: the blood splatter samples were mostly from a bird—right—we knew that... and some were from a human... but the blood didn't match the tongue... in fact, there was no blood in the tongue at all. It was from a cadaver... like... pickled in formalin already... the lab in Los Angeles didn't even bother with DNA testing, and they're laughing their asses off at us."

Chapter 14
Juliana's Café

Simms was off his game, and to make it worse, the start to his morning was going downhill faster than usual. Macina had already derailed his morning plans in more ways than one, and now he owed his partner a rundown on the adventures in Nassau and the Keys. His intention to share his findings with Gino and Captain Whitehead at the same time was now suddenly a bad idea, and they agreed on the need for a new strategy. Simms' instincts now told him that he and Macina should get away from the police station and avoid any encounter with the chief. "Gino, let's go get breakfast somewhere... you *are* hungry, aren't you?"

Macina, who never needed convincing when it came to food, was of a like mind, and volunteered to drive, "Let's go over to West Palm to a little café I like, and you can fill me in on your trip down south. And what's up with the sister?" It soon became clear to Gino that disappointment was in store, however, when Simms' account was not in any sense salacious when it came to Trinity, and so he silently vowed to wheedle the details out of his partner later. For the time being, though, he pretended to be content with Stevenson's tales of the two people of interest in the murder investigation at Giuseppe's restaurant, Valeria and Joe Di Rossi.

At the end of Simms' account, Macina found his partner's conclusions lacking. "So listen here, Stevenson... you say that Valeria and Di Rossi have alibis for the night of the murder... but it's all based on her sister's statement... what if that's a bunch of crap?"

"No, look... that bandleader—the guy who flew me down there—Jimmy Daniels... he also told me that he'd seen them both at the Drunken Chicken, and I didn't even ask him... see? So, I'd have to think he was somehow in on your little conspiracy theory... see what I'm sayin'? Why are we hung up on this?"

"Oh... well, that... uuhh, I was just thinkin' about something that Ricardo Avila told me the other day—I went by the restaurant to go over some of the stuff we'd gotten from him before, and he just said something about Valeria being Cuban, and being into voodoo and shit, and in view of some of the evidence at the scene..."

Simms thought for a few seconds while Gino exited the interstate to head into the heart of West Palm Beach, then said, "Context, Gino... what were you talking about when Avila brought it up?"

"I might have mentioned the vinegar shit we found spread around the kitchen..."

"Before? Or after he mentioned voodoo?" persisted Simms.

"Geezus, Stevenson, does it matter?"

"Maybe... maybe a great deal..."

"After, I guess... what's the issue?"

"Well, mainly, it goes back to the first time I spoke with Ricardo, and he brought up Valeria... he said he didn't know her well except that she was a pretty woman... he thought she was Puerto Rican or Jamaican, or some ethnic mix... he spoke of her derisively in those terms when I asked. And, see, this morning, you said that Ricardo told you that Valeria was Cuban... and then he told you she's into voodoo. See my problem?"

"Yeah, I guess... well, no... maybe I'm just thick..."

"Well, first, he lied to me. Second, he's Cuban too... and Cubanos don't practice voodoo—if they go in for traditional spiritual stuff, they go for what they call *Santeria*... he should know this."

"So? Isn't it all the same shit? And when did you become an expert in such things?"

"Yesterday..."

Macina just shook his head, scoffed, and then chuckled, "I'm still not sure what the big deal is—it all sounds like semantics to me... anyway, here we are... let's have breakfast and figure out this Whitehead thing." Simms only sighed and got out of the car into the thick morning air, and wished for more coffee and a less thick partner.

The early morning work crowd had already thinned out of the diner, and Macina headed for the vacant tables in the rear, ushered by a waitress with a name tag that read 'Emilia'. Simms caught Gino winking at the young woman, and quickly understood why they had driven all the way out to West Palm Beach. "So, Gino, how long have you been coming to this café?"

"A few months..."

"So, ever since you met Emilia, then?"

Macina blushed, "You could mind your business, unless, of course, you wanna tell me about Trinity..."

Simms laughed, "Maybe later, Partner, but right now, we should get down to business... Whitehead. Here's what I think... this morning, we'll go to meet with him... I'll say that I got a good lead on the waitress and the owner of Giuseppe's— reliable info that they've been seen in the Bahamas... and nothing more. If he asks, I'll just lie, and say I'm still working on things with some contacts I have. He won't ask questions..."

"Okay, what about the forensics stuff. We can't hide that from him..."

"Nope, we don't want to. In fact, we should lay it all in front of him, so that even he can't miss it—we've got no fingerprint matches yet, we do have human blood splatter and some kind of bird blood, along with a black crow's feather, and a broken flagon of vinegar or salad dressing or something... and still no corpse—just a tongue from a cadaver somewhere—a medical school or someplace like that."

Macina listened, then responded, "Yeah. But you know he's gonna ask what we think... he always does, then he either argues, or acts like it was all his own deduction..."

"Yup, so here's where you tell him about the technician who talked about voodoo and conjure and shit like that, and the vinegar concoction... and tell him that you think we might be dealing with a voodoo ritual or something weird along those lines. Say it just like that..."

"Do I really think that?"

"How the hell should I know, Gino... do you?"

"Not really..."

"So, sound skeptical when you say it... the main thing is to let the old bastard think he's on to something... or that we are... that'll give us some time..."

"So *you* don't think it was a ritual, then..."

"No... not at all. It was staged... but not for a ritual, or else it would all have been cleaned up,"

"So, you think Maria isn't dead?"

"I don't have a clue whether she's dead or alive, but I'm pretty sure that the evidence at the scene has nothing to do with answering that question directly. We'll want to see who we think might be responsible for a mucked-up crime scene first, and go from there..."

"Okay, I'm all in... let's see what Whitehead does with the info..."

"Right, meanwhile, we need to apply a little pressure elsewhere and see how Whitehead reacts... when are you supposed to have lunch with Minerva again?"

"In a few days... but we agreed to stay in touch if something came up..."

"Good. After we meet with the Captain, why don't you call her to confirm your lunch date. Say that you're in the area, and ask if you can drop by to clarify something..."

"Yeah, okay... I told her I was workin' on a murder case of a hobo over near the Wells... But, so... why can't I just ask her on the phone what you want to know?"

"Because you're gonna take me and introduce us, and you're gonna ask her if it's okay with her for us to go out to the old shark factory..."

"Do we really want to go over there today? I mean, she'll probably stall... besides, she doesn't like... as she put it, 'colored folks.'"

Simms laughed a low laugh, "Yeah, that just adds to the fun, right? I mean, there was a reason Whitehead told me not to go over there and investigate this case..."

"Well, you know she's gonna tell him... oh...," said Gino laughing. "You're pretty twisted..."

"Yeah I know, and guess what I'm gonna tell him when he bitches about me not obeying orders... I'm gonna blame you... See, your orphan kid, Davo, told you that his bunch had all been living at the shark factory... including old Rodney... so, we're investigating <u>that</u> murder, not the one at Giuseppe's.

"How long do we have before he catches on?"

"Maybe forever... at least until we solve this fuckin' case, anyway."

"I'm onboard... and, look, you've raised a question or two about our man, Ricardo Avila. Shouldn't we put a little pressure on him too?"

"Yeah, after we're done visiting Minerva, let's go see our favorite chef. I want to ask him if he's seen Valeria recently... I heard she was back in town," he said with his tongue in his cheek.

After breakfast, Stevenson waited outside to give Macina a few minutes to flirt with Emilia. As he gazed at the row of palm trees lining the street, and allowed himself to be calmed by the fronds waving in the humid breeze, his mind wandered down to the Keys for a brief visit. The interlude was long enough to imagine what Trinity might be up to so early in the morning, but not so long that he appeared to be drifting far away when Gino came hurrying to the car. He needed time to sort through this complicated attraction he had to Trini without Gino prying, and now he realized that the new girl, Emilia, would provide a way to keep his partner distracted and off his back.

Whitehead proved to be a pushover for their tag-team strategy and, without any coaching, began tacking notes to his office bulletin board and stringing pieces of yarn together for a voodoo conspiracy theory. Simms and Macina sat back in their seats, offering suggestions here and there, and rolling their eyes behind the chief's back. The plot to send Whitehead on a wild-goose chase succeeded so easily that, when they left the station, Simms began to wonder if it hadn't been too easy. Yet, by the time they'd driven two miles down the highway toward Manatee Wells, Simms let go of his doubts.

His next concern was whether Gino could handle the old lady when they arrived on her doorstep. Macina's call to Minerva had sounded amiable enough as he eavesdropped what little he could hear, but he needed to be sure. "So, Gino, are you certain that you can charm old Minerva? We don't want to spook her, see what I'm saying? It's important that she keep trusting you... so don't act too disappointed when she won't let us onto the property over at the shark factory..."

"Yeah, I get it. Should we let on that you have any information about Joe... or... what do you have in mind?"

"I'll play it by ear, depending on how our little visit goes... but I don't think it's a good idea to say too much, given what we just told Whitehead... right?"

"Right, good point," said Macina as he parked the old Dodge right in front of Minerva's house. Simms waited at the foot of the steps, while Gino went up to ring the doorbell. A long time passed without anybody answering the door, and Gino began to doubt that the bell actually worked. But just as he was about to knock, Minerva opened the front door and greeted Macina with a charming smile, "Detective... Gino... nice to see you... won't you come in?"

"Thanks, Miss Minerva, but I'm with my partner—so we won't take up much of your time," said Macina stepping to one side so that she could see Simms. "Miss Minerva, this is Detective Simms—he's working on that case I told you about... the dead hobo..."

Minerva's hospitable smile disappeared when she saw Simms, but Stevenson just smiled and said, "Good Morning," then tapped his forehead as if to salute her very being.

"Why did you bring *him* here?" she said in a whisper, a tone that Gino thought sounded distinctly like a hiss.

"Detective Simms is the lead investigator on the case, and I'm trying to help him out if I can," said Gino as pleasantly as if she hadn't just sounded like an angry cat. "Do you remember when I told you about that hobo case? We had witnesses who said that the dead guy had been with a group of itinerants living over there at the old shark factory?"

"Yes, but I..."

"Well, I was wondering if we could get your permission to go onto the property to look around—see if any clues might have been left when all of those people were taken away. And you seem to be the only person who could give us permission, given that your nephew isn't around..."

"I don't know why you need permission... you could just go over there..."

"Well, the road is chained off—there's a fence and locked gate, and such... so... it seemed reasonable to ask permission—that's all..."

"Well, I don't have a way to let you in," she said defensively.

"Okay, well, thanks for letting us interrupt your day, Miss Minerva. Do we still have a lunch date next week?"

Minerva's smile returned for a few moments, "Of course Gino!"

Her smile disappeared when Simms stepped forward, cleared his throat, and said, "Thank you, Ma'am. Oh, there's one thing Gino and I were wondering— about this affair with your nephew... have you heard from him, by any chance? We were told that his mistress was back in the area, but apparently, nobody at the restaurant has heard from Joe."

Minerva looked a little confused, perhaps a bit offended, then glanced around as if to determine if any of the neighbors were hearing any of this. Then she looked at Gino and answered, "No, I, uuhh... no."

"Okay, well thanks anyway," said Simms cheerily. "C'mon Gino, we've wasted enough of this nice lady's day. We've got to go meet with that County Sheriff's deputy, right?"

Gino said his farewell to Minerva with as much charm as he could exude, considering that he wanted to break into laughter, hurried down the steps, and with a final wave, got in the car and drove away.

As they headed down A1A toward Giuseppe's, Macina began to see the angle that Simms was working. "So, how do you want to play this with Ricardo? Are you still thinking we should let him believe that the waitress is back in town?"

"Absolutely. Did you see Minerva's face a while ago? She obviously thought that if the mistress was back in town, that Joe should be back too... and she didn't know..."

"So, what, you think we'll get the same reaction from Ricardo?"

"Yeah, I mean, unlike Minerva, Ricardo *knows* where Joe is—or was... they spoke to each other while I was in Nassau... but, Ricardo wouldn't know that I was there, or that I'd spoken with Joe... so, if he thinks his boss is back in town and he hasn't heard from him, he might worry."

"You think he's hiding something?"

"Yeah, I don't know exactly what he's up to—but look, he didn't tell his boss that the wife was missing, right? And he's acted as if he doesn't know much about Valeria, when in fact he knows a lot about her *and* her relationship with Joe. So, on the one hand, I can see that he might have been less than honest with us to protect his boss, but if he's protecting him from us, why not tell him about Maria?"

"Right... so, do you think he's up to something with Minerva and the chief?"

"Good question, but I've got no answer, and I don't want to speculate. I'd like to ask Joe Di Rossi some questions about now, too, but he's disappeared again—as near as I can tell anyway."

"All right then, Partner, I'll follow your lead with Ricardo... here we are."

When the two detectives walked in the front door of the restaurant, they spied Ricardo in the back, and the chef waved them in the direction of his office. Once inside, Ricardo said, "Gentlemen, you should have called ahead, and I would have prepared a special dish or two for your enjoyment..."

"Thanks all the same, Ricardo, but we've got a busy day ahead of us..."

"Oh?" interrupted Ricardo, "Some new developments?"

"You might say that—but nothing we can talk about right now. We came by with a couple of questions though. Have any of Giuseppe's relatives been in, asking about him or Maria?"

"No... I can't say that they have..."

"Doesn't that seem a little odd? I mean, he's got an aunt that lives with them, and cousins by the dozen... I'd think they'd at least come by to see how things were going..."

"Well maybe, Detective, but they've never had anything to do with running any of his businesses, let alone the restaurant... Joe relied on me when he wasn't around."

"Okay, I guess that makes sense... So what about Valeria? Have you seen her since she got back in town?"

Ricardo looked a little surprised, but answered coolly, "No, I hadn't heard she was back—so who said she was?"

"Oh, we interviewed her roommate," Gino answered before Simms could respond.

Stevenson hid his grumbling thoughts behind a poker face—now was no time to contradict the story, but Gino was out of line in naming a witness. He could only hope that there was no damage done, because he still had one more question. "So, you haven't heard from Joe either then?"

Ricardo still hadn't entirely recovered from the previous exchange, but he said, "Well, I spoke to him briefly by phone a couple of days ago... he said he'd be gone for another week or so..."

"Did you tell him what was going on here at the restaurant..."

"Well, I didn't need to—he'd already heard, and that's why he called me..."

"So, you did discuss the whole thing, then..."

"No, I just gave him a quick overview of what I knew... he seemed in a hurry to get off the phone."

Simms noted a few things on his pad while Avila was answering, then said, "Well, Chef, if you hear from Valeria, would you let us know right away? So, thanks for your time... we have to get going."

Chapter 15
Busy Morning

Simms and Macina ambled across the parking lot behind the Third United Baptist Church, headed for Gino's broken-down Dodge, when Gino's mobile began ringing again. "Good lord, Gino, can't your girlfriend wait an hour without calling you? That's like the tenth time your phone has gone off since we got here."

Macina, who had been ignoring his phone for a half hour, stopped to check the call, "Hold on a second, Stevenson, I need to return this call—it's from Ike Harris over in the Sheriff's office..."

Simms nodded apologetically, and took a walk around to the back of the building. His thoughts jumped to the security videos from the day of the murder, and so he began one more time to reconstruct the recorded scene that had caught old Rodney's exit behind the restaurant. Nothing changed—at least to Simms' eye—it seemed obvious that, after leaving the back of the restaurant, the hobo would have made his way down the alley, and then headed a few hundred yards directly out into the oak hammocks. Nobody in the parking lot could have seen him—it was only luck that the camera perched on top of the church had caught Rodney's exodus that day. Satisfied that he hadn't overlooked something earlier, Simms returned to the car, where he found Gino scratching his head.

"Stevenson, we need to go over to Dilly's Tavern and meet with Deputy Harris. Get this... the Sheriff hasn't had any communication from Whitehead or anybody else in our department about Manatee Wells—ever! Harris was checking out what he needed to do to get a warrant for us and... well... I'll let him tell it. C'mon."

Dilly's Tavern was a throwback to an earlier time, housed in a building which had been old when Truman was President. It was a saloon where law enforcement officers could come to drink and celebrate or commiserate with fellow officers without much interplay with ordinary civilians. Simms had hung out in the joint in the early days of his career, but in recent years, he had largely avoided the scene whenever possible. As he and Macina headed for the front door now, Stevenson laughed at a few of the memories that were resurrected by mere sight of the old door itself, still hanging crooked after taking a beating in a storm decades before. Macina, on the other hand, was a regular and knew exactly in which booth Ike Harris would have hunkered down, and he led Simms directly past Al the bartender to the back of the bar.

"Ike, you remember Stevenson Simms?"

Harris gave a friendly smile and extended his hand, "Yeah, been a minute, Simms... how's it goin'?"

Simms shrugged and said, "Never a dull moment—I think the last time I saw you, you were buyin' rounds for every cop in the house, but I can't remember why..."

Harris blushed, "Must have been when I was celebratin' my divorce..."

"That good, huh?"

"Absolutely... expensive but worth it..." The three men laughed, even though it rang of a bitter irony.

"So, how's life been since then?" asked Gino.

"Peaceful—at least at home—the streets, swamps, and backwoods are treacherous as ever, but I'm not tellin' you anything you don't already know."

"Well, we coulda been librarians or something safe, secure, and useful," quipped Simms, getting the desired laugh from both of his companions.

"So, Gino told me that we might have a political or jurisdictional problem—what, with him looking into stuff over in the Wells?"

"Nah, I wouldn't say that exactly," said Ike. "The Sheriff doesn't give one shit if you guys are over there talkin' to people of interest... it's just that Gino said your Captain had cleared it with my major, but, truth is, nobody has heard anything at all... so maybe it just slipped his mind... or... Gino said it might be something else..."

Simms looked at Macina reproachfully, but without missing a beat, said, "Maybe, maybe not, but I'm not gonna speculate on anything without evidence. If we're right, and if word got out, this case would slam shut in our faces—and if I'm wrong, it'd hurt an innocent person... and get our asses kicked—big time."

Harris laughed a little nervously and asked, "So what can I do to help?"

"Any chance you can finesse a warrant without getting too specific? The property is that old abandoned shark factory north of the village—out in the swamp. Here are the particulars," he said, handing an envelope to Harris and adding, "So, it's not like there's a bunch of people whose civil liberties are gonna be sacrificed here... an anonymous tip said that a murder victim used to hang out there with a large group of homeless folks—who were bused out of there a few months back... we just want to look around to see if there are any clues as to why those people were herded onto a bus in the middle of the night, and if there's a connection with his death..."

"Maybe I can finesse the warrant," said Harris. "Depends on the judge... anonymous tips aren't real strong... but you don't think it was the crime scene?"

"No, the guy was killed down our way... and I guess it really wasn't an anonymous tip, right, Gino? It was one of your trusted informants." Macina nodded and looked at the deputy earnestly.

"Okay," said Harris, "I can try an end run with my major... meet me back here about ten-thirty tonight... we might still have an old judge who gets sleepy and loosens the rules late at night."

"Cool, Ike, but... we must keep our P-D out of the loop... we'll take the heat if it blows up... but it's gotta be this way," said Simms. "Now, we're buyin' lunch... so what'll it be?"

"Thanks, but I should get back and work on this warrant for you guys—how about a raincheck—or you guys buy the drinks tonight? Say, nine-thirty?"

That night, Simms and Macina arrived back at Dilly's half an hour early, expecting the place to be full of half-buzzed veteran peace officers. Instead, it was deserted. Macina looked at the bartender, "Where is everybody, Al?"

The old barman just shrugged, "Happens sometimes... who knows?"

"Have you seen Ike?"

"Not yet... he called a few minutes ago and wanted me to make sure you guys didn't leave before he got here."

Gino ordered two cups of the leftover morning coffee and two shots of Irish, then sat down with Simms to wait. Sipping at his whiskey, Macina tried to ask nonchalantly, "Did you get ahold of Valeria's sister this afternoon?"

The subtlety was lost on Simms, "Nah, I didn't try. I asked Baxter to check in at the Drunken Chicken to see if Trinity was doing okay—he can do stuff like that, real low key. He called back just before I left my house—she's fine. There was no sign of her sister or our main man, though."

"Yeah, I guess you're in a tight spot until this case gets resolved..."

Simms poured the whiskey into the last half of his coffee, took a sip and wrinkled his face. "You actually drink this stuff and expect to see retirement age? Jesus."

Gino started to say something, but Ike Harris strode through the door right then, and headed to their booth. Before either of them could say anything, Harris plopped a brown folder down on the table, "Well, you guys can sure pick a doozy when you want to..."

"Judge didn't go for it, then?"

"Oh, yeah, that's your warrant... it was a piece of cake, but not for the reasons I'd expected."

"So?" said Gino.

"The judge said we didn't really need this, because the Feds were gonna be there tomorrow—along with the Florida State Division of Historical Resources— and get this—it's at the request of the owner's agents. The entire property is an open book right now. He said we could just show our badges and walk in. But I asked for the warrant anyway, just in case there's ever a question that pops up in your case later on. So he signed it."

Simms looked at Gino, then back at Harris, "So, obviously... what the heck are the Feds doing there?"

"Well, the best guess around our office is that it has something to do with Indian artifacts— usually, you won't see the Feds and D-H-R show up unless it has something to do with Native American antiquities or sacred burial grounds and such..."

Gino had an epiphany, "That's gotta be it... my informant says that there's an old graveyard back in the palmettos— away from the shark factory buildings... so maybe if they were going to tear down the old factory, they discovered something of historical value. You know, there's a lot of new laws about artifacts and shit like that... they'd want to notify the right people."

Simms was trying to figure out how Macina knew anything at all about such matters, but gave up and decided to ask later. Instead, he asked Harris, "So, did you guys get called in to help out or to provide security or something?"

"No, there was just a courtesy heads-up to the Sheriff, but it was the old judge who told me when I went to his house tonight—that's when I first heard of it."

"So, you want to go with us tomorrow morning? Seems like your major would have a vested interest in having a deputy on site..."

"Thanks, I think I will—nothing else is going on anyway, and you two seem to have a knack for getting your noses into interesting stuff."

The three men had agreed to meet at the old shark factory at 8 AM, since there was no reason to try to beat anybody else to the property. But when Simms and Macina finally rumbled to the end of the pot-holed road in separate cars, they found a half dozen County Sheriff's vehicles on the scene. And Ike Harris was pacing around the perimeter, which was now cordoned with yellow tape. "Hey... good morning guys... Gino, I was about to call you... just to prepare you for a different kind of day."

"Why? What's up with the manpower? Got a war goin' on?"

Ike shook his head and laughed, "Well, the D-H-R guys... you know, the archaeologist types—they were here at first light, all gung-ho to get started. But one of their minions got curious about the buildings and such—and went exploring. He didn't get far before discovering two dead bodies in front of the main factory. So, they called us out—first thing this morning." Harris pointed toward the white shrouds on the ground, "Looks like these two dumb-asses got into an argument and shot each other late last night or early this morning... the bodies were barely cold."

"Well, what in hell's name were two guys doin' out here in the middle of the night—and what could they possibly have found to fight about?" asked Simms.

"Exactly to the point, my friend..."

"How'd they kill each other?" asked Macina

"Looks like shotguns at ten paces... and you gotta check this out," answered Ike. Simms and Macina followed Harris past the covered corpses inside the near end of the main building, into what looked like an old storeroom. Harris pointed at brown bales stacked several feet high, "Marijuana—ganja! A ton of it at least, according to our guys. And look back here..." Inside a closet was a pallet of white bricks wrapped in plastic. "Field tests say it's cocaine... but we'll have to have the lab confirm it... maybe fifty-sixty keys worth."

Simms just stared at the stash for a few seconds, rubbed the back of his head, then looked at Macina and started to laugh. Gino blurted, "What's so funny?"

"What's funny is that none of this makes any goddamn sense. Why would Giuseppe invite the Feds out here if he was hiding narcotics on the fuckin' property? I mean, we don't even know why *these* people were invited, right?" he said, pointing to the DHR crew members, all of whom were now being herded behind the yellow tape by Ike Harris.

"Right," said Gino, "but now I know..." his voice trailed off to avoid revealing that he'd already been on the property, "why the fence and locked gate are here."

"But do we? I mean about the fence and all—let's find out who installed the chainlink... that should give us a clue who..."

"So, not Joe Di Rossi, then?"

"Maybe... but, that doesn't necessarily connect him to the dope and the two dead guys, right? I mean... look, your witness told you who ran them outta here, and it wasn't Joe, right?"

Gino nodded, started to say something, then thought better of it as Deputy Harris walked back over to them and broke the silence, "So... is this shit related to your dead guy, or not?"

Simms started to laugh again, "Maybe, maybe not! If so, it's a new twist on our case-—maybe more than one twist." Simms thought another moment, then said, "Okay, look, Ike... for now, these dead guys and the drugs are not our business... this mess is in your hands. But... let's see if we can find out from the State or Fed archaeology guys why they're here and who exactly they've been dealing with in the owner's family. Ike, can you do that quietly while Gino and I snoop around—you know, like we were gonna do with this warrant originally? We'll try to stay out of the way of your forensics team."

"Sure, no sweat... I'll tell 'em that this may be related to one of your cases..."

"Tell them it's two of our cases... oh, and look, this shitshow will hit the news sometime today... can you see if you can keep our faces out of the story for a little while?"

Harris agreed and left Simms and Macina to regroup. Gino waited until Ike was out of earshot, then asked, "So where do you want to start... I mean what clues could lead us to Rodney's..."

"Rodney?" interrupted Simms, "Good god, Gino, keep up, would ya. His murder was just a subterfuge for us being here... we want to know if Maria was hiding out here..."

Gino's face reddened, "Well, obviously, she's not here..."

Simms chuckled, "Not now... but let's see if there's any evidence that somebody—*anybody*—was livin' here. And either way, we want to find out why old Aunt Minerva and Captain Whitehead were here chasing out the homeless folks a few months ago... doesn't that event seem connected to all this? Clearly, there were no drugs stored here then."

Gino nodded, "Well, Davo said that his bunch was told that there would be some construction going on here..."

Simms started to rebuke Gino one more time, but his cell phone rang, interrupting his train of thought. "It's Whitehead— I better take it," he said in a whisper, as if the chief might somehow overhear him before he even answered the phone.

"Morning, boss, what's up?"

"Where are you, Stevenson?" demanded Whitehead.

"I'm with Macina..."

"Well, there's a very hysterical woman trying to reach you... let's see... yeah, her name is Scarlett. She said you told her to call you if anything turned up in the restaurant murder case... her house was burglarized last night, and she says it's connected... So, when you and Macina finish your breakfast, go pay her a visit..."

Simms wondered why Whitehead hadn't already sent a couple of uniforms over to secure the scene, but responded, "Got it, boss... thanks for relaying the message."

Simms clicked his phone off, then looked at Macina, and Gino said, "No need to tell me, I heard him bellering."

Simms laughed, "Cool... look, I should go see what this woman is all worked up about... it can't be too big of a deal if the chief didn't send somebody straight over. Can you check this joint out here, deal with Ike... follow up on the chainlink fence—there's usually a metal tag with the company name on it... and maybe go visit your little pal, Davo? See if you can get him to remember any more details of what this property looked like when they were all living here. I'll call you after noon... maybe we'll come back out here again later... or? I dunno..."

"Got it, partner... I'll be curious to see what this supposed burglary is all about too..."

Simms guided his car carefully along the sorry excuse of a road, away from the shark factory, until he got to good pavement. He stopped, got out to check his tires, and swore at the layers of salty marsh mud that had now accumulated on the undercarriage and bumpers. He made note of the chainlink fence company, figuring that Macina would forget, then headed for a drive-through car wash to remedy the mud-caked appearance. So far, there was still nothing in his morning that had gone according to plan, and now he was trying to be flexible and still stay in control. His method of dealing with the laws of chance usually proved frustrating, no matter what tactic he used, but it didn't ever stop him from behaving as if he could steer the fates his way.

After the carwash, he went through a drive-through for another cup of coffee and a breakfast sandwich. But he was just stalling now, and he knew it. Why was Scarlett so frantic to reach him? "*It can't be that big of deal, and there's no way it's related to this case... what's her game? Maybe she's got something about Valeria, and this is her way of getting attention.*" In the end, he could muster no real answer, and decided that there was only one way— he'd just have to face her and be surprised.

This time, he parked right in front of her house instead of down the street. She'd called *him*— that was his personal protocol with witnesses when they called. Park in front and make it obvious to the entire world.

The grass was still scraggily where it was overtaking the fenced yard, and the gate was still stubborn to open and quick to snap closed. But today, the front door was locked tight and the window shades were drawn shut. And, on the front door was a pentagram sloppily painted in red and a crow's head nailed in the middle of the scrawl. *"Oh, no shit... that's not ever a good thing to come home to..."* Simms muttered to himself before knocking firmly three times. He could see movement in the curtains on the front window, then the sound of a deadbolt clicking before the door opened.

"It took you long enough to get here... what if I was being murdered or something?" demanded Scarlett.

"Well, I am sorry, but if you have an emergency like that, you'd better just call 911," he said. Then he added, "I was investigating a crime scene about an hour from here... so now, tell me what's going on."

Scarlett's eye shadow was smeared as if she'd been crying, or as if she'd been out partying all night—Simms couldn't discern. "Detective, somebody broke in last night— and—you saw the front door!"

Simms' tone changed sympathetically, "Where were you when this happened, Miss Scarlett?"

"Uhh, I was staying over at my boyfriend's place..."

"And the baby?"

"With me and his daddy..."

"Okay, so besides the front door, any other damage? Anything taken?"

Only in Val's room... well, they trashed mine, too, but nuthin' is missin'. C'mon, I'll show you..."

"Okay, have you touched anything, Scarlett?"

"Not in her room... just mine... c'mon in and see."

"Okay, good. I'll get a forensics team over to... oh, shit!" said Simms when he saw Valeria's room. "Sorry, that was unprofessional—I didn't expect this." Simms stood and gawked at the red paint on the walls, and was nearly knocked over by the smell of feces and a dead animal. He couldn't tell which smelled worse. In the middle was a stick figure about three feet high made of dry tree branches with a rope around its neck tied to the rest of the dead crow, which hung by its feet in disgrace.

"Miss Scarlett, do you have any place you can stay out of the way while a forensics team pores over this room? Then I'll help you get this cleaned up as soon as possible..."

"Yeah, thanks... the kitchen, or I can stay over at my boyfriend's house... but look... there was some antique stuff of Val's that is gone—old mother-of-pearl brushes and combs and stuff, and a little wind-up clock that belonged to her mama or grandma... Why would they take stuff like that... it's just mean."

"I don't know, Miss Scarlett... have you talked to Valeria lately?"

"A few days ago... she said she was still waiting on word about that job in Key West..."

"Okay, well, if you can get a message to her, you can tell her what's happened here, and let her know that Detective Simms is on the case."

Scarlett's blushed, "So, you've talked to her since..."

"Since you talked to her about my last visit? Yes, we've spoken a great deal..."

"Oh... well, I uuhh..."

"Don't worry, you didn't do anything wrong, and nothing that I wouldn't have done for a friend. So, look, do you need a ride, or... I'll have to go as soon as forensics arrives, but I'd be glad to drop you and the baby somewhere..."

"Thanks, but Charlie should be here any time..."

"Okay... well, if he can stay with you after forensics gets here, that'd be a good idea... the kitchen is fine... but please don't let him touch anything in Val's room..."

Simms called the forensics team and stayed with Scarlett until they arrived, examining the mess, taking notes, and sketching the crude artwork in his notebook. As he drove away from the house, he had no idea where to go next, so he headed for his office.

Not wanting to have a confrontation with Whitehead, he tried slipping in a side door of the station and hurrying down the corridor without encountering anybody important. But no sooner had he sat down at his desk, then a red-faced police chief was standing in his doorway. "Simms," said the chief in a hoarse voice, one that Stevenson knew meant was a sure sign of anger in the old man, "I thought I told... no! I know I told you to stay out of Manatee Wells and let Macina do the investigating over there!"

Simms feigned surprise, "Have you been talking to Macina?"

"Last time I checked, I don't answer to you... so, what the goddamn hell are you up to?"

"Uhhh, Chief, Macina *is* investigating the murder at Giuseppe's with those folks over in the Wells—just like you said—but I was tracking down a lead on the murder of that old hobo, Rodney... we never discussed that case, did we? Anyway, that's why I was with him over there... I sure wish Gino would have let me tell you about it first... I didn't think it'd be a problem."

Whitehead blustered some more, but then went away in a stream of profanity, confirming what Simms already suspected— the now certain knowledge of exactly where the chief had gotten his information. After checking for messages and rustling through paperwork for a few minutes, Simms decided to find a quiet, anonymous place to have lunch.

Chapter 16
Busy Afternoon

Macina stepped through the open doorway of the Third United Baptist Church Wayfarer Shelter, hoping to surprise Davo with an invitation to lunch. "Sorry, Detective, he's still doing his chores... we'll get him out here in about fifteen minutes," the matron told him.

"Chores?" Macina let that notion float around in his brain while he waited for the elderly woman to fetch his young informant. "*I think I'll ask about that situation before the day is out... he should be getting lessons, not work details,*" he told himself as she disappeared into the shadows of the building.

Presently, the matron ushered Davo into the reception area, and the boy greeted Gino like a long-lost friend. As it turned out, of course, Davo was eager for lunch, although he looked as if he might have welcomed almost anything except what he'd been doing. "Davo, do you like pizza? I know a good place not far from here..."

"Davo likes it when we can get it," the boy replied.

"Good enough, then... we'll go over to this Italian restaurant where I know the chef. He'll fix us up with something special, I'm sure."

Davo had little to say on the short drive, choosing instead to peer out the window and catalog everything he saw on the short route. When Gino turned in at the Third United Baptist Church sign, the boy laughed, "Davo knows this place, Detetive... we could get leftovers in the back sometimes. But we ain't never been inside. Is it really okay?" Macina just laughed and nodded.

They had arrived after the main lunch crowd, so Gino pointed at a table near the front window when the hostess greeted them. She smiled, "Welcome back, Detective, I see you have a new partner. I'll let Ricardo know you're here," she said in a lilting Caribe accent.

Gino laughed and opened the menu, "What kind of pizza do you like, my young friend?"

"Any kind is good," said the boy with all sincerity. He just nodded as Gino read some choices from the menu, only shaking his head at the sardines, "No, suhr... Davo don't eat fish bait, 'specially on pizza."

Macina laughed, then looked up to see Ricardo approaching the table. He never saw the smile fade from Davo's face, nor turn into a scowl while the two men exchanged greetings. Ricardo looked at Davo and said, "Lizzy told me that you had a new partner. How about a root beer, young man?"

Davo looked a little confused, then resolutely claimed, "No, suhr, Davo doesn't drink alcohol..."

Gino stifled a laugh, "Well, my friend, I think you misunderstand Chef Ricardo's offer... root beer is a soda—no alcohol involved. I'd recommend giving it a try, and if you don't like it, well, you can try a coke or something else."

The boy fidgeted in his seat, but agreed. Then he sat quietly and studied Ricardo while Gino discussed the pizza options, wishing that the chef would soon disappear. When at last, Ricardo headed back to the kitchen, Davo cleared his throat and leaned toward Macina to whisper, "Detetive, Davo knows dat man..."

Taken by surprise, Gino asked quietly, "How?"

"He come to da camp over yonder to see the Monk—ol' Rodney. He come two— nah, three times. Dey say 'ol Rodney does things fo' him, and dat's why we gets food from da kitchen sometimes."

"What kind of things, Davo?"

"Davo don't know... just what we done said, is all."

"Well, he didn't seem to recognize you..."

"No, Suhr... Davo don't exist when strangers come to camp. You unnerstand?"

"Yeah, I think so... well, you've nothing to worry about here." Gino changed subjects, and quizzed the boy about life at the shelter, his chores, and whether or not there was any schooling available at all. Davo cheerfully explained the way of things as if it were all a great adventure, but to Gino, it sounded more like a 19th century orphanage.

By the time the pizza arrived, the pair seemed to have run out of things to chat about, except for root beer. It required a refill to finish explaining how the stuff was made and why it wasn't beer at all, but eventually it grew quiet except for the noise of eating pizza. Presently, Davo stopped eating altogether and leaned back in his chair, "So, Detetive, you ain't asked Davo nuthin' about nuthin' yet. What does ya need to know from us— for lunch and all?"

Gino was taken aback, "Well, I don't have anything in particular—you've been most helpful so far, and you did surprise me about recognizing the chef here. I just wanted to see how you were doing, so I asked you out for lunch."

Davo was quiet for a while, then said, "Well, you can ask Davo anything, anytime—no need to feed us..."

Gino laughed, "Only a boy can eat the way you do... it makes me happy to see it." The table went quiet again as Davo nibbled at a bit if crust, then Gino said, "As I sit here and think about it, can you tell me more about how things were when you all lived out by the old shark factory in Dago Bay?"

"Like what?"

"Well, like, did you all live inside the old factory, or tents, or...?

"In da buildings—all of 'em. But not dat ol' shack out past the graveyard... we dint go near it."

"I remember we saw the path out to the graveyard, but I must have forgotten about another building out there..."

"No, Suhr, Davo didn't say nuthin' about it..."

"Did Rodney stay out there, or...?"

"Nope, he was in da main building wit the rest of us, I guess... he never said nuthin about going into da shack."

"Well, you didn't say much about the graveyard, either... how was it like... haunted, or...?"

"Nah, Davo doesn't think so... dem people all been dead long enough to sort der crap out— least dat's what everybody said. Dey was all pirates, anyway... we all knows dey went straight to hell right away."

Gino laughed, then asked, "Who said they were all pirates— and not Indians or something else?"

"Dat's what everybody said, dat's all."

Simms met Macina back at the shark factory by mid-afternoon, and found the crime scene already cleared out. Ike Harris was almost ready to leave too, but stayed to brief the two detectives. "Our forensics guys have finished processing the murder scene as best as possible. There were so many sets of footprints and tire tracks around here, that it's unclear if anybody else was present when these guys were shot. Our guys are skeptical now, though... it may be that these two didn't kill each other... but I can't say more until they're done."

"And the dope?" asked Simms.

"It's all in custody... my major has to decide whether to involve the DEA or not. He's already annoyed that the Feds are here with the State gravediggers."

"Where are those guys now?"

"They'll be back tomorrow, first thing. We're trying to reach the owner's agent—some guy named Zevon Harmon—but no luck so far. The info they gave us was a dead end."

Simms brightened up at the recognition of Harmon's name, and said, "Yeah, well, maybe not... We think the property owner is also the owner of the restaurant where one of our homicides took place..."

"No shit!?" Said Ike. "Do you know where he is right now?"

"Nope. Last we heard, he was in Nassau on business... he might be in the Keys by now... but nobody has seen him around here for nearly three weeks."

Ike scratched his chin, "So, when were you gonna tell me this?"

"Sorry, Ike... it didn't seem relevant until now... he wasn't a suspect in our case," Simms lied.

Harris looked at Macina for a tell-tale of some sort and, failing, said, "Okay... what else aren't you telling me, then?"

Simms answered, almost too quickly, but Ike seemed not to notice, "Well, the owner—Giuseppe—is Joe Di Rossi—he's got a large family in Manatee Wells, so we've been thinking that somebody like that might be involved in our case—and now maybe yours too."

"Wait... Di Rossi? That's not the name we were given... Joseph Rossini... or something like that, and you've been referring to him as Giuseppe."

Gino laughed, "Yeah, like the restaurant. Same difference... Joe changed his name to distance himself from the family's history over here in the Wells... it's the same guy, though."

Ike nodded as if he understood, "Thanks, I'll keep that info in mind... now what else? I mean you two are awfully interested in what's going on here over a dead itinerant that wasn't killed here..."

"Right you are, Ike, and we're getting around to it now... it's a bit touchy—I've alluded to our suspicions and so forth this morning... so this needs to be on the down low..."

Ike stepped back a couple of steps and looked around to see if anybody was watching them. Then he said, "Okay, just hold on to it right now. If you find out anything concrete that might connect to this case, you'll let me know, right?"

Once Harris was assured, he got in his car and left. As the Deputy's car disappeared down the dirt road, Gino said, "Partner, we're walking a thin line with Harris..."

Stevenson nodded, "And with Whitehead, too, Gino. We'd better get on with our walkabout here, and leave this place to Harris if we can't find anything related to what we're after."

"Right, so... about that shack the kid told me about..."

"I've been all ears since you called me..."

"Well, it's out in the hammocks— out that way past the palmettos—we've got maybe three hours of daylight."

The path from the factory buildings toward the graveyard was easy to follow through the saw palmettos and squat cabbage palms, where the archaeology teams had already trod the course many times that morning before the dead men were discovered. But for the path to the shack, Gino was navigating with Davo's vague directions, and this led the detectives off on a fork in the trail that almost immediately melted into dense woods. Even then, though, the white sand path was clearly visible. The main problem for the two partners was avoiding the sharp fronds of palms and cactus, and the gnarly tree roots rising from the earth in the shadows.

"Why would anybody build a cabin way out here in the middle of all this?" wondered Macina aloud.

"Maybe it's had a half century or more to get hidden," answered Simms, ducking under a low hanging oak limb. "Although, I have to say, these trees look way older than that—by centuries."

"Maybe so, Stevenson, but somebody has been on this trail recently—there's plenty of footprints in these sandy stretches." They kept walking, silently now, looking into the densely packed woods for any sign of a building. Eventually, they crossed a small clearing and saw the trail lead under the perfect arch of an ancient oak. Ducking under the massive limb, avoiding the snarl of wild grapevines dangling from all angles, they emerged into another tiny clearing. There, nestled in a tangle of green, covered in moss and yellow lichen, was a cabin. "That doesn't look like what I'd call a shack," said Simms.

"Nope, but that's what Davo called it... but he never saw it—or so he said..."

"Maybe it was a caretaker's cottage or something..."

"Yeah, but who's been taking care of it recently? I mean, it's not run down liked the factory buildings..."

"No, but it's not a five-star, either. Let's see if anybody's home."

After calling out and getting no response, Simms gingerly went up the steps, noticing that the shutters had been painted at some point in the distant past. The porch creaked under his weight, and he stopped short of the door sill, then reached out and rapped on the door. It creaked open slowly under the impact, inviting him to peer inside. "Somebody has been living here, Gino... let's look around."

Macina followed Simms inside the dim room and looked around. "Somebody keeps it pretty tidy. Except for the dishes in the sink… they look pretty crusty…"

Looking around some more, Simms went into a back room, "Well, here's a cosmetic bag of some sort. Bed's not made up." He opened an antique wardrobe and peered inside, "Ladies stuff…" he said, returning to the main room. "Okay, well… don't touch anything else, Gino. We better call Ike and tell him to turn around. His forensics people will want to give this little hideaway a going-over."

Chapter 17
Earlier That Morning

Captain Albert Whitehead clicked off his phone and slouched back in the seat of his car in disappointment. Maybe it was confusion that controlled him now, that's all he could feel through the paralysis. Minerva was willing to let it all go, rather than take this new risk with him. "*Minerva, my lady,*" he had whined, "*we are into the Colombians for a million or more if we lose this shipment! At least help me get part of it back tonight so we can cover our losses.*" But the old dame wouldn't make the call to her two cousins, and Whitehead knew why—she was suspicious of his story. After all, even he hadn't believed that Federal antiquities authorities, nor even the meddlesome State bureaucrats, were suddenly about to begin an investigation of an old graveyard in the swamps of Manatee Wells.

It was only Lady Luck who had dropped the information in his lap in the first place, sheer serendipity. When Minerva had called him to say that two of his detectives were snooping around the old shark factory, including the fact that one was an imposing black man, Whitehead knew he could control the situation, but it meant getting out in front of any problem. First, he had to cover his tracks with the County Sheriff, because he had intentionally *not* contacted his counterpart out of concern that the Sheriff would grow interested in a murder case with ties inside his jurisdiction. But Whitehead had lied to his own men about it too, and they were now poking around. And if Minerva had complained to *him* about a black cop, he could bet that somebody else in her neighborhood would call the Sheriff with the same complaint. And this is where Lady Luck stepped in. The Sheriff had just laughed at Whitehead when he called, *"Boy, Albie, you're late to the party—the Feds and the State boys are also interested in that property, and one of my deputies is getting a warrant over there to investigate some murder case... so, yeah, go on over too, if you want! It'll be quite a party in the morning."*

That conversation had been at dinner time, but now it was after midnight and Whitehead was out of resources and time. And he knew it. He made the short drive to the old factory road, unlocked the gate, and slowly navigated the rutted track out to the factory. The two guards wouldn't be alert for trouble—most likely, they'd be sleeping instead. So he counted on surprising them, then expected he could proposition them to help him move the cocaine if they understood that the place was about to be raided. Whitehead reasoned that it wouldn't take much convincing because they knew he was Minerva's partner in the operation. All he'd have to do was make up a story about why Minerva hadn't called them herself. He cursed her once again for her stubbornness.

As he slowly steered closer to the factory, he decided that surprise in the middle of the night was not a good thing. *"Best to make a noisy entrance—lights, horn—I'm less likely to get shot,"* he reasoned. To a certain extent, Whitehead's strategy was successful. The guards were alerted minutes before his arrival, and they didn't shoot him on sight. But they proved intractably opposed to his offers to let them make off with as many bricks of coke as they could carry, in exchange for their help in loading up his trunk.

"Look," he told them, "we need to salvage at least fifty kilos of this load before the Feds get here—just to break even. You boys can have as much of the rest of it as you want—just make sure that you're out of here before dawn." But when they insisted on an approval from cousin Minerva, Whitehead tried to talk them out of it.

"Don't bother calling her on your phone at this time of night—she won't answer. She's got a different mobile I gave her... I'll get mine from my car and call her on that one—she'll answer *me*—then you can speak with her yourself." When they agreed, he disappeared into the shadows where his car was parked, and returned with his riot gun instead.

"Boys," he said, having gotten the drop on them, "I don't have any more time to argue! Either help me or, I swear to God..." He shot them both in succession when one reached for his shotgun. Then he spent a few haphazard minutes staging the scene to look like the men had killed each other. Once satisfied with the makeshift scene, he drove to the rear of the storage room and loaded his trunk with bricks of cocaine, and then drove into the night.

It had all happened quickly, and Whitehead felt no remorse. He'd given the two knuckleheads plenty of opportunity to help him—and themselves. Now they were dead, apparently by their own hands—if he'd staged the scene convincingly. There was enough coke left, not to mention a warehouse stacked full of ganja, to keep the drug agencies happy, and there was nothing he could think of that would tie him to the scene. His tire tracks would be overrun by a bunch of new vehicles soon enough, and he had enough product to keep the cartel at bay. And if his luck held, Minerva would never find out.

Chapter 18
Progress, Signs, and Confessions

Simms threaded his way along the white sand path, now illuminated only by the narrow beam of his tactical flashlight. The canopy of oaks and vines swallowed the starlight before it reached the floor of the woods and, more than once, he avoided sprawling on his face when a tree root evaded his beam and sprang from the shadows. Why he had volunteered to stay at the shack until Ike Harris' deputies arrived to secure the place was beyond him now, and he had no brain space available to second-guess his decision. At the moment, he was more than annoyed at his skittishness in the dark, berating himself for being spooked by a palm frond here, or a snakelike vine there, when they popped out of the night air.

Finally, Simms reached the clearing where the old factory buildings stood as silhouettes against the deep purple of the midnight sky, free of the tangles and shadows of the oak hammocks. He imagined that Macina was already entwined in the arms and legs of Emilia somewhere in the outskirts of Palm Beach, breathing restfully without a care for the revelations of their day's investigation. *"That's fine,"* he concluded under his breath, *"Gino did volunteer to stay, but there was no reason for us both..."*

Mercifully, there had been no rain that day, so the road out to the pavement was not as tricky in the dark, allowing Stevenson to exhale once he hit A1A and turned for home. On the drive, he searched the recesses of his memory for some image of beer bottles in his fridge, but the hunt was fruitless. Imagining a cold draft beer or two, feet up and shoes off in front of his television, he made the detour to the corner market near his home for emergency rations.

Now, fully expecting the day's miles would fall away with little prodding, he edged his car into the narrow garage and headed for his front porch. Only when he fished his door keys out of his pocket did he notice the newly scrawled artwork on the doorway. There, big as a basketball, was the image of an eye. It was unmistakably an eye, brushed in blue paint and framed inside a six-pointed star. Above the image arched the words, ***Il Malocchio.***

Simms set his bag of groceries and briefcase down on the steps and drew his pistol before unlocking the door. As quietly as he could, he pushed the door open a crack, then wider, then flipped on the light switch. Nothing. Mail on the floor, windows closed... no sign of entry. "*Shit, first the swamp, then this. I must be losing my nerve.*" Once he retrieved his belongings from the porch, he found his camera and took a few photos. "*The lab can print these in the morning,*" he told himself calmly. He knew the door art was a message from one '*admirer*' or another, but which one? Was this the same shithead who smeared Scarlett's place? Or a different one? They seemed quite different to him, but all he could surmise was, "*Hell, I'm no expert... I need an expert opinion...*" He kicked off his shoes, popped a beer, and slouched down on the sofa, pistol within reach.

When he opened the second beer, he muttered, "*Screw it. I'm gonna call her.*" It'd only taken one beer and 10 minutes to overcome his hesitancy about calling Trinity. Sure, he might be pulling her back in to his investigation, but it didn't seem inevitable. At least, that's what he told himself as the alcohol took effect. He let the phone ring until an answering machine picked up and a recorded voice sweetly suggested that he might want to leave a message. He hung up. After two more tugs at the beer, he called back and left a message. *"She's probably working,"* he reasoned before falling asleep.

Gino Macina was late. Well, he was late by Simms' standards, but it was only 7AM and, shortsightedly, they'd made no plans to actually meet early. Simms sat at his desk and stared at the photos of his front door. *Il Malocchio*. *"Macina might know what it means. Or Trinity. Or Madame LaCroix."* Simms was impatient to find out so he could speculate on the origins of the artist. At the same time, an internal clock told him that he should get out of the office and drive out to the old shark factory before Whitehead showed up. The last thing he wanted right at that moment was for the chief to start micro managing his day. Then he remembered Scarlett's break-in. *"Shit, I need to get that report before Whitehead sees it. It's not all about you today, Stevenson,"* he muttered.

A forensics tech gave him a rough cut of their findings along with a few photos, and he ducked out the side of the building, headed for Manatee Wells. On the way, he called Macina and told him to meet at the shark factory at 9AM.. "I've got to attend to a couple of things before I get out there. Wait... do you know what *Il Malocchio* means?"

Gino got him to spell it out... "Oh, *Il Malocchio..."* he laughed. "It's a reference to the evil eye or bad spirits. Why do you ask?"

"I'll explain when you get there," he answered impatiently.

First on his list was breakfast, but he hadn't invited Macina because what he really wanted was a solitary bit of time to look at data from Scarlett's break-in. Waiting for his breakfast, he sat hunched over a cup of coffee perusing the photos of the red paint scrawled on her door and in Valeria's room. Then he took a close look at the blue handiwork on this own door. In his opinion, they were entirely different. Fingerprints from Val's bedroom were mostly hers and Scarlett's, "*but there were some unknowns too...*" His mind jumped around until he focused back to the evil eye. Then he noticed that the stars were different. One—the red scrawl—was a pentagram, while the "evil eye" was set in a six-pointed star formed from two triangles. *"That seems different, or maybe not. Who knows?"*

Then his phone rang.

It cost her a week's worth of tips from The Drunken Chicken, but Trinity had made a decision: she was going to fly up to see Simms. The notion had emerged in the middle of the night and she wrestled with it in the dark, weighing the sound of his voice against the content of the message. "*Val and Scarlett's house ransacked? Val's heirlooms stolen? Where the hell is Valeria now, anyway?*" Then the graffiti—she had to see it, and the message was vague. She couldn't quite visualize what he'd told her, but maybe she could decipher the meaning if she saw it. *"Or maybe Auntie Sonia can, if I can show her photos."* But what was she doing, inserting herself in Simms' case? *"After pitching a fit about him involving me just a week ago, I'm going to his rescue?"* There was more to it than that, and she knew it. She'd tried to book an afternoon flight from Key West to West Palm Beach late in the night, but couldn't get through to an agent. She went back to sleep, leaving the ticket until morning. The wrestling match was over for the night.

Her morning phone conversation with Simms revealed many more details about events, and it galvanized her decision to fly north.

It was personal now, on more than one level. But first, she had to go see her Aunt Sonia, Madame LaCroix.

Simms and Macina arrived at the shark factory within minutes of each other, and found the Deputy falling all over himself to relay his latest information. "Here's a photocopy of what the D-H-R sent over regarding their project here. Basically, it says that a member of some obscure Indian tribe has asserted that this is a Native American sacred site, and is filing a claim against the owners to have the land turned over to the tribe under provisions of a Federal law."

"What tribe?" asked Macina, his interest again piqued by the subject.

"Uuhh, I'm not sure how to pronounce it—it's in the report... J-a-e-g-a, I think it was."

Macina laughed, "Well, if he's from the Jaega band, he's about two-maybe three- hundred years old by now... the rest of 'em disappeared or became extinct in the seventeen hundreds..."

Ike laughed, "Yeah, the head honcho with the State is skeptical about all of it... he said the same thing—this guy wasn't old enough to be Jaega."

Again, Simms was curious about Macina's knowledge of Native American antiquities and made a mental note to get to the bottom of that one day soon. Instead, he asked, "So, why now? Why make such a claim now? I mean, this place has been vacant for half a century..."

"Well, apparently, the hurricane that came through a couple of months ago washed out some of the underbrush and moved a lot of sand that revealed the graveyard. Per the owner's agent—that Zev Harmon character—the owner will not contest the Jaega Indian claim if the D-H-R scientists can validate whatever it is they have to find... the owner will simply ask the State for some tax considerations going forward, and some other stuff... it's all in there."

Macina listened patiently, then said, "That's kinda weird, Ike. Our information is that the graveyard was an old pirate burial ground from the Spanish gold days... after my source told me this, I did some checking— look, the State already knew of this site, but since the graveyard is on private land, they decided against making any efforts to control it. Apparently, the regs already require a number of things from the owner if he wants to disturb the antiquities, and it's not considered that important of a site anyway."

Harris shrugged, "Right, so this Indian's claim is something new... nobody saw it coming."

Simms silently debated whether to add anything to the conversation, but finally decided to ring in, "All very interesting, to be sure, but we also have it on good authority that Joe Di Rossi ... or Rossini... whatever name we're gonna use for this owner— Joe— he had plans to tear the old buildings down and build something new out here. That intel seems at odds with what you're saying, Ike. Had you heard any rumblings about any building plans? Or, Gino, was there any recent permit application in the records?"

Gino said, "I didn't see anything like that, but I didn't really look either."

Simms nodded, "Okay, but, how do we reconcile all of this with a ton of dope being stored here with two dead men guarding it?"

Harris interjected, "I don't know the answer to that, but our forensics folks think there was more coke in that shed on the night of the killings than what we found in the morning. There were tire tracks in front of the door and a set of shoe prints going back and forth between the car and the shed... like seven or eight times... and nothing was tracked over the top of 'em."

"So, you think there was another guy here?"

"Yeah, for sure... the shotgun shells at the scene were ejected from the same gun, and it wasn't one of the dead guys who did the shooting... both of their guns were unfired."

Macina laughed, "Well, Ike, looks like you boys have your hands full."

Simms shot a glance at Macina that Gino missed; not wanting to give Harris the idea that the Treasure Coast PD was bailing out of the case, he asked, "Ike, what about the cottage... what've you guys found out there?"

"Not much more than what you and I talked about last evening, Simms... it seems obvious that a female was living there... our guys know a professor up in Jacksonville that can test hair and stains for DNA... we found two types of hair in the bed. That's gonna take some time, though. Fingerprints are all over the place, and it's gonna take days to sort through all of that, too."

"That's cool, Ike. Let us know if you find anything... oh, I got a call from a source earlier this morning—we might have a lead on the whereabouts of the property owner. I think we both want to speak with him at length."

Ike's mobile buzzed right then and he excused himself, so Simms and Macina began walking back to their cars. "So, Stevenson, we've told Ike that Joe Di Rossi is also the owner of Giuseppe's, but not a key person of interest in our murder case... at some point, he's gonna put two and two together... about Maria and all. What are you gonna say then?"

Simms scratched at the back of his neck, "We're gettin' close to that time, Partner. We've all but told him everything, but...

"Right, but he thinks we're investigating the hobo's murder."

"Yeah, I know, and somehow, I'll have to connect the two cases if he asks. I did tell him that we had two cases, and he's smart enough to put this all together... he probably already has, but if we come right out and tell him, he might have to keep us away from the case 'cuz it's out of our jurisdiction now. But look, I really do have a chance to find out where Joe is first... otherwise, they'll put out a warrant, and we'll likely never find him if he heads for Venezuela or someplace. See, I'm picking up Trinity from the airport in a few hours..." Gino laughed and started to say something, but was interrupted.

"Simms! Macina! Don't leave yet! You're gonna want to see this!" The detectives turned to see what Deputy Harris was hollering about. Ike beckoned, "Hurry up! The State boys found a grave."

Simms laughed and started walking toward Harris, "Right, well, it *is* a graveyard."

Harris waved him off, "This is a fresh one." The detective picked up the pace.

"Doctor Chen, this is Detective Simms... and Detective Macina... we're working a case together. Boys, Dr. Chen is head of this project and he's a... uuhh...

"Forensic anthropologist," said Dr. Chen.

Ike said, "Right, the Sheriff's coroner and Dr. Chen are good friends, and so he's given the go ahead for the exhumation..."

"Right," said Chen, "It's not much of a dig... you can see... she was in a shallow grave over here on the far edge of the old graveyard..."

"She?" queried Simms.

"Yeah, she hadn't been in the ground long... a week or so, from our first look. The body wasn't too far gone."

"But not two-and-half or three weeks?"

"No... no way," said Chen. "We'll see if we can still get a decent set of prints, do a dental records check..."

"Can you do a DNA test on her hair?" asked Harris.

"Sure, we'll send a sample up to Jacksonville... and it'll perhaps take longer to determine cause of death," replied Dr. Chen.

Simms cleared his throat, "Ike, can we talk for a moment? Gino, stay here with Doctor Chen and watch what they're doing... take notes, yeah?"

"Okay," said Gino knowingly, as Simms and Harris walked 50 feet away.

Once they were out of earshot of the others, Simms said, "Ike, you aren't gonna be happy with me, but I need to clear up a few things I've been vague about..."

Harris chuckled, "I was pretty sure... but decided you had your reasons, so no harm, no foul. What's up?"

"Macina and I have been investigating two homicides, not just one..."

"Yeah, you've said that..."

"Well, we think that the hobo's killing was related to the first one... remember a few weeks ago... the murder at Giuseppe's restaurant?"

"Yeah, the one where there was no body," said Ike sarcastically.

"Right... well, but we had three missing people, though, a husband, wife, and a waitress who was the mistress. The wife's family said she—the wife—was shacking up with *her* lover too while the husband was off with his mistress... but..."

"You think she's dead, the wife?"

"Right now, I'd say it's almost certain."

"Why? Just because we found a dead woman... wait... who is the wife?"

"Maria Di Rossi... "

"The owner's wife? The guy who owns this land?"

"Exactly... and the owner of Giuseppe's restaurant. We think Giuseppe's wife Maria has been hiding out here—based on what a family member told us. But there's a great chance that she's the actual murder victim. And, I really don't want to say more, Ike, because..."

Harris shook his head and frowned. "I guess you've been telling me this all along. So, you think he killed her?" he interrupted

"Well, no, I mean, we didn't before, because he has a strong alibi for the night of the incident at Giuseppe's Restaurant..."

“Wait? You’ve talked to him?”

“Yeah, I tracked him to the Bahamas a couple of weeks ago...”

“So, where is he now?”

“I don’t have a clue... he left Nassau in the middle of the night after I talked to him.”

“But you said you might have a lead on him...”

“Yeah, I’ll know more this afternoon when I speak with a source I trust...

“So, if this body is that of his wife, and it’s only a week old, then...”

“He’s gonna need a new alibi...”

Chapter 19
Speculations

Stevenson Simms sat quietly in the airport lounge waiting for Trinity's plane to arrive, and contemplated the morning's events. It was another day that had gotten out of his control way too early and now he was suppressing some anxiety that the next phase—the arrival of his last-minute visitor—might go sideways too. Still, he was able to rationalize the outcome, if not the order of the morning's events that had unfolded. "*Ike Harris wasn't pissed at me for withholding information, so that's good,*" he told himself unconvincingly. The near certainty that the buried corpse was that of Maria Di Rossi was, in itself, not good, but at least they could stop looking for *her.* However, that was small consolation in light of the twists her death presented. If she wasn't the one murdered in Giuseppe's restaurant, then who was that? And where was the body? There were no more missing people that they knew of. "*Maybe I was right all along—nobody was killed in that kitchen. But if I'm wrong, if old Rodney's murder was connected to the one at the restaurant, then how? Or, maybe they aren't,*" he reasoned to himself. "*Perhaps Rodney was just bashed in the head by somebody in the homeless camp... we hadn't even considered that possibility earlier because he was a witness in the restaurant killing—or so we were told... by three dozen biased observers... shit.*"

Then, there was the issue with Whitehead and Minerva. Simms rolled that around in his head for a few minutes. *"Minerva said Maria was hiding out somewhere, and she had a lover—at least that's what Macina says... well, in all likelihood, we know where she was hiding—the shack was almost certainly her hideout. But why hide, unless she was in danger? But from whom? Her husband, Joe? Or her own lover—who is he? And why not just stay at his place instead of some remote shack? Yeah, maybe she was hiding from her lover too, and by hiding out in that old cabin, she stumbled onto the drug dealers, and they whacked her. That'd be too ironic... well, Minerva and Albie Whitehead are up to something... but cocaine? That's a pretty wild notion... would he murder somebody like Maria to protect his ass? Yeah, probably... there are two more dead bodies at the site... gotta think that through, though."*

Simms looked at his wristwatch, and saw that he still had ten minutes before Trini's plane was due to land. He began to wonder what info she had that was so important that she just had to fly up from Key West to deliver it in person. *"It's gotta be about Val and Joe... she's gotta know where they are and where they've been for the last couple of weeks. Doesn't she? She seemed very concerned about the break-in at her sister's house and the graffiti. And how does that break-in mesh with the case? Or the artwork on my front door? Gino and I must have stirred up somebody's hornet nest... we deliberately tried to aggravate Minerva, Whitehead, and who else...? Oh, yeah, Chef Ricardo."*

And, as for Joe... Giuseppe himself... what's he up to? Hobnobbing with that South African guy, Zev Harmon... Val said Joey was gonna build something... Davo said the White Witch—Minerva herself—told the homeless people that the old shark factory was going to be razed for a construction project... surely, there can't be two projects that Joey was working on—and now, he's gonna give the land to the Indians? No way... unless... unless Minerva was just bullshitting the homeless people so they wouldn't ask questions and return... that would've interfered with the drug stash and such. And maybe Val was out of line... maybe Joey is just investing in one of Harmon's projects somewhere else... No that doesn't make sense, because the Florida State's report said that Zev Harmon was acting as the agent for the land owner, who is—Joe. So, why give the land away? He can't have known about the drugs... or maybe that's where he was getting the cash to build... build what? Nah, he didn't know about the drugs. Did he know about his wife's affair? So fuckin' what? He's shacked up with his girlfriend... he wouldn't murder Maria over that. Shit, I'm missing too many puzzle pieces."

Simms saw the small turboprop plane land and pushed all of his conjecture into a waste bin in the back of his brain. Then he stood up, stretched, and waited for Trinity to materialize from the small crowd of passengers. When he recognized her and saw her smile, it brightened his day in a heartbeat. Moving toward each other like two magnets, they nearly collided, but before there could be an awkward moment, Trinity put her arms around the back of his neck, stood up on her tiptoes, and gave Simms what he later thought was a pretty decent hello kiss, given that there had only been one real kiss before, and that had been a 'goodbye'.

She blushed a little and stood back as if to survey him, to see if he measured up to what she'd remembered from a little more than a week before. Seemingly satisfied with the reality in front of her, she took his arm and headed for baggage claim. "Surprised to see me, Simms?" she asked coyly.

"Here, and now? Yeah, certainly... it wasn't on my horizon for the week." He stammered a little, "I knew I'd see you again, though—or I hoped to, anyway. I'm sorry it's under these circumstances..."

"Yeah, well, we have to adapt on the fly, Simms... you know, take advantage of situations when they happen along. Hey, you know..."

she stopped mid-sentence, not knowing what might come out of her mouth next.

"What?"

"Nothing... I was... well, can we just go to my sister's place? I need to see what's happened there?"

"Sure, have you heard from her?"

"No, damn her. She hasn't answered any of my calls. I know she's getting the messages on her mobile."

"Maybe she's just scared about the break-in..." he offered vaguely.

Trinity just shrugged and pointed to her small suitcase, and Simms retrieved it. Once they were in the car, he handed a stack of photos to Trini, then he headed out to the highway. "Those are the shots our forensics team took of her front door... and Scarlett's room and Val's room... I tried to describe them over the phone, but these tell the story better than I can."

Trinity pored over the photos for several minutes, then said, "I tried to tell my Aunt Sonia what you'd told me on the phone, but she was kind of non-committal. She said they might be some amateur voodoo or something... witchcraft, I think she said. I told her about the missing mother of pearl hairbrush and accessories, and she just laughed."

"Laughed? Why?"

"She said they weren't worth anything... she's the one who gave them to Val. They were so fragile, they couldn't be used..."

"But Scarlett said they were heirlooms... she thought Val... "

"Yeah, they were our mama's. Still had strands of her hair in the brush, you know..."

"And Madame thought that was humorous?"

"Yeah, see, if this was some voodoo shit or amateur sorcery or something, they would want the hair from the hairbrush to cast a spell... see, it's what you would say... well, a sorcerer would need hair or fingernails, or spit, you know, something personal—belonging to the subject. Then he—or she—could mix up whatever kind of spell..."

"So, that works?"

Simms was only half serious, but Trini missed the irony in his voice.

"Well, that's the thing everybody thinks... but no. Auntie tries to tell her clients this too... if the spirits determine that the spell isn't just, then it won't work..."

"I still don't see the humorous part..."

"Well, it's not Val's hair in the brush, silly. And Mama has been dead for years... so..."

"So the burglar is wasting his time... I can see why Madame would get a chuckle..."

"Yeah, she did... oh, and she said to thank you for the cigars. Baxter brought her a box, he said it was fresh from Cuba... but how?"

"He has to smuggle his wife back and forth to Cuba every so often—he says it's either to see her sick mother, or her other boyfriend..."

Trinity laughed, "Seriously?"

"You never know about Baxter... he might be Madame's client one day."

"Oh, stop."

"Okay, okay, did Madame have anything else to say?"

"No, not really... she *was* curious about the evil eye on your door..."

"Those photos are in that other envelope..."

"Okay, I'll look at them. She says that if somebody plasters an evil eye like that, they might be trying to scare you... or they are very scared themselves, and it's supposed to protect them from you..."

"How can I determine which?"

"Hell, Simms, I don't know. I wouldn't worry about spell-casting if I were you! Oh, Jesus, these photos look a lot more serious than you described. Somebody put a lot of time and effort into the details. This isn't just angry graffiti... it's quite artful."

"Right, I had the same feeling about the little wicker shrine that was erected in Val's room. Did you look at that closely?"

"Yeah, I wish Aunt Sonia could see these pictures..."

"I'll get copies made, and you can take them back with you..."

When they arrived at Valeria's house, it was locked up tight, but that isn't what surprised Simms—it was the red graffiti still scrawled on the door. He looked at Trini and said, "I gave Scarlett a number for people who clean up this kind of mess after a break-in... I wonder why she didn't?"

"Oh, she did, Simms, but the people refuse to work on the place..."

"You've talked to her?" he interrupted.

"Yeah, this morning—after I had my plane ticket... anyway, she said they were too superstitious to touch anything, and they just scurried off like rats. She said she cleaned up her own room, but Val's is still a mess..."

"So, she's still at her boyfriend's place? He should've helped her..."

Trinity knelt down and looked amongst the potted plants on the front porch, then stood up with a triumphant look and a key and said, "Well, he's a tool, you know what I mean? Maybe good for one thing, and one thing only."

Simms laughed, "Yeah, I get the idea. So, you didn't answer my question earlier—does Val know about this mess?"

"Well, I told her a little bit in a message, but like I said earlier, she hasn't responded. But Scarlett told me this morning that she's talked with Val and gave her the gory details..."

Simms nodded, but his look was stern now, "Trinity, you have to try again, leave a message and try to convince Valeria to get back home. She needs to be here, and so does Joe. The Sheriff has found a body they are pretty sure is Joe's wife, and if he doesn't get his ass back here with some pretty good stories, he's gonna be in a lot of trouble. Look, I'm not supposed to say this, 'cuz it's not certain yet... but you can see the problem, right?"

Trinity was absorbing Simms' speech at the same time she surveyed Val's room, then stopped and looked at Simms. "This is a bigger fuckin' mess than I thought..."

"The room?" asked Simms, seemingly confused by Trinity's lack of focus.

"No, Simms... well, that too, but this mess that Val's gotten herself into. Yeah, this room is... I can't stay here tonight... Simms, can I stay with you?"

Simms felt his head nod up and down while his brain thought it was shaking side to side. "Right, you can't stay here... this still looks like a crime scene out of a bad movie. But..."

"Great, that's settled. I'm gonna go out to the living room and call Valeria again. I'm not cleaning up her shit."

Simms spent the next several minutes looking at the dead crow hanging from the stick figure in the middle of the room, and trying to decipher the red painted graffiti on the walls. *"And what's up with the dogshit spread around the room? I forgot about that touch... I need to ask Trini about that too."*

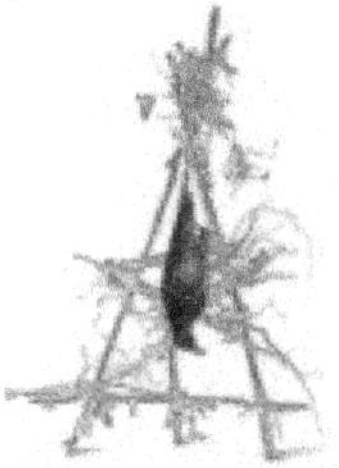

"Simms, do you have any wine at your place? Or food?"

"No, but I can take you out," he said, while they drove toward his side of town.

"Nope, you're gonna take me to a supermarket and buy a reasonable supply of groceries so I can make you decent meals, and you're going to lay in a supply of half decent wine so that the cook is a happy worker. Got it?"

Simms laughed good-naturedly. It had been a long time since anybody had bossed him around in such a pleasant manner, and he kind of liked the banter. "Okay, but..."

"But what?"

"Nothin'... I've got a pretty good market near my place..."

"Nice, now please tell me that your house is tidier than my sister's..."

"Always," he replied convincingly. "Now, what are the odds that your sister will call you back."

"Ha!" she scoffed. "Good question... my guess is that she'll call... well let's say she has a crappy knack for poor timing. It'll be inconvenient, you can be sure of that."

"Well, keep you phone handy while we're here in the market..."

They spent nearly an hour in the market, she flirting, he acting incredulous at the amount of supplies she piled into the cart. She picked out the wines to go with the meal that night, and a few extra bottles just in case she might have to prepare more than one meal. He just laughed, and hoped he had rum in his cabinet at home.

When they finally arrived at his front door, Simms put down the bags of groceries to fish for his keys. But Trini stopped chattering and set her bags down too, "Simms, this is... beautiful!" she exclaimed, surveying the blue-eyed art work. "Maybe you'll start a new trend in the neighborhood..."

Simms looked to see if she was serious, "I'm glad you think so... but it's probably a little too pagan for my neighbors' sake."

"You were right, though, this is entirely different from the graffiti at Val's place. And, yeah, this isn't a pentagram like on Val's door... it's called... well, it's a rendition of a talisman... Sonia's got one like it... she calls it a pentacle..."

Simms unlocked the door and pushed it in, "What's the difference? They sound the same..."

"Right, well, a pentagram can be pentacle... it has special meaning... different from this hexagram here... see... six points..."

"I still don't get it, and... I thought you said you didn't know anything about voodoo and stuff."

"Well, look, different practitioners like different symbols for their special meanings and the spirits they rely on... if they make a talisman out of one, it's just called... well Aunt Sonia calls 'em all pentacles... she said the hexagram might be used to summon spirits to protect against the evil eye... see, it's caged in the middle... and to answer your last question, I was interested in this as a little girl. It seemed like magic and fantasy and such. But I lost interest..."

"But Val didn't?"

"No, but she should have... she got stuff all mixed up and had a falling out with Mama and Sonia, and, well... she was just a brat. She didn't want to put in the time and effort to learn the craft—or that's what Sonia says."

"So, do you think she'll be freaked out when she sees her house?"

"Maybe, but she'll most likely just be pissed."

Simms thought a moment, "Has she ever spoken of enemies around here? You know, people who would do her harm?"

"No... well Val didn't speak fondly about Joe's wife, but then she's dead... it seems that the lady is beyond suspicion now."

"That's what I was thinking, too," said Simms, finally closing the front door and locking it. "So, I tend to live on the ground floor—there's an entire upstairs with a couple of bedrooms and a bath... take the one just to the right of the landing—it's all made up."

"Okay, I can go up in a minute... show me your kitchen and stuff, we'll need a corkscrew... and then you go clean up. You smell like you've been in a swamp all day."

"Well, that's because I was," he answered defensively. When they were finished sorting the groceries, Simms opened a bottle of wine for Trinity, grabbed a cold beer and headed for the shower.

Trinity milled about the kitchen, drinking her wine and planning the steps she'd need for cooking. When she heard the water running in the shower, though, she stopped what she was doing. "*What the hell, LaCroix, why not?*" She started undressing in the kitchen and finished strewing her undergarments by the time she reached the end of the hall way. She followed the sound to the master bath and, stepping into the shower, she said, "You don't mind, do you, Simms?"

Chapter 20
Davo's Dilemma

"Cleanliness is next to Godliness," echoed in Davo's brain. He'd heard the admonishment daily from the matron at the tenement house and dormitories that made up the Third United Baptist Church Wayfarer Shelter. It was her refrain when she made the daily rounds to inspect the toilets and showers at the shelter, and it was her criticism for whatever suspicious speck or yellow stain that might've remained after he was finished scrubbing. In Davo's mind, all he could wonder was why these so-called holy people were so filthy in the first place, so poorly skilled at taking care of their own business, that he had to clean up after them. They were the ones. God should be preachin' to them— or at least the gray-haired matron should be—about cleanliness... in Davo's opinion.

They had taken his shoes away. Well, the shoes had grown too small too quickly anyway, but the confiscation was supposed to keep him from running away. Davo had never let on that he'd escaped from tougher facilities than this one. Besides, he preferred bare feet. They were quieter when he made his stealthy way around the place in the middle of the night, mapping out the corridors and pacing the escape routes. No, taking away his shoes wasn't what kept him from leaving. It was that cop. He'd promised Detective Macina that he wouldn't run away and, for some reason, the promise meant something to Davo, although he didn't have the words to piece it together. He knew the word 'trust', and that seemed enough.

Davo had begun to overcome many his fears since hanging out with Macina. Yes, Rodney was dead and, yes, the band of homeless folks had run away, leaving him behind and alone with the Monk's zombie. But he wasn't afraid of anything when he was with the cop. Not the White Witch, not the old fat man who bellowed like a cow, and not the dark-eyed man from the restaurant. Davo wasn't afraid of the matron, either. She was too fat and slow to stop him if he decided to dart out of the shelter. So for now, cleaning toilets, sleeping out of the rain, and getting an occasional lunch date with Macina all seemed like an okay bargain. But at some point, he was going to have to come clean and tell Macina the rest of the story about the Monk, and what all he knew. That was a fear yet to be conquered.

Davo couldn't answer his big question just yet, did he trust Macina *enough,* have faith in the cop to protect him if he told everything? In Davo's experience, it seemed unlikely that a bunch of old white men would believe his story, and they almost certainly wouldn't believe what the Monk had told him. So, this would be serious business, and he could end up like Rodney—a zombie in the swamp—if Detective Macina let him down. Every time he thought about it, he got the same feeling as when he stepped in the swamp mud near the mangroves and began to sink... the muck pulled at him as if to suck him down. But the muck always stopped at his ankles and he could pull free. In his nightmares now, the mud kept pulling him down. Maybe he'd have to run away just to escape the dilemma. But not today, because today, he was going to lunch with Macina again.

Macina had phoned ahead this time, and the Third United Baptist matron had Davo ready to launch as soon as Gino arrived. Except the kid was barefoot. "No, Suhr, dey got too small for Davo's feet... like in one night... Davo likes it, tho'."

"Well, that may be, but no friend of mine has to go barefoot when we go to lunch... we're going to that Sears out on A-1-A and get you some good sneaks... and socks... Davo, you'll want socks with new shoes."

"New?" Davo choked up, "We don't 'member new ones fo' long time."

"Well, then, it's about time... then we're going to a place where a friend of mine works— her name is Emilia, and her auntie owns the place. It's called Juliana's Café down in West Palm."

"Dat's a ways, Detetive... why we... oh... she more than a friend?"

"Very sharp, you are, Davo. Yes, Emilia is more than a friend..."

"You gonna marry her?"

Gino laughed, "I haven't asked her yet, but I suspect her mama's expecting me to ask her someday soon... and if I don't, well, I'll have to find another place for lunch... okay, here's our turn for Sears..."

Davo was working on the last half of his sandwich and a second root beer, while still keeping a side-eye on Macina and Emilia. The cop hadn't asked him any questions about the Monk, or the encampment, or the shelter— yet. But the boy couldn't help wondering what was coming. It wasn't an uneasy feeling, just an expectation hanging out in plain view, matter-of-fact-like. Still, Gino's question interrupted the boy's musing, "Davo, Miss Emilia wants to know if you'd like some ice cream, or a piece of pie?"

It wasn't the kind of question he was expecting, "Davo is kinda full, but reckons pie would be good anyway."

Macina laughed, and Emilia hurried off to the kitchen. "She real pretty, Detetive... maybe ya'all shouldn't wait too long to ask her..."

"That may be good advice, my friend," said Gino. But maybe not today... I have to get you back to the Third United Baptists, and then I have to go back to work."

Davo nodded as if he understood the complications involved in Macina's problematic life. He was spared further excuses when the pie arrived as if delivered by an angel. Davo watched her float back to the front of the café, looked at the pie, took a bite, then put his fork down. "Detetive, Davo need to tell ya'all something... it's about ol' Rodney and dat otha' fella, da chef..."

Gino looked at him intently, "Chef Ricardo? You already told me that you recognized him, and that Rodney did things for him... is there more?"

"Yes, Suhr, Davo didn't say all he knew and hears about dem two." He took another bite of pie, as if it gave him the courage to keep going. Once swallowed, and thus fueled, Davo said, "'Member dat night when da commotion was at da Italian place? Davo seen 'ol Rodney running away, and dat chef Ricardo looking fo' him. And Davo thinks dat ol' fat man was theah too, yellin' at people... you know, da man I seen wit da White Witch."

"You were there, Davo?"

"Uh-huh... we was hiding behind dem dumpsters... We's afraid da chef seen Davo, but don't think so now. And he come to da swamp later, and Davo hears 'em from the bushes, talking about a fake murdah plot, and such. Da chef, he tellin' Ol' Rodney how he spread voodoo crap all 'round da place. On an' on he went. Da Monk said da chef done good... Den, he was kilt... next day or day aftah. But befo' bein' kilt, ol' Rodney tells Davo... he says stuff about crows and blood and crap, and not to tell nobody—like he knows Davo was in dem bushes all da time."

"Davo, my friend... I'm going to write this down in my notes so I don't forget anything... but you have made my day! Can you remember any details about the voodoo stuff? It's kind of important if you can..."

Davo ate another bite of pie, "Yes, Suhr, Davo has a pretty good memory. And we ain't afraid when we's wit you."

Chapter 21
Digging Around

Macina was waiting impatiently at the police station for Simms to arrive, quite full of confidence that he'd solved their case. For over an hour, he walked down the hallway to Simms' cubicle every five minutes or so, expecting to find his partner juggling a half-empty Styrofoam coffee cup and shuffling through the papers stacked on his desk. The paper-shuffling was a habit that Simms had perfected to annoy Gino, and Gino knew it, but right now he would have welcomed Simms and his fidgeting.

Finally, exasperated at finding Simms' vacant office once more, Gino sat down at his own desk and went over his notes again. It was all there. The kid knew about the blood, the crow's feather, the four thieves vinegar, the tongue. The tongue had freaked the boy out the most, because it really had to have come from a dead person, and he couldn't imagine how that was possible. Neither could Gino, but for different reasons.

After poring over the details yet again, it dawned on Gino why Simms was late. He'd forgotten all about Trinity's visit. Now, distracted by another fascination, he tried to imagine how he could torment Simms for the rest of the day. Simms gave few chances to be needled by anybody, let alone Macina, and Gino wasn't about to let the chance go by.

Then his phone buzzed, but it wasn't Simms. It was Ike Harris with another distraction. "Hey, Ike... what do ya know this early in the morning... you can't have a positive I-D on the body already..."

"No, Gino, I'm out here at the shark factory— and look, you and Simms might want to come out to the old graveyard right now. Doctor Chen's people have at least a half dozen places that he thinks were just recently covered-up. There's fresh diggings scattered all around the site. They're not quite as big as the dead woman's grave, but he's waiting on our forensics guys to show up before they touch anything."

"A half dozen?"

"Yeah, probably more, now that they're looking around a little closer—we gave them the go ahead to work on their project, and this turned up first thing..."

"Shit... I'm on my way... thanks Ike."

Macina called Simms and left a message on his mobile, then headed for his decrepit Dodge. *"Things couldn't be simple, could they? No. They never are... if this were easy, anybody could do it—even you, Macina,"* mumbled Gino, reciting a mantra he'd often used after jumping to conclusions too early.

Simms beat Macina to the shark factory by five minutes. "Thanks for the message, Partner," he told Gino. "Ike is over at the graveyard, but I told him I'd wait here for you."

"Thanks, Stevenson," said Macina coolly. "I thought you'd be in early today, but I forgot about your girlfriend..."

Simms chuckled, "You have no idea... but let's go see what Ike has."

Macina tried to find his edge on Simms during the brief walk to the graveyard, but it eluded him, "What'd you do with her—she didn't leave you already, did she?"

Simms laughed out loud this time, "It's not gonna be that easy, I'm afraid... she's taken control of my upstairs rooms, and..."

"She's not staying at her sister's place?"

"Nope, it's still a mess, so she invited herself over... well, taken over is a better way to say it. So, what's up here? You said you had news, too?"

"Yeah, it can wait, I guess... Davo had some info that I thought was important, but if these guys from the D-H-S find more bodies, my info might not be worth snot."

Ike Harris waved them over to where a shallow pit was being excavated on the edge of the site, and then he pointed out a series of yellow flags that dotted the clearing that defined the graveyard. "This is the first dig," he explained. "Doctor Chen says there are patches covered up by dead palm fronds and debris... see—all of those flags inside the evidence tape—it looks like a crazy quilt when you stand back. But under those dried palm fronds, there is a layer of clean white sand. See—every place you see a flag, it's the same."

"This pit doesn't look big enough for a body..."

"No, but forensics is worried there might be body parts scattered about in all of these spots..."

"That'd be pretty gruesome... what about the actual graves, though? I'm not seeing much that looks like a graveyard," asked Simms.

"No, right... Chen says this is a very weathered site, which is typical for newly discovered spots... so he'll look for mounds of stones... they have metal detectors too... he thinks there won't be any traces of wood markers or anything of the sort, given the centuries of storms and such..."

Ike was interrupted by Dr. Chen, who called out and waved them over closer. "Officers, this is one of our technicians, Aretha Cooper... This is Detective Simms, and Detective Macina... you've already met Deputy Harris, I think. So, what have you there, Aretha?"

The technician looked baffled as she stood up and wordlessly handed a plastic container she'd filled with colored beads to Dr. Chen, who was chuckling, "Keep looking..." he said to Aretha.

"What?" asked Ike, squinting at the jar.

"Let's just say these aren't Jaega Indian beads..."

"Fakes, then?"

"Well, not necessarily fakes... you can buy these by the bag full on any reservation, or any roadside trinket stand between Tamiami and Fort Pierce... so, they're not necessarily fake, but I wouldn't call them artifacts... see what I mean?"

"Sooo...?" said Macina, "this isn't a graveyard?"

"Be patient, Detective," answered Dr. Chen with a grin.

Once Aretha finished sifting through the top layers of sand, she'd found two arrow heads, a few more beads, and a pottery shard. Dr. Chen told her to probe deeper to see if there was an older grave beneath the shallow pit. Then he turned to his group of technicians that had clustered around the dig, and pointed out to the field, "Let's get to it, folks. Don't get sloppy, let's be meticulous..."

Then he turned to the three investigators, "I'm certain that these trinkets were planted, but I can't for the life of me think why... I mean, unless this man who claims to be a descendant of the Jaega people is a complete moron... surely he can't think that anybody is going to fall for this ruse..."

Simms offered, "Maybe he didn't plant this junk himself... what if he's just a stooge? Or, maybe he was supposed to do it, and paid somebody else instead of following orders."

"But from whom?" asked Dr. Chen. "I mean, this land is obviously valuable... I get that, but why would the owner agree to give it up? Did he fall for the ruse himself, or what?"

Simms chuckled, "I doubt it... but I think I may know why... let me make a phone call to verify something... and meantime, Ike, might I suggest that you and Doctor Chen invite this self-proclaimed Jaega man out here or into the office, under the premise that you want him to inspect the artifacts you've found and verify that they are from his ancestors. Then you'll have him close by."

Ike laughed and agreed, "It'll be worth the charade, Simms."

Simms started back toward his car, then turned, "Gino, when I come back, can you tell me how you know so much about Indian antiquities and such... the short version, maybe."

"Trini, it's me, Simms... how's it going this morning? Have you heard from Val yet?"

"Nice to hear from you too," began Trini in an annoyed tone. "How are you this lovely morning? Oh I'm fine... thanks very much... can't walk very well at the moment... but fine, all the same. Thanks for asking, though."

Simms groaned, "Sorry... I'm surrounded by cops at a murder scene..."

Trinity laughed, "I know, I'm just busting your chops... so, nope, I haven't heard from her, but I tried another tactic... I had Scarlett leave her a message, and told her to let Val know that Maria was dead..."

"Well, it's not for sure yet, I mean the body might not be Maria's..."

"Maybe not, but it should get Valeria's attention if somebody besides me tells her... even if the info is wrong, she needs to get her ass back here. And Scarlett will be just theatrical enough..."

Simms sighed, "Okay, maybe it will work... look, the reason I called is to ask you about something I thought... well, I think I remember something you said to me when we were in Nassau..."

"Geez, really? I could have said anything then..."

Simms laughed a little, but got back to business, "Did you tell me that Val had said something about Joey wanting to build a casino somewhere, and that's what the wheelin' and dealin' was?"

"Well, if I did, I shouldn't have..."

"But it's true, then, I didn't dream it up?"

"It's true as far as I know..."

"Thanks, lady, you made my day... see you soon... gotta go..."

Simms called Macina on his mobile, "Gino, can you meet me at my car?"

Sensing a note of urgency in Simms' voice, It only took Macina a few minutes to jog down the trail to the parking area. "What's up, Partner."

"So, you know a lot about native American antiquities and such..."

"Yeah, my brother studied it in college, and we used to go out looking for treasures in our spare time... it was a way to make a little cash and..."

"Right, I get it, but you were talking about the antiquities laws and such too..."

"Well, we had to be careful with the new Federal and State laws that were passed back then—and he was all about protecting real

Indian heritage and antiquities, and stuff like that. We had to stop what we were doing, actually."

"Oh... well, maybe you know... why are all the casinos in the state owned by Indian tribes?"

"Their tribal lands are sovereign, so they can do whatever they want... it's Federal law... so outside of the lottery, dog tracks and bingo parlors, nobody else in this state can have gambling operations..."

"Right, I guess I knew that... so, Joe Di Rossi couldn't build a casino here on this property, unless..."

"No, he couldn't do more than a bingo hall except on Indian... oh, shit... Really?"

Simms laughed, "Yeah, well, I'm just as thick... when I was in Nassau, Trinity told me, and I forgot—Joey was working on a deal to build a casino, and that guy, Zev Harmon? I met him too. He's not just Joe's agent... he's done this kind of thing in South Africa, and in Nassau... maybe even in New Jersey... it's all coming back to me now. That's how Harmon fits into the picture..."

"So, if Joe quit claims the property to a native American... that's not good enough! He needs the State to declare it tribal land or something like that..."

"Yeah, something like that— let's go talk to the good Doctor Chen to see what he thinks, and let Ike in on our theory..."

"Okay, said Gino," as he started walking, "but why murder Maria? And the drugs and dead drug guys—how do they fit in?"

"Try to keep up, Gino... they aren't necessarily connected... let's get our facts straight on this graveyard thing first, before we start speculating on the rest... it may not even be our case anymore... or, if we pull a few threads, it might all lead right back to Giuseppe's."

"About that," began Macina, but then he stopped himself. "Okay, let's go find Ike."

"Look, you guys, it's not my call," explained Ike. "It's up to my major and the Feds what they do from here on out. But, a lot has happened since this morning's events. Doctor Chen's team has excavated all of the shallow pits, and they were all salted with the same kind of trinkets. It looks like Chen wants to take a hard look at the real graveyard for historical purposes—you know, once and for all... and my guess is that they'll likely go after the owner—Joe Di Rossi—and this guy, Harmon—for antiquities fraud or something... however, they're trying to figure out if any laws have actually been broken. But they got the Indian fella to come in right away, around lunch time, which is surprising, and he's either pretty stupid or a good actor..."

"So, will it be fraud if Doctor Chen's people determine that it's really a good historical find, you know, like an old pirate camp or something?" asked Macina.

"That's what I'm trying to explain, Gino," said Ike. "We have to determine if it's criminal either way. But right now, we still have to investigate the two killings by the factory storeroom... and the Di Rossi woman's murder..."

"So, it is Maria Di Rossi, for certain?" asked Simms.

"Yup, dental records are a match... hair test results aren't back yet..."

"Okay, Ike," replied Simms. "I guess we'll see how that plays out... I still don't have a location on Joe yet... maybe by tonight, though... I'm workin' on it. Zev Harmon could be more difficult to pin down... he's a South African, and from his reputation, he doesn't stay in one place very long. If he gets wind of Doctor Chen's findings, he'll likely vanish... you guys might want to keep a lid on your Jaega friend as long as possible so word doesn't leak out.

"Yeah, I agree, but so far, we don't have any charges to hold him on. Maybe we'll just keep playing charades as long as we can."

"Okay, I get it... look, we'll catch up with you tomorrow, Ike. Gino and I need to check in at the station, and then I need to entertain one of my leads," said Simms, giving Macina a chilling glance before his partner could chuckle.

After leaving Harris to confer with Dr. Chen and his crew, Simms and Macina headed for their cars. Before Gino could say anything, Stevenson asked, "Gino, earlier today, you said you had some info...?"

"Nah, it can wait until tomorrow... oh, I have a lunch date with Minerva... what are we... uuhh, is there some strategy I should take with her? I mean, she's gonna want to know what we've found out about Joe and Maria..."

"Yeah, crap! I dunno... tell her that we have leads on their whereabouts, I guess. If she asks for more details, just say that we have sources who believe they know where to find them... it's not entirely a lie, is it?"

Macina laughed, "No, it's pretty cold, though. Well, I could ask Minerva if she knows anything about the shack out by the old shark factory... or, maybe I should steer the conversation toward the menu at Giuseppe's... or maybe I should take her there for lunch. Don't we want to know if she's been there recently, or maybe see if she knows the chef? She might tip her hand if she thinks we're suspicious..."

"Or, just the opposite... we still have to deal with the fact that she and Whitehead are connected, don't forget that... Just use your judgement, Gino—she seems to like you, so you'll have some leeway in chatting about things."

"Okay, Partner, see you tomorrow morning."

Chapter 22
Friends and Forensics

For once, Simms had the good sense to use his mobile phone to head-off hard feelings with a woman—he called Trinity to say he was heading home, and asked her if he could pick up anything at the market on the way. For her part, Trinity was pleasantly surprised, but told herself not to get used to him being on his best behavior when it came to balancing work and personal life. He'd already warned her of his past record on that account, and it hadn't taken long for her to see that the line between his work and his home was blurry at best. However, she was already in a good mood with news she was nearly bursting to share, so she put a CD in the stereo, opened a bottle of wine, chopped vegetables, and stirred the skillet to the beat of Latin drummers.

When Simms walked in the door, he was nearly knocked down by the smells of good food flooding the house. The kiss she planted on him was a sweet end to a long afternoon and the beginning of what he readily imagined would be a memorable night. "Simms! Come sit in the kitchen and have a glass of wine... and for God's sake, put away your phone and take off that stupid gun... and your shoes... look at the mud! Have you been in the swamp all day—again?"

Simms laughed at her brash hectoring and did as he was told—he hadn't noticed the caked-on mud clods when he got in his car earlier, and now he had a momentary pang of regret knowing that the inside of his car would need cleaning—again! But he let it go as quickly as it had stung him. Trinity wouldn't stand for his fussing about his floor mats, and he knew it. He really wanted a beer, too, but instead, wisely accepted the wine with grace.

"Guess what, Simms!" she said when he sat down on a stool at the counter to watch her cook. "We got through to her, me and Scarlett... Val's gonna meet us at our Aunt Sonia's tomorrow afternoon..."

"Us?"

"Yeah, you and me, Simms... that is... can you drive me down to Key West tomorrow?" Now her tone had changed with her entreaty.

"Uhhmm... I guess, maybe around lunchtime or so... it's a four or five-hour drive—or more, maybe six if we hit traffic—but... yeah, where is she? Is she with Joey?"

"Well, she was kinda vague on that... but she wants to talk with you, okay?"

"Okay... we don't have to take Scarlett too, do we?"

Trinity laughed, "Hell no... that'd be torture... no, Scarlett's just happy she could help out— oh, and I hired a cleaning service from the yellow pages—they started cleaning up the mess at the house this afternoon. They said it'd take a week or so, with the painting and all... Val said she'd pay for it."

Simms laughed, "Nice work, lady... and for your latest accomplishment—what's for supper... what is that you're stirrin' up here?"

The pair chatted while she cooked, easily finishing the first bottle of wine by the time the meal was on the table. Simms had no time to let his mind wander to the events of the day or the murder cases that dangled tauntingly in the wind, for every few minutes, Trinity would kiss him or brush his cheek, or cozy up to him. It was his mobile phone that broke the spell.

"Sorry, Trini-—I should take this call..."

"But your dinner will get cold," she pleaded pointlessly as he walked to the living room to fetch his phone.

"Stevenson, hi, it's Ike Harris... sorry to bother you at home, but we got the forensics back on the gunshots and the two dead guys at the shark factory. Look, we need to meet—tonight, if you can—I can't sit on this after tomorrow morning, and I think you have information you've not shared— but it's time— before any shit hits the fan..."

"Okay, where?"

"Dilly's Tavern—in an hour? How's that? I'll call Gino if you want."

"Good, see you then," said Simms without hesitation, and hung up.

There was no way that Trinity could help but overhear his end of the conversation in the next room, and she mustered her spirits to hide the disappointment, "When do you have to leave, Simms?"

"In a half hour or so, sorry, Trini... the County Sheriff has something that he's gonna show me and Gino before... well, I don't know what all. But he wouldn't have called me instead of Gino unless it was critical..."

"About Maria?"

"I don't think so... not directly, anyway... I can't say more. Sorry," he said, and he meant it.

"It's okay, Simms, eat your meal... I'll still be here when you get back," she said, and gave him a kiss as a promise.

Gino was already at Dilly's talking with Ike when Stevenson arrived. They were in the back corner of the nearly deserted joint, and Ike got right down to business when Simms slid into the booth. "Stevenson, at the beginning of our little project, you implied that there might be a sensitive link to your department, but you wanted to be sure before saying anything out of school..."

"Right, I remember..."

"Well, you might want to let us in on that bit of intel about it now... the forensics came back on the two dead guys at the dope cache..."

"Well, you mentioned that your guys thought there was a third guy—the shooter..."

"Yeah, well, there was, and he knew what he was doing. First thing... decedent number one was shot from less than twenty feet away... one-inch shot pattern, center mass... double-ought buckshot, all eight pellets recovered from his chest cavity. Number two, probably shot from thirty or forty feet away... shot pattern about two inches, only six of eight pellets recovered—the guy was likely trying to reach for his gun or duck down behind something..."

"Sooo...?"

The shot was all copper-coated... flight-control wads were recovered at the scene along with the empty shell casings... these were Federal duty rounds, Simms—not the cheap ammo some rando gets at his local hardware store..."

"So, Ike, you think it was a cop?"

"Yeah, and my major will think so, too."

"We think it was, as well," said Simms. Then he looked at Gino and took a deep breath. "We know that our chief, Albie Whitehead, has a relationship with Joe Di Rossi's aunt, a woman named Minerva Rossini... Minerva lives in Manatee Wells with Joe and his wife—or did until they disappeared..."

Ike scratched at his ear lobe, "So, I can see the complication for you guys and why you wouldn't want to tell us about it—sort of. But what's the connection with the murders at the factory..."

Simms nodded, "Well, we were investigating the murder of one of our witnesses—the old hobo—and Gino learned that Minerva and Whitehead ran a bunch of homeless people out of the shark factory a few months ago—in fact, they brought in a bus to take 'em away. And Whitehead apparently threatened them with jail if they returned—he told 'em that the place was gonna be torn down... then Gino found out that a man resembling Whitehead paid cash for the fencing and gate around the entrance to the property..."

Macina added, "We're pretty sure that Whitehead and Minerva were operating the drug warehouse at the shark factory..."

"So, that seems like a pretty long bow to draw, I mean that's all circumstantial," said Ike, "especially if you want to publicly implicate the police chief... yeah, I'd say you had a problem".

Simms said, "Ike, I think *WE* have a problem, now, because you've got the forensics that pins suspicion on a cop killing two drug dealers under pretty odd circumstances... see, now the scope of the problem just got a lot broader if that cop is a local police chief? And look, your forensics are no more definitive than our circumstantial connections... I mean, twelve-gauge duty loads aren't unique to law enforcement, so by itself, that bit of evidence isn't conclusive."

Ike drank the last of his coffee, mulled over what Simms asserted for a few moments, and then cleared his throat, "You also said that Joe Di Rossi had plans to build a casino on the site... so he's a suspect in these murders too?"

"Maybe not, Ike... why would Di Rossi invite the State and Feds out to his property, or be running a scam to give the property away if he was dealing drugs out of the place?"

Harris nodded, as if he'd already come to the same conclusion. "So, what else do we have? I mean, by process of elimination..."

Gino interrupted, "So, I have a lunch date with Minerva Rossini tomorrow, and..."

"What?" said Ike, incredulously. "How... why?"

Gino laughed, "I've been trying to curry favor... see?" He then blurted, "We had to investigate the disappearance of her nephew and his wife... and then the hobo was murdered, and that hobo was the original connection to the restaurant murder... our only potential witness—but he was also connected with the homeless bunch who got run out of the shark factory..."

"Jesus!" said Ike "But lunch?"

"Well, it's the only way we could get the old lady to open up," interjected Simms. "Turns out, she likes ol' Gino's genes better than mine..."

Harris laughed and Macina blushed a little, then got back to his point, "I assume, Ike, that your Department hasn't notified next of kin on Maria's death, yeah? Otherwise, you'd already know about Minerva..."

"True enough—we've been sitting on it like you guys suggested, since no relative has reported her missing... so what?"

"Well, I am supposed to pick Minerva up for lunch at noon tomorrow... why don't we time it so you or your boys arrive about one minute before—or after—I get there... you ask for Joe— he's not there, obviously, but she'll say she's family and Joe can't be reached... then you regret to inform her that a member of her family is deceased. See, this is our best chance to catch her with her guard down. She'll ask where, when, and what all. Then you tell her that Maria's body was found near the old shark factory, and she's been dead for a few days... maybe add that it coincides with two other recent homicides on the property... Then you leave, and I can console her. She's not stupid... if she and Whitehead are involved in the drug ring, she'll have to have some doubts and concerns about him right about then... let me work it."

Simms said, "I like it. Meanwhile, why not put a tail on Whitehead? I mean, he might just be arrogant enough to carry the missing cocaine around in his trunk... and even if he isn't doing that, if Minerva brings him up to speed, he might get nervous and lead you to the dope. And, if he doesn't, well, he doesn't... but at this stage, it's easier and less likely to blow up in our faces than trying a search warrant."

Chapter 23
Manipulation

Simms and Macina had little trouble in convincing Deputy Harris to go along with the plan. One the other hand, Simms had a much more difficult task convincing Gino that Minerva was going to be a lot tougher to unravel than he imagined. The pair spent the morning at a coffee shop on A1A near Manatee Wells going over different strategies. For his part, Macina hadn't even considered that Minerva might withdraw entirely when she heard the news of Maria's death, but Simms knew instinctively that they'd have to back off for a time if that happened. In that case, all the focus would then be on Ike's job of tailing Whitehead, because if Minerva called the chief instead of leaning on Macina, the chief might panic and lead them straight to the missing drugs.

Simms emphasized that, if the old lady was indeed in some mild state of shock, but did agree to spend time with Gino anyway, then it was all up to Macina and his ability to charm the woman and play up to her emotions. Simms wanted nothing left to chance. "Look, Gino, we might only get one shot at this. Obviously, I can't be there—she hates the sight of me and, besides, I think I've got a meeting with Valeria LaCroix lined up. So, you're on your own once you set foot on Minerva's front porch."

"Valeria? Where?"

"Key West... but stay focused here, Gino... what's your angle with Minerva if you spend time with her today? Let's go over this again."

Macina scoffed, "Easy, Stevenson... her biggest concern, so she says, has been the neighborhood gossip mongers and the rumors that Joe killed his wife... she seemed convinced that they were both involved in their own outside affairs, and that exposing that fact would be preferable to the murder gossip. But with Maria dead, her hopes are up in flames on that front... so if she knows anything about Joe's whereabouts, I'll convince her to tell me..."

"Beyond that, we need to ascertain if..."

"...She has any inkling about what's going on at the shark factory," said Gino, completing Simms' sentence. "So, I think I just have to be direct and tell her that we know that an agent of Joe's has been working on a deal with the State of Florida to turn the factory property over as a Native American heritage site, and it was those people that found the body."

"Yeah, I was hoping that Ike would be the one to divulge that bit of info... maybe call him this morning and work that detail out..."

"Right, but then, I'll want to ask her if she knows anything about those plans, or if she'd heard anything about tearing down the old buildings..."

"I think you should pursue the point that there were two other murders on the property in the last few days... Ike seems to think it's okay to mention drug deals and a drug ring, too."

"Yeah, I think we all agree on that point, 'cuz that's the leverage point on Captain Whitehead... even if she doesn't crack on the drug business, we want her to wonder if the chief had anything to do with Maria's killing ."

"Exactly, Gino. So, the game's on the line, Partner, and you've got the ball."

Minerva was softer than they had hoped, at least at first. Her knees buckled when Ike broke the news about Maria, and Gino kept her from falling down. He helped her sit back down on her rocking chair where she'd been waiting for him in the warm morning air, then he smoothed the folds of her flowered dress and helped her put her hat back in place. He picked up her purse, put it in her lap, and looked straight into her tear-filled eyes. There was no sign of deceit there, he decided, and turned to Ike, "Deputy, where was the body found?"

"It was in a shallow grave out by the old shark factory, in an old graveyard... I understand that it's family property?"

Minerva, nodded affirmatively, but remained mute except for the sobs she was trying to control. Macina asked Ike, "Deputy, how long ago do you think...?"

Ike said, "The medical examiner thinks a few days... same time frame as two other homicides out there... Ma'am, do you know if Maria had any reason to be on the site? We know that the husband-—Joe Di Rossi—he's your nephew, you said? He had some people from the State antiquities department examining the graveyard as a potential Indian heritage site... would Maria have had anything to do with that negotiation?"

Minerva finally spoke, stammering, "I've not heard anything about that, Deputy. I've stayed out of the family business affairs for decades, ever since my brother died and left it all to Joey."

Ike said, "Okay, well, the reason I asked, is that the other two killings were linked to a large stash of narcotics in an old storeroom attached to the abandoned factory building, and we think it's possible that she may have stumbled onto a drug ring, and gotten killed in the process."

Minerva rubbed tears from her eyes with a small hankie, "Drug ring? How... I d- don't know... that can't be..." she stuttered.

Ike said, "Well, the drugs were real enough, that's for sure. So listen, I won't bother you anymore for now, you have a lot to process, Ma'am. I'm sorry for your loss. If you hear from your nephew, please make sure that he understands—it's imperative that he contact the Sheriff's office. Here's my card."

After Ike left, Gino asked her, "Minerva, do you have any idea... was Maria hiding out there? You once told me that you thought she was hiding somewhere..."

Minerva just shrugged, "Maybe... but where would she have been living?"

"Well, there are quite a few buildings scattered around the property. But it doesn't seem like any of those ramshackle structures would be suitable for a lady like Maria..."

Minerva studied Gino's face for a few moments, "Well, Gino, there is a caretaker's cottage in the middle of the hammocks that has been maintained... that's where I thought she must have been all this time..."

Gino realized that she was fishing now. "Miss Minerva, that sounds pretty isolated, and look, I'm a cop, so I've been wondering since we first had lunch... what—or who—was Maria hiding from? She'd have to be pretty scared by something to stay by herself in such a secluded spot. Is there something to all of this that you weren't telling me? I mean, it's kind of important now—if we're to catch her killer."

Minerva sighed, wiped away another few tears, then answered, "I told you I thought she was having an affair. Remember?"

Gino nodded, "Yes... so did Joe find out and threaten her?"

"No, no! Absolutely not. She told me that she had a lover, but he turned out to be a horrible person, and when she tried to break it off, he threatened her... threatened to expose the affair."

"Did she tell you who the man is?"

"No, she just went into hiding... to the cottage, I guess. It was just supposed to be until Joey came back from his whoring... Two of my cousins' boys—young men—they were taking supplies to her."

"So, she knew about her husband's affair?"

"Oh, most certainly... he was a serial cheater, I've told you this... but she long ago quit having relations with him, you see? That's the way of it... but he was supposed to keep his shenanigans discreet."

"About your two cousins... the Sheriff might want to speak with them..."

"I haven't seen them in several days, but they live here in the village. I'll write down their names..."

"Okay, Miss Minerva, I can pass the information on to the Sheriff's deputies... it's their case now. Are you going to be okay? Do you have friends and family...?"

"Yes, Gino, I'll be needing to make some calls... you can go now... although I'm sorry our lunch has been spoilt... will you still come again?"

"Yes, of course... I'll check in on you real soon."

"Hey, Ike, it's Gino..."

"What've you got, buddy?"

"I just left Minerva's place... I think you'd do well to keep a tail on Whitehead... I'm pretty sure that the old lady will call him soon. She confirmed that Maria was living in the cottage out by the factory. Two of her cousins were ferrying supplies to Maria, who was supposedly hiding out from a threatening ex-lover."

"Did she give you any hint about drugs and such?"

"She's pretty reserved, but I think she was hiding something there... and, as for the rest of it, well, she's pretty cagey, like I said. She said she didn't know who Maria's lover was... and as for the drug operation, I think she's fully capable of deflecting all this shit onto somebody else—like Whitehead—if she gets cornered herself. And listen, you might want to have somebody check on these two cousins... they might be the dead guys... if I'm right, it could be enough to turn Minerva against Whitehead in a heartbeat."

All right, let me have the info..."

Chapter 24
Road Trip

Trinity chattered Stevenson's right ear off almost all the way past the Ft. Lauderdale exit. When the Turnpike jogged east, she grew quiet, then asked, "Isn't this the wrong direction, Simms?"

"Nope, this is the way the Turnpike goes... we have to go around Miami, and this is usually the fastest route. We'll turn back south again in a few miles—see the signs? Don't think like we're going to Miami"

"I'm sorry, this is a lot longer drive than I remembered..."

He chuckled, "We've only been on the road for three-quarters of an hour... there's still three and a half to go... Just let me know if you have to pee— but don't wait until the last minute unless you wanna take your chances behind a saw palmetto..."

Trini laughed, "It wouldn't be my first time..."

"So, I called Baxter... I can stay at his lodge..."

"Why not at my place?"

"Well, I thought it'd be best if the neighbors didn't have too much to talk about... plus, where's Val staying? No, it'd be best this way... see what I'm sayin'? This is still a murder investigation. It's sketchy enough that you and I are..." his voice trailed off.

"Are what, Simms? What are we...?" she prodded with a sly look.

"Lovers. How does that sound? Lovers."

"But you're all business today anyway, right..."

"It has to be..."

She was quiet again and he was sure she was pouting, but he couldn't deal with it and stay focused on the traffic too. So, he let her stew all the way past the Everglades exit. The traffic had thinned by then, and in the silence, he'd puzzled-out what this trip must mean to her— not just to himself and the case. His problem was stringing the right words together to soften the reality, and no amount of mental rehearsing seemed satisfactory. Finally, he just blurted out, "Trini, I'd like to meet with your Aunt Sonia again while we're down here... I brought the photos of the graffiti, and I..."

"Of course, Simms... she'll be glad of it. You got her all interested in your case, what with the last meeting and me trying to explain what you told me about the graffiti."

"But, I need to speak with her alone this time, not with you, and especially not Valeria as part of the conversation... and when I talk with Val, you can't be part of it either. Believe me, it's for your own good."

"Are we suspects?"

"No, not in my book, anyway, and the more independent my sources of information are, the better the chances of keeping it that way. Eventually, this case will be scrutinized, and the fact that I've gotten help from three family members—independently—Look, this is an example of what I'm trying to get you to understand... Remember, before you even knew who I was—down in Nassau—you gave me info about Val and Joey that proved their alibi... see? Without that..."

"Yeah, I get it..." but her voice didn't quite sound like she was okay with what he was saying. "Listen," she said, "Val should be at my place when we arrive. I'll let you into the apartment, chit-chat for a few minutes, then I'll walk over to Aunt Sonia's. You can meet me over at her house when you're done... that way, there's no corruption... or whatever you wanna call it."

He chuckled, "Thanks... this is all gonna work out... I just really need Joe to voluntarily return home and answer questions before this blows up all out of proportion. Actually, we all need that to happen—it's just that Val and Joe need to believe it. With Maria's death, there's a lot of suspicion, and it's gonna keep mounting..."

"Right... it's always the husband—or the butler, right?" she quipped.

Simms could tell that she was trying to lighten the mood, and he chuckled, "Right, but we don't have a butler in this story, so all eyes are on the cheating husband..." Trinity went quiet again for another hour.

True to Trinity's prediction, Valeria had settled into her sister's apartment, and she was obviously laying low. The curtains were drawn, there were no television or radio programs blaring for the neighbors to hear, and only one light was on in the corner. And that's where Val was when they walked in, sitting in the corner and simply reading a book. When they unlocked the door and walked in, she didn't do more than say 'hello' in the most casual way. For Trinity, though, the scene was too unnerving, and she began to fuss over her sister. "How long have you been here? Have you eaten anything? Does Auntie Sonia know you're here?"

Valeria stood up and stretched, then hugged her sister, "I'm fine, Trini. Calm down, okay." She held out her hand to Simms, "Detective, we meet again..."

"Indeed," said Stevenson. "Thank you for agreeing to a meeting..."

"Well, there's really no choice now, is there? Not if I want my life back, anyway..."

Trinity interrupted the flow, "I'm gonna go get some take-out and bring it back..."

Simms looked at her, "I thought you needed to check on your Aunt Sonia? Why don't you do that first? We can all go get a meal somewhere after Val and I talk for a bit."

Trinity meekly said, "Okay, yeah... that makes more sense... I'll go see her, then... well... uuhh, I'll see you two in a little while."

Simms waited for Trinity to extricate herself from a drama of her own making before sitting down at the dining room table. Val moved over to sit across from him, folded her hands in her lap, and said, "Well...sounds like Maria must have finally pissed-off the wrong people..."

Simms ignored her play at humor, "Or the wrong person... so where have you been?"

"We've been staying on Exuma, near Dunmore Town... Zev Harmon has a friend with an estate on Pink Sands Beach... do you know it?"

"Of course... a little rich for my pocketbook, but a sweet spot if you can swing it. I assume that you have all the people in the world to vouch for you..."

Valeria said, "I suppose so, but that wouldn't really let us off the hook would it? I mean, won't somebody try to say that her murder was a hit, you know like in the 'Godfather'?"

Simms shrugged, again ignoring the innuendo. "That scenario is always a possibility that any investigation would look at, but without evidence it's a weak thread to pull on. And for the record, Maria's death didn't look like a mob hit in any way. Is Joey still on Exuma?"

"He was, two days ago, but Zev might've convinced him to move..."

"Why? Harmon doesn't trust you?"

"He doesn't trust any woman when it comes to serious shit... and, after all, here I am, talking to you. Listen, Detective, let's cut to it. Joe didn't kill his wife, and neither did I, and we didn't have anybody else do it either. There were plenty of people that hated her... all you need is to figure out which one fits the evidence... So, have you realized that Maria was sleeping with Ricardo Avila?"

Stevenson's eyes widened, the only giveaway that he'd entertained suspicions about Ricardo Avila's involvement in any of this. But he hadn't considered Valeria's assertion until that moment. "The Chef? Did Joe...?"

"Yeah, Joey knew... and he didn't much care as long as they kept it secret, and as long as Maria wasn't harping at him all the time."

"So, how long was that going on?"

"I don't know for sure... Joey told me when we came down here to Key West the first time... a couple of months ago, I guess. But my sense was that it'd been longer."

"Did Maria know about you and Joey?"

"Well, yeah..."

"Is that why she fired you this last time?"

"Probably, but I kind of asked for it... I got snotty with her... and afterward, I decided that I shouldn't keep working there..."

"So you didn't go back when Joey rehired you?"

"He didn't rehire me..."

"But Ricardo said..."

"Detective, you might want to take a step back for a second... if you're relying on anything Avila has told you about this whole affair... look, he's a gifted con man. About a year ago, he convinced Joey to let him buy into the restaurant... some cash down payment... then payments against salary or some shit... I don't understand all the side hustles..."

"Why...?"

"...Why did Joey agree? He wanted to pursue this casino venture, but he needed somebody to keep the restaurant running smoothly... I think he also promised Ricardo a piece of the action in the casino too—you know, down the road-—food services and such..."

"So, what? It went sour somewhere along the way..."

"Well, yeah, Ricardo started screwing Maria..."

"Geezus... I thought nobody liked Maria... even Ricardo bad mouthed her..."

"See, there you go again, Detective... what'd I just tell you about Ricardo Avila... he didn't like her either, that's true, but it didn't keep him from..."

"Pursuing an affair..."

"Now you are starting to see the picture..."

"So... I don't see a motive for Ricardo to kill Maria..."

"I didn't say he did..."

"Well, you led me right to the conclusion..."

Valeria frowned, hesitated a moment, then said, "I can't tell you how to do your job, Detective Simms. I'm sure you have access to much more information than I do... but maybe you need to begin with the time discrepancy between the murder scene discovered at the restaurant, and the time frame when Maria died... from what Trini said she's been told, it's like two weeks different..."

"Yeah, I'm aware. Okay, so look... is Joey gonna come back and answer questions, or is he gonna become a fugitive?"

"Well, Harmon is advising him to stay out of reach because of the casino deal... he says it'll be difficult to go forward if Joey is in jail or on trial..."

"Maybe, but if there's a warrant out, there's no way the state of Florida is gonna sign off on a casino license... so, Harmon's advice isn't worth swamp mud. At least if the restaurant is still viable and if Joe returns, he'll have income... but if Ricardo Avila is up to something, that could all be in jeopardy in Joe's absence."

"I know all this, and I agree with you. I think Joey is on the fence—at least until I report back to him on what you and I discuss..."

"Well, I hope you don't wait too long, Val. So, look, I'm going to call Trinity and ask her to meet me at your aunt's house, then she'll come back over here to stay with you. I'll see you tomorrow, and maybe you can tell me something more concrete about Joe."

Simms drove the few blocks to Sonia's, and met Trinity on the front porch. The slight tremble in her hands told him she was on the verge of losing her composure again, so he wrapped his arms around her and whispered, "It's going to be okay, Trini... Val's going to be fine."

Trinity pushed back just a little to look into Stevenson's eyes, as if trying to read a poker hand. Then she asked, "What'd she say?"

"I think she's gonna convince Joe to return home and deal with this mess like a grown-up. Now, why don't we go in and greet Madame LaCroix, and you can take the car somewhere to get food. I'll catch up with you back at your apartment..."

"Okay, she's waiting..."

"Does she know that Valeria is back, and why?"

"Yeah... well, not why."

"Any advice before I go in?"

Trinity chuckled, "You already know the drill..."

After Trinity excused herself, Simms sat with Sonia in front of her homemade shrine, sipping the dark rum offered by Madame. Sonia studied the photos of the graffiti painted on Val's front door, and then the blue artwork from Simms' own entryway. She looked at Simms, then examined the photos again. "Señor Simms, I want to understand... Trini says many things and I do not always follow... where was this painted... the red one?"

"Madame, that is Val's house... and those are the pictures from inside her bedroom... the dead crow, the feces..."

"Yes, yes. I did understand, then. And the blue paint?"

"That, I'm afraid, is my own front door."

Sonia shook her head, "No, my friend, you do not be afraid... the one who painted this is afraid of you... much skill went to painting this... see? The evil eye is to protect from you... you have made great fear in somebody, and they are asking a spirit to protect them from you."

"So, isn't it a warning to me?"

"Yes, well, it warns you that whomever you have threatened now has protection..."

"And the red painting... is it not the same..."

"No, it is poorly made... not the same person... not even the same beliefs... perhaps *aficionados*—or fakers ... It is to make Valeria afraid of somebody. If there were a spell cast, there would not be this mess. It is some warning, I think, made to cause fear, only fear."

"Is it possible that this red paint and all the rest was simply to make it look like a Voodoo curse had been cast by a sorcerer or something? What I'm asking is whether somebody who was not an initiate might think a real priestess had done this..."

Madame puffed on her cigar, then put it back on the edge of her ashtray, sipped at her rum, then picked up her cigar again and repeated the steps. Simms watched the smoke curl upwards out of the dim light while Madame sipped her rum one more time. Finally, she said, "Yes, that makes more sense than a sloppy *aficionado*. Señor Simms, I think you have more understanding than most..."

"So, if my suggestion is true, then Val should not worry... but the vandals should worry that I'll discover who they are..."

Madame LaCroix smiled, poured another dram, and said, "Indeed. Now we must talk about my other niece, Trinity."

After leaving Trinity and Valeria, and while driving out to Baxter's fishing lodge, Simms began second-guessing his actions. He was glad to be free of Trinity and her nervous drama for a few hours, yet he missed her already. He wanted her to spend time with Val in hopes that she'd finally push her sister over the edge on returning home with Joe, but there was a chance of collusion between the two that would wreck the investigation. By the time he reached Baxter's driveway, however, he'd convinced himself that he'd made the right choices. Besides, he wanted to talk to Baxter about the case, and he couldn't do that with Trinity hanging out with them.

It didn't take long for Baxter to chime in with his opinions, although he'd later say that Stevenson was the one who opened that particular door with his whining. "I dunno, Baxter, something in this case is missing."

"Simms, my friend, are you putting too much faith in the sisters? I mean, are you seeing things clearly?"

"Yeah, Bax, I've looked at that from every angle. Trinity's been forthcoming, and I just stumbled into her by accident—you're the one who set me up with Jimmy Daniels, remember?"

"Okay, that was then. But after that, the mistress, Valeria... she could sway her sister, don't you think?"

"Oh, sure, but Trinity's the one trying to convince Valeria to come home. I mean, no doubt that Val's clever enough. And no doubt she was sizing me up this afternoon... but that's to be expected if she's gonna trust me enough to tell her boyfriend to go home and face the music. Right? I think I'm right. I think I've read her correctly."

"But you told me—not five minutes ago—that she led you right to the trough—right up to pinning it on Ricardo."

"Yeah, she did, but she pulled back from an accusation..."

"But she played it well, clever girl, yeah?"

"Oh, certainly. But here's the rub: she's the one who told me that Ricardo started shacking with Maria right in front of the husband—after Joey cut him in for part of the restaurant. Even she admitted that she couldn't see a motive for murder— only if Joey had killed Ricardo... see?"

"How clever is she, then?" continued Baxter with his challenge.

"I guess it's still a possibility, but it doesn't feel right. Look, I want to see a way for all four murders to be connected, and it'd be convenient enough to pin it all on the husband. But, why would the chef, Ricardo, start up with Joe's wife after being cut into a partnership? Especially if he really hated her like everybody else says. Makes no sense."

"Maybe. Maybe not. Some guys will do anything for a sniff. Or, maybe it was a macho thing for Ricardo— getting' into the boss' wife's panties... Or, maybe it was a thrill... you know, a James Bond kind of thing, gambling, taking a risk... maybe he was hoping Joe would have a jealous fit and whack his wife, but at the same time, there was a risk Joe would come after him instead."

"Geezus, Baxter, that's a lot of 'ifs' and 'maybes'. And none of it explains a motive for murdering Maria. And who got killed in the restaurant? Where's the body—nobody else is missing?"

"Maybe that's the answer, Buddy. Nobody. Maybe nobody was murdered in the restaurant, and Macina and the boys at the station got it all wrong."

"You mean it was staged to look like a murder scene? Why the fuck would anybody do that?" Simms now found himself arguing against a theory he'd had from the beginning, and shook his head at Baxter's skill. Now there was no way out but to keep on, "And look, Gino wasn't involved in the scene that night. Sure, he sometimes acts like a nervous squirrel on the highway and gets distracted, but he's not been too bad on this case. So, back to my question—I mean, nobody would stage a murder scene without a murder..."

"Well, maybe..."

"Stop it! No more 'maybes'. You're fuckin' exhausting. Pour me another tequila, and tell me why your new bride is still in Cuba..."

Chapter 25
Returns of the Day

"Good morning, Simms... how are you doing? Too early to call?" Trinity sounded too cheerful for the hour.

But Simms mustered his best, "Good morning, my Lady... I'm a little slow thus far— first cup of coffee in hand now, but that goddamn Baxter was up and out on the water at dawn. He had this really nice tequila from Jalisco and, well... you get the idea."

"You boys! Honestly, I thought you'd be talking about us girls, but I suppose it was all about fishing."

Simms laughed. "Well, we did talk about his wife," he deflected, then changed the subject. "So, what time do you want me to come over? I told Val that I'd be by early— I want to hear her decision—or, rather, Joey's decision..."

"Well, you can relax—she told me last night—they're coming back—Joey is flying to Key West as soon as he can make arrangements, so I'll stay here with Val until then. Besides, I need time to go see my boss at the 'Chicken'. So you might as well head on back north as soon as you feel like it this morning."

Stevenson was caught off-guard by her short speech, and fumbled for words, "Oh, uuhh, really? That easy, huh?" A hint of suspicion crossed his mind, but he let it go. "Any idea when you will be coming north, then? I mean, the sooner the better as far as Joe is concerned."

"That's it?" she scolded playfully. "I hoped you'd be interested in when you could see me again..." She'd caught him off guard again, judging from his silence. So she laughed and said, "Hopefully, Joey will see it your way... Val seems to think so... and she trusts you for whatever reason I can't figure out."

Simms' headache wasn't allowing him to process her irony just yet, and he curtly answered, "Okay, Trini, just so you understand the situation I'm in. I've put myself between a rock and a hard place as far as Joe is concerned, and I don't have any control over the Sheriff... you know, if—or when— he might issue a warrant for Joe. And, as of this morning, I have no idea what might have developed back in Manatee Wells. If something happens... if there's anything I should know that pops up today, let me know right away, okay?"

Trinity did promise. However, there hadn't been much more to their conversation that morning. She had tried to keep the tone light, and it failed in distracting him, so she just gave up on the effort. As for Simms, it'd taken an hour of driving up U.S. 1 and processing their morning chat before he realized he'd quite entirely missed her intentions. But he did put a lot of faith in the integrity backing up Trini's words, and her promise stuck with him for most of the drive north up through the Keys. Normally, he might have dawdled somewhere like Islamorada or Key Largo for lunch, exploring some obscure roadside dive or oyster bar for stone crab sandwiches, just to extend the sense of freedom that being in the Keys gave him. But not on this day, for his work life had now stretched clear into paradise and back again, tainting the charm of peeling paint and rickety saloon doors, so there was no reason to linger over his favorite roadside attractions.

Near the turn-off to the Everglades, he laughed at the "**Casino and Resort**" signs that beckoned travelers from their northward course to the lands of the Miccosukee tribe. He was half-tempted to stop and gawk at the Indian artifacts displayed from the back of the dozen awning covered pickups that formed a small shopping bazaar dominating the intersection, but the signs for deep-fried gator-on-a-stick turned his stomach and he continued northward. The thought of such displays haunting the Old-World inhabitants of Manatee Wells did touch off a bout of laughter as he sped by. *"Joey will be safer in prison than on the streets of Manatee Wells, if they ever find out what he has planned for that shark factory land,"* muttered Simms to himself.

He stopped for gas just north of Miami and called Macina. Because neither man wanted to risk an encounter with their police chief by going to the station, they agreed to meet at Juliana's Café in West Palm. In fact, just as he surmised, Macina was already there when he called, and was more than happy to wait a while longer for his partner to arrive. When he rolled into the lot a half hour later, Stevenson recognized Macina's dilapidated Dodge and chuckled at the Departmental joke, then walked in and found Gino in the back of the diner. Emilia recognized him immediately, smiled, and followed him with a pot of coffee, then left the partners to their business.

"Damn, Stevenson, you put some miles on in the last twenty-four. Was it worth it? I don't see the woman..."

Simms grimaced at the implication, "She'll be coming back with her sister and Di Rossi... he's agreed to return to the States."

"Does he know what's waiting for him?"

"Only the part about his dead wife— nothing was said about the shark factory bullshit. You said earlier, you haven't heard anything from Ike Harris?"

"Nah... they have a tail on Whitehead, but unless something happened last night..."

"Do you think Minerva called him out?"

"I don't know if she even called him at all... maybe she's afraid her phone is tapped or something. I saw Whitehead back at the station yesterday afternoon late, and he didn't bat an eye... didn't ask me where you were... nuthin'."

"Okay, well, that buys us a little time, then."

"For what?"

"So, I have some new info—Valeria LaCroix told me that Ricardo Avila was screwing Maria..."

"Bullshit! That can't be true. Can it?"

"Why not?"

"Well, Ricardo said...," then he hesitated, "... ooohh shit! Really? He's that clever? But, did he kill her? I mean, why would he?"

"Apparently, Maria wanted to break it off, but he threatened her with something... that's Valeria's guess about why she went into hiding."

"Yeah, Minerva said something like that too, but... so why does Valeria think Avila killed Maria?" Macina's tone was more of a demand than a question.

"She didn't actually accuse him... in fact, what she told me after that little bombshell made it all the more confusing. Get this: a few months ago, Joe made Avila a partner in the restaurant so he would have more time to pursue the casino deal."

"Hell, that makes no sense... why would Avila then risk it by having an affair with Maria? I mean, he really seemed to detest her, as near as I could tell."

"Exactly what I thought... I mean, there are several weird explanations, if you want to believe that Avila is really twisted. But, I'm at a loss as to how it connects him to her murder... I'd rather suspect that she got herself killed by the drug dealers... I mean, the murder scene investigation at the restaurant hasn't turned up a body, and no one else is missing... and we've been chasing old Rodney's murder like it was connected to the restaurant. But, there's no real reason to connect the two..."

Macina interrupted Simms, "Hold on to that point for a minute, Partner." Now his voice turned apologetic, "Remember a couple of days ago—the day that Maria's body was discovered? I told you I had some info? It seemed important at the moment, but not so much after the body turned up."

"Yeah, yeah... so spit it out, Gino."

"Davo—I had lunch with him earlier that day, and he dished up something he'd been holding back. He overheard—down in the hammocks— before Rodney was killed... Avila was out there talking with Rodney in the swamp... Davo says they were discussing a fake murder at the restaurant, and Avila was giving Rodney the details on how he planted voodoo signs around the kitchen... Rodney told Avila he'd done it right. Davo knew the details, Simms! That was the night after all hell broke loose at the restaurant. Look, Davo saw Rodney running away from the front of Giuseppe's that night. Next, chef Ricardo came looking for the Monk, but a fat man with white hair called the chef back to the crowd."

"Whitehead?"

"Yeah, I'd say so... and so did Davo... Davo said the fat guy was yelling orders and stuff at the cops"

"And Rodney turned up dead the next day?"

"The day after, according to my notes," said Gino. Simms started laughing and Macina, amazed, asked, "You aren't pissed at me?"

"No, for what? Being distracted by a dead body out at the shark factory? No, I was distracted too. Look... this info is one of the missing pieces... the way I see it, Ricardo Avila staged a fake murder scene, and planted stuff to make it look like some kind of voodoo killing— that would point the finger at somebody in particular, right?"

"Yeah, go on..."

"He knew Maria was in hiding somewhere... maybe even knew where..."

"Okay."

"He knew Joe had run off with Valeria, the Cuban waitress, who, only days before, had been fired by Maria... and whom Ricardo knew dabbled in some kind of Cuban voodoo stuff..."

"Maybe..."

"He did... Valeria told me so herself... Now—one day after we tell Avila that we heard that Valeria was back in town, her place is vandalized and a bunch of fake voodoo shit is smeared all over her house."

"Fake? How do you know that?"

"I showed the photos to a real *Santera*—a priestess. She just laughed... she said it was an amateur trying to scare somebody..."

"Yeah, so, let's say you're right... why? What's the motive behind all of this, even if it's all connected as you say?"

"You mean besides framing Joe and Valeria for the murder? I don't have a fucking clue."

"Oh, I see... but I'm not convinced that I see a motive for framing Joe that makes sense in terms of actually murdering one—or two—people, if you count Rodney... and I assume you'd say Rodney was killed to keep him from blabbing about the fake murder."

Simms nodded, "I would say that, yes."

"And, look," said Gino, I don't want to be argumentative, but Maria seems to have been killed more than a week—maybe two—after the incident at Giuseppe's. So, if Avila was planning on murdering her and blaming somebody else, wouldn't he have done it right away?"

"Not if he thought the body wouldn't be found for a long time... as long as Joe Di Rossi was missing and Maria was hiding out and considered missing, he had time on his side. And look, Maria's body might not have been found for a very long time—if ever—out there in that old graveyard, then nobody would recognize a time discrepancy... Look, Ricardo couldn't have had any idea that the State people would be digging around out there..."

Gino poured another cup of coffee, then said, "And neither Minerva nor Whitehead would have known about that either, or else they wouldn't have been storing drugs out there... but, Stevenson, suppose the two dead drug guys actually did kill Maria, then..."

"Well, first off—it's likely that these two dead guys were Minerva's cousins she told us about... so they would've known Maria... and would have no reason to whack her—none that I can see, anyway. But, if they did kill her, it certainly would have been a happy accident for Avila if he truly was up to something. And the more I think about it, the more I'm convinced that he was up to something—remember, he didn't even tell Joe that Maria was missing—but he did tell us, right?"

Simms let that point sink in with Gino for a few seconds, then continued, "I see your point, though, Gino. The District Attorney isn't gonna take this case against Ricardo Avila the way it stands. There's more than reasonable doubt—as you have suggested... so we need something more."

"Right, and remember that our star witness about Avila planning a fake murder scene is a homeless kid who overheard something in the middle of the swamp one night.. I think we need to have a lot more... let's ask Harris to see if Ricardo's fingerprints or hair turn up at the shack... our people finally got his prints a few days ago, along with the rest of the staff at the restaurant. At least see if we can place him in that cottage..."

"Or in the bed in that cottage... that'd be even better, 'cuz it'd corroborate Valeria's story without having to rely on anything she or Joe Di Rossi says about it."

"Okay, I'll call him now... meet you out at the dig..."

Ike Harris was sitting in his car waiting for Simms and Macina to arrive at the old shark factory, when the usually taciturn Dr. Chen hurried over to his car, waving his arms to get the deputy's attention. "Deputy Harris! Deputy Harris! Come quickly! You must see this!"

Ike popped out of his car as if he'd come under fire, and faced Chen with his open palms out to his side as if to question the nature of the emergency, "Is somebody hurt?"

"No, no! But Come! Come! My technician has found something amazing." Then he turned and trotted back toward the graveyard, expecting that Harris would be at his heels. Harris, who hadn't trotted anywhere for months, reluctantly followed. It was only a few hundred yards, but Ike was out of wind when Chen stopped next to a group of his team members. Still, what he saw next left him breathless. "See, Deputy? Gold coins. Many coins!"

At first, all Ike could see were a few coins nestled in the dirt with some old rusted metal pieces, but where Aretha Cooper was kneeling and sweeping away the sandy soil with a small brush, a larger pile loomed out of the ground. "Holy shit, tell me that isn't a bunch of trinkets from the dime store!"

"No, Deputy, this is the real deal. We got a strong hit on a metal detector, and started investigating... see? The treasure was near the head... the skull is right there... I think the rest of the old skeleton must have been laid toward the west—there," said Chen, pointing. "We already found the brass hilt of a cutlass or something similar... looks like the coins were in a wooden chest, long since rotted away. Only some pieces of the metal edging or hinges were still in place."

"So, this isn't even an Indian graveyard?"

"Likely not, at least not this plot we've been working. But see that little hilltop poking up over the palmettos out that way? We've been exploring around that this morning, and I think it's probably a midden which, if I'm right, will prove to be full of Native American pieces. We just didn't notice it at first because we were so focused on this graveyard..."

"So, the knuckleheads who were planting beads and arrowheads and such crap in this graveyard were just..."

"...Ignorant crooks," piped in Aretha Cooper, looking up from the hole in the ground she'd been excavating. "It's happened a lot," she chuckled.

"Indeed," said Dr. Chen. "Now, what does that do to your murder case, Deputy Harris?" he asked.

"I don't know—maybe nothing except add color to the story, however it turns out. Look, I need to make a call to find out where my two colleagues are... they've gotta get out here and see this." Chen smiled and turned back to watch Aretha brushing away dirt from the remains of an ancient human spine.

It took another half hour for the two detectives to arrive on the scene, and when they finally strolled up to the dig, Harris nearly knocked them over, "Hey! About time! You gotta see this..."

Arriving at the dig, Simms had to blink twice for the scene to register, "Geezus... tell me that's not fake!"

"Nope... Spanish coins... all of it..."

"So, no chance it's Jaega Indian..."

"None," laughed Dr. Chen. "Now, that over there," he said pointing at the top of the mound that jutted above the palmettos, "that midden might be Native... but I doubt it's Jaega in this locale... likely one of the other extinct bands, I'd guess it's of the Ais people."

Macina looked at the mound and started, "That rock? It's a...?"

"Not a rock," said Chen. "What made you think it was a boulder? There's nothing about the geology of this place that would have a boulder that size..."

"I dunno," said Gino, and swallowed the urge to say that he and Davo had climbed that 'boulder' a week earlier, using at as a lookout to spy on the shark factory and drug dealers. "I guess it does seem out of place..."

Ike herded Simms and Macina away from the group, "So, what was so urgent earlier that we had to hurry up and meet clear out here?"

"Oh yeah," said Simms, "Listen, Ike, we may have a suspect that links our restaurant murder investigation to Maria Di Rossi's murder over here in your backyard. I'm going to ask our forensics lab to send over fingerprints from a person of interest, and we'd be surprised if they didn't match some stray fingerprints your folks have from the shack. And look, if any of the hair you found over there is other than Maria's, you might wanna get it checked to see if it's male... we think we know who she was having an affair with. So check the sheets."

"Who?" blurted Ike. Then, on second thought, he waived his demand, "Never mind... you just tell me when you think it's the right time... more objective that way. Do you have hair from this person?"

"Nope, but if the fingerprints match, we'll get the hair when we make the arrest."

"So, not the husband?"

"Nope. He's been in the Bahamas the entire time... but he's coming back to answer questions, or so I'm told."

"So, you haven't spoken with him?"

"Not since all of this transpired. He knows his wife is dead, but nothing about what you all have been doing out here."

"Okay, then. Great. We've detained the fake Jaega Indian this morning... we can hold him incognito for a day or so, then we'll have to charge him with something, and he'll get a lawyer..."

"Well, stall as long as you can... we don't want Zev Harmon to catch wind of this until Joe Di Rossi is back in town... we really don't want him to discourage Di Rossi from returning."

"Yeah, no worries... apparently, Jaega Indian-boy's cell phone got broken, so, unless he can remember Harmon's phone number, he's shit outta luck on that account."

"Broke, you say?"

"Yeah, fragile things, aren't they?"

"Right on..." chuckled Simms. "So, one more thing... I'd like a word with Doctor Chen when he has time."

"Sure, let's go ask right now."

Dr. Chen, now buoyed by the morning's discovery, was more than happy to consult with Simms, who got right to the point, "Doctor, I know your team specializes in Native American stuff, but do you ever run across other cultural or ethnic artifacts or..."

"Oh, certainly, Detective Simms... we're still exploring what was likely the first freed slave town in Florida... you mean something like that?"

"That's interesting, but, no, not exactly... we have a case with some evidence purportedly linked to voodoo rituals or some such thing..."

Chen chuckled, "Well, Detective, this must be your lucky day... one of my technicians did her doctoral dissertation on such beliefs and practices... let's go talk to Aretha back over at the dig..."

Chapter 26
Albie Fails

Aretha Cooper patiently listened to Simms explain the evidence from Giuseppe's kitchen, nodding with each item—the black feather, splatters of blood—both human and avian, and remnants of 'four thieves vinegar'. She laughed out loud when he described the cadaver tongue, "That's an old medical school stunt," she added. She asked about the actual details and ingredients of the 'four thieves vinegar', then frowned, "Maybe it's not authentic," she posited, "I mean, strictly, the ingredients aren't correct." Her eyebrows raised at the red pentagram scrawled on the wall, but she said nothing.

Without further explanation, Simms pulled the photos of the vandal's artwork from Valeria's house out of a manila envelope and let Aretha study them, then he repeated with the photos from his own front door. "What do you make of those?" he asked.

Cooper compared the two sets of photographs, then said, "Well, it's difficult to be certain... I mean, there are so many crackpots who think they can become vodoun practitioners by reading a little bit on the internet or listening to their grandmas talk about the old days... but in my opinion, the evidence you described from the restaurant is a hodge-podge of some amateurish prank." Simms nodded, and she continued, "Now here... the first set of photos—that's somebody's home, yeah? Probably some amateur trying to scare the residents, or kids messing around to cover up that they broke in... but no serious practitioner would do anything like that."

"Thanks, Aretha... what about the second set?"

"They're different, for sure. I mean, the person who painted that evil eye was an artist and took care in creating it... but I've never heard of... well, where did you say those photos were taken? I'd have guessed it might be found on the doorway of a priest or priestess, you know, to protect their home from harm."

"Well, in actual fact, somebody painted it on my door one night..."

"Really?! That's... well, I'm surprised, Detective... there was a lot of effort put into painting that image to ward-off evil... normally, I'd say it was to protect you, but maybe it was aimed at protecting somebody from you..."

"Would you say it was voodoo... or something else?"

"Not in my experience... it's not islander style... it's not Afro culture, at least none based on any of the sects I've studied."

"Well, I don't want to put words in your mouth, could it be European?"

"Perhaps... but, I've not studied or seen that kind of witchcraft or magic. Sorry. My focus was on derivatives of island spiritual practices— it's way more complicated than black magic and popular movie lore."

"That's okay, you've pretty much corroborated what an old cigar smoking Cuban *Santera* told me... so you've been quite helpful."

"A Cuban Santera? How on earth did you get close to somebody like that? I mean, I struggled getting by all kinds of crackpots... what? Did you pay her? I mean it must have cost you something?"

Simms laughed, "Well, the cost may yet need to be determined..."

"So, you knew someone close to her... a girlfriend, maybe?" she fished.

Simms laughed again, "Seems so..." then he deflected, "What about your work, though... Crackpots and all? How'd you finally manage?"

"Well, I started with an old Mexican *Brujo* in Monterrey, Mexico... he wanted to be paid in *ganja...*"

"Did you?" Simms asked, and she looked at him hesitantly, unsure if she should answer his question. But he persevered, "I would have... but of course, you'd have to deal with a cartel down there, I suspect."

Relieved, Aretha laughed, "Yeah, but that wasn't the worst part... he took me to see an old hag he said was his sister, and left me there with her. But she was preoccupied casting spells on her neighbor's chickens and told me to come back later."

"Did you?"

"Hell no! I got on the first plane back home, and thought about changing my major. I finally got a break with three hoodoo sisters in Baltimore, and then they put me in touch with somebody in the boondocks of Virginia, and so on. I worked my way down the southern states to see the various ways these folks practice their religion. But once I got down into parts of the deep south, it got hairy. I had to get my brother and his friend to go with me for protection in a few places—they're both Navy Seals... anyway, the Louisiana bayous were interesting... Sadly, I didn't have the funds to travel to Haiti, Cuba or Jamaica, though... I had to rely on word of mouth and written testaments from people who'd lived and practiced there. I visited Little Haiti, Little Havana, The Big Easy. Eventually, I got enough material to write my paper."

Simms held out his hand, "When this is all over, if I have anything more definitive, I'll send it along. And, if you don't mind, I'm going to put you on a list of expert witnesses in case my findings turn up in court—you'll get paid, of course."

Cooper chuckled, "That'd be interesting..."

Simms had one last thing on his mind, "But I wanted to ask—you went through all of that effort to research your paper got a doctorate... how did you end up digging in the dirt for Doctor Chen and the State?"

Cooper laughed, "I needed a job..."

Simms walked Cooper back to the dig site and grabbed Macina, "Come on, Gino, we've got work to do." Gino nodded, shook Ike's hand, and started to leave with Simms.

About 20 yards away, Harris hollered, "Wait up!" Simms started to ask "*what now?*" But Harris saved him the effort. Waving his mobile phone in the air, he said, "One of our deputies followed your chief to a self-storage compound... you know the one over by the private jet strip off A-1-A?"

"Yeah, let's go..."

"Okay, backup is just arriving and they've gained entry through the front gate... they should have him pretty much red-handed by the time we get there..."

"Well, only if he's our guy," said Simms, not believing his own words for even a moment.

Albert Whitehead sat sullenly in the back seat of his own car. For the moment, out of courtesy, he slouched without handcuffs. Deputies had relieved him of his pistol and confiscated his police-issue shotgun and ammunition, however, and a single deputy stood sentry. The dark blue Dodge was hemmed-in by several Sheriff's vehicles, while a handful of deputies examined the contents of a storage garage that now stood wide open. Harris, Simms, and Macina arrived on the scene just behind the Sheriff's forensics team. One glance at the inside of the garage and they knew that Whitehead was in trouble.

Simms, on the drive from the shark factory, had wondered exactly what he would say to Whitehead, but had not found the words then. Now, as he slipped away from the crowded storeroom to confront his captain, a wave of sympathy hit him. "Chief... what the hell? If they find what I think they're gonna find... Geezus, I hope this storage room isn't in your name..." Whitehead started to speak, but Simms put up his hand to interrupt him, "Don't say anything that I'll have to testify to, Chief. Just wait for your lawyer. You know that."

Whitehead's jaw went slack, and he resumed staring out through the windshield, as if to imagine himself flying away. Simms turned his back, walked over to the garage, and stood between Macina and Harris. Harris told him, "At least a hundred kilos of coke in here, and a safe full of cash. One of my team told me they've got a file box full of papers, too, along with a ledger of some sort. It's gonna take some time to go through everything, but we've got enough here to lock up your chief while we examine the rest."

Macina asked, "Is there anything that connects Minerva or Di Rossi to this operation?"

Harris smiled, "The facility is in her name, although the owner told my guys that he's never seen a woman come here... so maybe Whitehead just used her name on the rental agreement. The owner's got security tapes back a couple of weeks, though, so we'll have to see how this plays out. Did Whitehead talk to you?"

"No, he didn't say a word... he started to, then clammed up and ignored me. I mean, what's he gonna say anyway?"

"Okay, well, now what happens over in your shop? Who's in charge? We'll want to know who to be in touch with..."

"Well," interrupted Macina, "Stevenson is senior..."

Simms countered, "Let's not get ahead of ourselves... I need to get back to the station and make a call to the mayor... he'll decide... but for now, I guess you can keep me in the loop."

"Right," said Harris. "I'll tell my major. You might want to hurry up and tell your mayor, though, 'cuz the shit's gonna hit the fan big time, and pretty quickly..."

"Okay," said Simms, "I'll call him on my mobile right now. "There's obviously gonna be drug charges... what about murder... the two dead guys at the factory?"

"Just say 'maybe' on that, pending further investigation of the drug stuff and the evidence at the murder scene. We'll take a look at his shotgun and ammunition to see what forensics can come up with. I doubt we'll speculate with the press about that... I think either the Sheriff or the prosecutor's office will have a more complete statement later on—it's not my call now, Stevenson."

Simms herded Macina away from the group and looked straight through him. "Gino, you need to keep this under your hat, and the hat pulled down tight. Understand? It's going to hit the fan in our office... all I'm gonna tell the mayor right now is that you and I had stumbled onto Whitehead when we were investigating the murder at Giuseppe's, and that the County Sheriff had been helping us out. I want him... No! We need the mayor to think this all just happened... just dropped into our lap... because if he thinks we were privy to anything concrete and didn't notify him that we were investigating our own chief, there will be hell to pay."

Macina grinned, "Well, that's pretty much what just happened, right? I mean, we were out in the field with Harris investigating the death of Giuseppe's wife with Harris when he told us..."

"Right... well, eventually, somebody's gonna hear about Davo and Minerva..."

"Okay, Stevenson, I get it. I really do. Nobody's gonna ask me anything anyway—everybody thinks I'm in over my head."

"Look, Gino, in the past, you've taken being in over your head to an art form... but really, you've done a great job on this... let's finish it up right."

Macina laughed, trying to figure out if that was a compliment or not, but pushed on, "I suppose... but we still have to solve Rodney's murder, too—Ricardo, Joe Di Rossi... they're on the menu at Giuseppe's, right?"

Chapter 27
Chef Ricardo On the Menu

The next morning, Simms rose an hour before dawn and hurried to his office to prepare for a meeting with the mayor and the city attorney. His news the previous afternoon about the arrest of Chief Albie Whitehead had been met with a cold telephone silence by His Honor, the Mayor, a reaction that Stevenson more or less attributed to shock. He'd alerted the man that the County Sheriff would likely be calling later on in the evening with a formal courtesy update. In return, Simms was gruffly ordered to report to City Hall promptly at 8 AM, and warned to be prepared for a detailed briefing. His Honor was not wanting to face a raucous gaggle of reporters under any circumstances, but certainly not without a chance to prepare.

After his conversation with the mayor, Simms had then worked late into the evening to craft a straightforward summary as preface to an eventual comprehensive report, sharing multiple phone calls with Macina to make sure his partner was looped into the storyline. His early morning goal was to outline the final report prior to walking over to City Hall, and he knew that politics made it imperative that he and Macina were in lock-step agreement on the details. Macina had told him, "Don't worry, Partner, nobody from City Hall is gonna ask me any questions about anything."

Simms let Macina's self-deprecation slide this time and, instead, simply replied, "Anybody associated with this case could be called as a witness, Gino, and this report, which will wind up before the court in discovery, had better match whatever we respond to at a hearing or trial. You are a principal investigator in this, so be prepared." After he got off the phone with Macina he thought to himself, *"I hope Gino's payin' attention to me and not playin' grab-ass with his girlfriend."*

At a quarter of 8, files in hand, Simms headed out the door of police headquarters. He immediately realized that he should have planned better, for the gaggle had already assembled on the steps of the mayor's citadel. Fortunately, Simms remembered the dank subterranean tunnel between the two buildings, a hallway that only the disgraced Whitehead used when called across the square on one errand or another. So, Simms retraced his steps, ducked back into headquarters, then scurried along the basement corridor like a gopher on a mission. And the mayor was no fool. He'd arrived at the back door of City Hall at dawn, while the reporters were still drinking coffee and stabbing out cigarettes in the remnants of their morning hash browns.

The mayor, like any politician, was more than happy to take credit for the hard work of his ace detectives in ferreting out the corruption in the Department. Of course, His Honor first had to know what Simms had to say, then consult with his staff, and then tell Simms how it was all going to go down. "Oh, and, Detective Simms," added the mayor just before Stevenson thought he was off the hook, "I want you standing by my side... be prepared to answer any questions I lob your way." Simms gulped a little. Even though he wasn't disappointed in the assignment, he was surprised by the mayor's gesture. Only later, in retrospect, did Simms realize that His Honor was not being entirely magnanimous in sharing the spotlight. If things got screwed up down the line, there would be a fall guy, and

Stevenson had just had a bullseye painted on his forehead, a target far less ambiguous than the evil eye on his front door.

When the dust settled on the morning press conference, the local story had been given enough spin to credit the Mayor and the Treasure Coast PD's 'special investigating team' with working hand-in-glove to crack the case and jail a corrupt cop. Or, at least it would have if Simms hadn't clarified that the case was a joint effort with the County Sheriff. If that little addendum of truth had caused a sour patch in the mayor's gullet, the etched movie star smile on his face didn't reveal a thing. But Simms did save His Honor the more acidic gastric distress of eating his own words later on after the Sheriff's press conference was staged down the highway a few miles, because that's where the bigger picture was splayed for the TV audience to indulge themselves in all manner of speculation.

Macina sat in the comfort of the police station and watched the entire performance on TV, then drove down to breakfast at Juliana's Café in West Palm. By the time he'd driven south on the interstate and parked his car, he figured Simms would have wrapped up his post presser meeting with the mayor, and decided to call him to invite him down to breakfast. For his part, Simms couldn't wait to get far away from the town square, but told Macina, "I'm with ya... but I gotta return Ike Harris' call first."

"Ike, it's me, Simms..."

"Nice work this morning, buddy," said Harris. "I hope your mayor appreciates how much grief and the never-ending shitshows you just saved him. Thanks from all of us over here, too. It would have looked like a jurisdictional pissing contest if you hadn't clarified the joint effort aspect, and my major already has one of those brewing with the State, so he's about on his last nerve ending."

"Yeah, I could see the 'gators coming for us at one point. The bastard... well, he gave me a chance to speak. Otherwise..."

"Yeah, we've all been there... look, the Sheriff is issuing another statement—it's a joint press statement with the State's D-H-R about the murders over at the factory, along with a blurb about the antiquities, the gold coins, and so forth... I wanted to let you know, too, that we got fingerprint matches from the cottage that match the set you sent over to us from the Giuseppe's Restaurant scene."

"Really?! That's great, Ike. That puts our number one suspect in Maria Di Rossi's murder in her cottage at some point."

"Who is it? Can you say?"

"Yeah, and it's not the husband. It's the head chef at Giuseppe's, Ricardo Avila."

"No shit? I can't wait to hear the details on that..."

Simms chuckled, "You'll have to wait, but I can tell you this to tickle your imagination... rumor is that he was having an affair with the deceased. Think about that for a bit. Anyways, look, I'm gonna get ahold of Macina, and we'll bring Avila in for her murder and also for the murder of that hobo, Rodney... when we get DNA from Avila, can we ask your contacts up in Jacksonville to check it against..."

"Yeah," interrupted Ike, "but maybe get a snip of his hair. It's faster to match what we found in the bed. We'll have time for the fluids and other stuff that the DNA guys like. So, listen, I need to be able to explain to my major why you guys are bringing Avila in, and not us."

"Right... So, about Avila's custody, I'm more than happy to turn him over to you guys when we're done with him. For now, though, how about you and I agree on the story that we're still trying to determine where Maria was murdered, even though her body was discovered in your territory-—we still have the messy scene at the restaurant as our main focus here."

"Okay, that works for now, especially since we've got our hands full with your old boss and his lawyers... and this thing with the State antiquities guys is ballooning... I've never seen so many bureaucrats in one room before."

Simms said, "Great... besides that, the hobo was murdered in our backyard, and we believe that Avila is the perp on that killing too. So look, about your antiquities case, I expect Joe Di Rossi to show up sometime later today. We're gonna take a shot at interviewing him about his wife, then I'm gonna encourage him to voluntarily go talk to you guys. I won't say anything about the State antiquities thing. So, Ike, thanks again... I gotta call Gino."

"Cool. Oh, then ask Gino to call me... we need to tell that old lady... Minerva Rossini... that her cousins are dead— definitely the two corpses at the shark factory. And then we'll need to ask her a few questions about Albie Whitehead. You guys might want to be part of that little charade."

"Yeah, for sure. When? We can be up in the Wells after lunch... we should have Avila in the box by then... Oh, wait. I gotta be at the airport to collect Di Rossi—hopefully—so Gino's gonna have to represent."

Macina met Simms at Giuseppe's, along with two squad cars of uniformed officers just about the time the restaurant staff was gearing up for the lunch crowd. Ricardo Avila's smile faded and the words welcoming Simms and Macina for lunch froze on his lips when he saw the uniforms. All that remained was a stark look of confusion when he heard the words, "Ricardo Avila, you are under arrest for the murder of Maria Di Rossi and related crimes. You have the right...."

Avila interrupted, "I didn't kill anybody..." Simms ignored his protest and placed the handcuffs on him, finished Mirandizing him, then escorted him to one of the squad cars. He told Macina to go in and explain to the staff that their head chef had been arrested, but not to answer any questions. Then he told the other officers to take Avila back to the station, book him, then put a guard in an interrogation room with the prisoner.

Simms waited for Macina outside the restaurant, and said, "Look, I know you want to be in two places at one time, but I think it's more important for you to meet Ike over in Manatee Wells... maybe try to get to Minerva's before he and his boys arrive. If she thinks she has an ally in you, she might be more cooperative in talking to Ike."

"Okay, I think you're right... and I wouldn't expect Ricardo to say anything without his lawyer anyway..."

"Yup, I agree... so get goin', Partner. I'll catch up with you later this afternoon... hopefully, we'll have Joe Di Rossi back in town and willing to drop by the station before evening time."

Simms sat across a small table from Ricardo Avila in a stuffy room outfitted with three remote video cameras. Avila sat uncomfortably on a folding chair, his hands now manacled in front of his waist instead of behind his back. Simms peered at a clipboard of notes, doodling for effect, as if he were making notes in preparation to interrogate Avila. Finally, he began, "Ricardo, just so we're on the same page here, you don't need to answer anything without your attorney present..."

"I don't have one... and I already told you, I don't need one. I didn't do anything."

"Okay. How long had you been carrying on an affair with Maria Di Rossi?"

Avila's jaw dropped, then he smiled, "Is that what this is about? Did Joe put you up to this? That was no crime... I was doing him a favor..."

"So, to be clear, you were having an affair?"

"Yeah, so what? It doesn't mean I killed her."

"Why would you think Joe—Di Rossi—that's who you're talking about?"

Avila nodded.

"Why do you think Joe would, as you say, put us up to arresting you?"

"Because the entire scheme was his idea... he wanted a divorce so he could be with that waitress, Valeria... so he... he made me an offer."

"A stake in the restaurant if you got his wife to commit adultery..."

"Exactly. How did you know?"

Simms ignored the question, "So, what went wrong? Why did Maria want to break off the relationship with you and go into hiding?"

"What? That never happened. And there was never any mention about offing her either."

"So, did you have her stashed someplace so you could keep the affair quiet? I mean it would have been a scandal at the restaurant..."

"No, we always met at my place... Joe was too busy to give a shit..."

"So, you never visited her at her place?"

"No... she still lived with Joe and his old aunt..."

Simms made a few notes, then his phone buzzed. "I'll be right back in, Ricardo, don't go anywhere," he smirked, then he stepped outside.

"Yeah, Gino, what's up?"

"Minerva wasn't home, so we're all waiting to see if she shows up... Maybe she went to lunch with a neighbor... How's it going with Avila?"

"He's talking a little... I got to go back in, though... I'll call you later."

Simms returned to the interrogation room and settled back into his chair, then looked at Ricardo with a hard stare. "So, you never spent time with Maria at a hotel or a bed and breakfast, or some lover's getaway?"

"No."

"Okay, I want to ask you about something else. Do you know a character named Rodney? Some called him a Tibetan Monk, or The Monk?"

"I don't think so..."

"Homeless guy, lived down in the hammocks with a bunch of others?"

"Who knows? Those creatures were always panhandling at the back door of the kitchen..."

"Oh, well, we have a witness who saw you conspiring with Rodney about murdering somebody in the restaurant... just prior to all the hullabaloo that night when we all came out to investigate a murder scene in your kitchen... Anyway, Rodney turned up dead a day or so later..."

Ricardo Avila looked silently at his hands for a few moments, then said, "I think, Detective, that you've been given bad information... but I'm not going to say another word to you until I have a lawyer."

Macina waited across the street from Minerva's house for less than a half hour after he phoned Simms, all the while, Ike Harris was parked a couple of doors down, waiting patiently. When Minerva did finally show, it was in the back of a black Cadillac with dark tinted windows, preventing Gino from seeing any other occupants. As the Caddie drove away, Gino hurried to get in front of her so she would see him walking toward her in plenty of time to avoid being startled. She didn't smile at him, but put her arm out so he could steady her up the steps. Once at the top, she said, "I've been expecting you Gino. Did you come to arrest me?"

"Nope. I came to tell you that the Sheriff is going to come see you with some distressing news, and he has some questions, too."

"I know about Albie already, Gino. That was my lawyer dropping me off. He said not to answer any questions without him being present."

"Makes sense to me, Miss Minerva... just tell that to Deputy Harris... see, here he comes now."

Ike walked up the steps, "Ma'am, do you remember me, Deputy Harris?"

"Yes, I remember when you were here a few days ago... I'm not senile yet."

"No Ma'am. When I was here, I mentioned that we were investigating a couple of homicides over by the old shark factory..."

"Right, Maria..."

"Well, two more besides her... we have a positive identification... they are the two young men whose names you gave to Detective Macina as your cousins..." Minerva trembled, and Macina, who was still supporting her arm, put his hand around her waist, afraid she's swoon any second. "We're sorry for your loss..."

Gino helped her over to a chair, but she declined to sit. Instead, she asked, "Do you know who is responsible?"

"Yes, we have very strong evidence, and a suspect in custody... you may have heard it on the news this morning..."

"I don't watch television much... who is it?"

"Our suspect is Albert Whitehead..."

Minerva sat down then and looked at Macina. "Gino... did you know?"

"Yes, of course... Whitehead has caused quite a scandal in our Department, and there's a fair amount of outrage now that it's out in the press."

Ike Harris said, "Ma'am, we have a few questions about your connections to Chief Whitehead..."

Minerva interrupted, "Deputy, with respect, I have a statement I'll make, but only with my attorney present..."

"In that case," said Ike, "we'd prefer that it be in our offices..."

"Fine, if you'll be so kind as to drive me there, we can call my attorney on the way so he'll meet us over there."

Gino cleared his throat and Ike raised an eyebrow, but Gino continued, "Are you sure about this, Miss Minerva?"

She replied, "Absolutely. I told that dog he was gonna get us in trouble, but I never thought he'd do something like this... so... are you coming or not, Gino?"

Simms was waiting for Trinity's plane from Key West when Gino called to inform him of the turn of events with Minerva. When he clicked off his mobile, he tried to formulate some brief, yet lucid explanation to present to Joe Di Rossi—that is, if Joe was even on the plane as Trinity had promised him that morning.

Simms' first priority was to get a statement from Joe about his agreement with Ricardo Avila, but that would require cutting Joe away from Trinity and Valeria. Next, he had to decide when to inform Joe that his Aunt Minerva was, at the least, involved in giving a statement about an illegal drug operation in Manatee Wells, and at worst—and most likely—in the Sheriff's custody for her involvement. If he blurted that out up front, Joe might not be focused on the Avila deal. If he waited too long, then he risked alienating Joe for any future cooperation.

It took Simms five minutes to see a solution. He called Gino back, "Gino, listen... timing is everything. At some point this afternoon, I'm going to call you for a minute and hang up. Then you're gonna wait three or four minutes and call me back to give me the news about Minerva. Got it?"

"How about, no? Did you lose your mind in the last five minutes?"

"Nope... I need a statement from Joe without him being distracted about his aunt. See? But, then I need to tell him... like I just found out... get it."

"Okay, got it... I'm just getting to the Sheriff's station now."

Chapter 28
Giuseppe Returns

To Stevenson's relief, Joe and Valeria were on the plane with Trinity. Trini exited the plane with a smile on her face, with Joe and Valeria in tow, and walked straight for him. Simms scarcely noticed that only Trinity had a smile, because he was self-absorbed in wondering if she was truly glad to see him or simply proud that she'd followed through on her promise. He scolded himself silently for parsing her motives as if she were some duplicitous suspect, and realized that she *was* glad to see him *and* happy that she'd been successful. *"They're all part of the same package,"* he concluded silently as the trio approached him.

Simms, finally recognizing the stress of the moment, broke the ice as congenially as he felt was appropriate by asking about their flight, level of hunger, need of a restroom, and spontaneous but forgettable chit-chat aimed at getting them to relax. While the women visited the restroom, Simms told Joe, "Ricardo Avila has been arrested for two murders, including that of your wife. I really would like to get a statement from you about a few key things having to do with Avila and the murder scene, which looks a lot like it was your restaurant."

Joe sighed, "Okay... do I need a lawyer?"

"Nope, we're not accusing you of anything here," answered Simms, again choosing his words carefully, "But if you want to call one, you can. I was really hoping that we could drop the girls off at my home, then go to my office for some privacy."

Joe scratched at his earlobe, "Yeah, okay, that's fine... I'm really... pissed... sad... shocked... all of it, I guess. I'd really like to know what happened. I mean, there was nothing sweet about my wife, but she didn't do anything to deserve this."

"Okay... well, let's collect your bags and see if we can get this over with before dark... I'll see if Trini feels like fixing us all a meal, or maybe we can go out—just not Italian tonight..."

Joe chuckled, "Okay, understood... let's get to it."

Simms took Joe in the side door of the station and gave him a seat in his office. Pulling out a cassette recorder, he apologized, "I hope you don't mind... routine protocol around here, and given what's been going on in this Department this week, I shouldn't leave any steps out."

Joe looked at him with a little suspicion, but said, "Nah, go ahead. If I don't like where something is going, I'll say so..."

"Good idea... Okay, so I'd like to know the nature of your agreement with Ricardo Avila, where you made him a partner in the restaurant..."

"Simple... I needed time to work on a deal to build a casino on my land in Manatee Wells, and I knew I'd be away, or at least pretty distracted by all of that negotiation, and I didn't want the restaurant business to suffer. He's actually the one who proposed some kind of arrangement. Ricardo has always been kinda of a partner anyway, I mean, he's a fantastic chef.."

"Yeah, but apparently not the best business partner...We did some digging... the restaurant is part of an L-L-C, but you're the only officer listed. Wasn't your wife part of the company?"

"No, we had a prenup on most of my family's property... I set her up with the ladies' salon next door as her own business, and she was a partner in a few other things we got going later on. She also acted as sort of a pit boss with the restaurant staff when I wasn't around—the staff knew better than to cross her."

"How does Ricardo's piece of the action fit in, then?"

"I had a separate agreement drawn up for him..."

"So, was seducing your wife part of the deal?"

Joe responded "Ha! Hell no, is that what he said? No, he just started up with her, but that was okay by me, it kept her from being so nosey about me and Val..."

"Did Maria know about this deal?"

"I didn't tell her... maybe Ricardo did..."

"Who else would have known? Your kids? How about Valeria? And did Ricardo know that Maria wasn't a full partner?"

"I only told Val recently... I don't talk to my kids about business—they've both moved far away from Manatee Wells. And... no, I don't think Ricardo knew anything about the overall structure of my LLC. There was no way he could unless Maria shared stuff. But, no matter how angry she might get with me, she was all businesswoman. She never would have divulged something like that."

"Not even if Ricardo had brought up your side deal? Wouldn't that have made her mad enough?"

Joe shook his head, "No, 'cuz it really had no effect on any of her business affairs... like I said, we had separate holdings."

"How recently did you tell Valeria? Before or after she got fired the last time?"

"I don't remember... where's this going?"

"I was just trying to figure out if... you know, if Maria had discovered the deal with Ricardo and knew about your affair with Valeria...if it had anything to do with Maria firing Val the last time that happened... and whether, if she got wind of the deal with Ricardo, it might have sent her into hiding."

"No, I just told you... wait... Hiding? What do you mean?"

"So, Maria, she'd moved out of your house, right?"

"No, of course not. People gossip enough as it is... she was still living there with my aunt when I left for the Keys. Why?"

"Well, it looks like she'd been living in an old cabin out in the palmettos near the shark factory for some time... you know the place?"

"Well, if it's what I'm thinking of, yeah, there's an old caretaker's cottage in the woods... but hell, nobody could live there..."

"Well, all the evidence says she was doing just that... and her body was found buried in the old graveyard nearby... you know where that is?"

Joe looked stunned by that news, "Well, yeah, everybody knows about the old Indian burial grounds by now... we notified the State about it recently—after that hurricane last year... they were supposed to come out and survey the site... "

"They did... they're the ones who discovered Maria's remains—that's where she was buried."

Joe sat speechless, contemplating the string of events he'd just heard. Finally, he asked, "So, you think Ricardo killed Maria at the restaurant and buried her way out there?"

Simms again chose his words carefully, "That was our first thought... but the Sheriff is investigating the cottage to see if there's evidence of violence there..."

"How do you know Maria was living there?"

"Fingerprints, hair... DNA samples are up in Jacksonville, too, but the other is enough... along with toiletries, clothing, food, and so forth."

"That's weird... you know, Ricardo didn't tell me she was missing either, but how does he tie in? It makes no sense that he would kill her?"

"That, I'm afraid, is more than I can share in an ongoing investigation—I told you what I know about Maria as a courtesy—we think you deserve that much. But I can't take the chance of jeopardizing the investigative aspects..."

"Okay, I get it," he sighed in resignation. "How did she...?"

"The coroner hasn't said, yet, Joe... I'm sorry."

Simms spent another half hour asking Joe questions about the band of homeless people at the factory, asked if they were the same ones that came for handouts at the restaurant, whether he knew Rodney, The Monk, and just about anything that might be randomly linked to all of the investigations. None of it went anywhere, but Simms hoped that it was suitably confusing to Joe.

When he was nearly finished obscuring the main details he'd wanted to get from Joe, he excused himself, "Joe, I was supposed to call my partner about something... can you hang out in here for a minute?" Simms left his office, called Macina, hung up and returned. "Sorry, his line was busy. Things have been a bit crazy around here... what with our police chief being locked up..."

Joe started to ask what that was about, when Simms' mobile buzzed, "Hey Gino, thanks for calling back... sorry I forgot earlier... what's up?" Simms listened to Gino repeat himself for several minutes, then said, "All right, well that's not good. Okay, thanks, Partner."

Simms clicked off his phone, took a deep breath, then started, "Joe, that was my partner, Detective Macina. He's been at the

Sheriff's office down by the Wells all afternoon... it has to do with your Aunt Minerva..."

"What? Is she okay? What happened?"

"Well, more or less okay... she's been arrested..."

Joe's face puckered into an odd grin of disbelief, "What'd she do, poison the neighbor's dog again?"

Simms shook his head, "No, nothing that simple... she's been arrested as part of a drug ring— run by, we think, our police chief Whitehead..."

"That can't be true!"

"Well, from what my partner just told me, she's pretty much confessed... see, two of her nephews or cousins... we're not sure which—maybe they're yours too—were murdered out at your family's old shark factory, where they were guarding a cache of drugs. In fact, the same people that discovered Maria's body found the two dead men and called the Sheriff, and they found the drugs. The evidence points to Whitehead as the killer and the ringleader of the drug distribution ring—although, undoubtedly, we'll find a supplier somewhere higher up the food chain. Anyway Minerva has apparently come forward once she heard about the killings... sounds like she's burned Whitehead, but she'll likely face some kind of charges herself."

Joe sat silently for what may have seemed like an eternity to anyone listening to the tape later, but he finally asked, "Whitehead? That's his name? Fat guy, white hair, goes by 'Albie'?"

"Yes, you know him?"

"Minerva introduced him once a few months ago... she's been carryin' on with him for a while..."

"By 'carryin' on', do you mean an affair, like intimate relations?"

"Oh for God's sake, I don't need that visual. Jesus!"

Simms put up his hand as if halting traffic and changed the subject, "Okay, can't say I blame you... So, about the shark factory... is that what you planned to tear down to build your casino?"

"Yeah, it's been a nuisance for decades... squatters, druggies, campers—all trespassing... you name it. Back in the day, rumors are that my grandfather used it to store marijuana for distribution up the rivers and inland to the swamp people... is that what you say she was involved in?"

"That and a few hundred kilos of cocaine..."

"How can that be?"

"Joe, I don't know, but the Sheriff is investigating all of that... it's out of my jurisdiction. I suggest you go up there first thing in the morning and see what you can learn from the Sheriff. He'll likely have more info on Maria's case, too."

"Can't I go try to bail Minerva out tonight? The idea of an old lady spending the night in the slammer is... well, it's not right."

"Her lawyer has been with her... he'll do all that's possible, but they'll have to get a judge to okay bail, and that can't happen earlier than tomorrow."

Joe leaned back in his chair and folded his arms, giving Simms the sense that he wasn't going to get more from the interview. Joe confirmed his body language, "Are we done here? I'd like to go back to your place and get Valeria... we'll get a cab to my home in Manatee Wells, and tomorrow, I'll go see the Sheriff, first thing."

Simms let the hot water pound him on the back of his neck until it felt like needles penetrating into his brain stem. Somehow, he couldn't shake the guilt of his duplicitous interview with Joe, and the pelting shower wasn't working fast enough, no matter how hard he concentrated. It was the surprise of Trinity's slippery body embracing him from the side that changed his focus entirely. "You don't mind some company do you, Simms?" She asked coyly in her soothing voice, knowing the answer to her question this time. He twisted to face her, and before he could answer, she pressed her breasts firmly against his chest and kissed him. "It'll be okay, they'll be okay" she said, pulling away a little and looking up at him. "Now suds me up before we run out of hot water, I've got plans for you from now until morning, so no more sulking over work."

Chapter 29
Last Puzzle Piece

Simms was never a strong advocate of sleeping-in late, especially when the noise in his head was drummed along by an army of clues and suspicions marching down main street. Trinity tried her best to keep him pinned to the sheets, but, at best, her efforts were only good for an extra half hour the next morning. Then, Stevenson made a purposeful effort that resulted in a two-minute shower, a gulp of coffee, and a wet kiss short of a clean getaway. Or so he thought.

The drive to work began with a mental punch list of things on the day's agenda, but it was an exercise interrupted at every stop sign and red light by a flash of vision involving bare skin, or wet tongue, or nibbled earlobes. He nearly turned around in defeat, when his mobile buzzed. "Good morning, Ike, I was just on my way to the office... you saved me a call."

"Stevenson, my friend," Ike began in an uncharacteristic display of camaraderie, "I've got a man named Joe Di Rossi out in the lobby... desk sergeant says Joe asked for me by name..."

"Yup, I told him to ask for you... Gino called me last night to say that you've got his aunt locked up."

"Well, that's true, and Mister Di Rossi is almost certainly going to join her, and I wanted to let you know what's going on..."

"Uuhh, well, it doesn't sound right... I talked with him at my place for nearly two hours, and I think he's pretty straight on the murders..." Simms pulled his car off into a parking lot so he could pay attention to Harris.

"You might be right, Stevenson, but here's the problem... the county prosecutor has come up with some vast conspiracy theory that the murders and the drug ring, and the hoax out at the old shark factory are all connected in one giant plot. Until he sees things in any other light, Di Rossi is gonna be in custody as a suspect in masterminding the whole deal... and I'm sure that's gonna cause you some fallout..."

"No shit, it is, Ike. There's no way Di Rossi had anything to do with the drug thing... he never would have invited Doctor Chen's bunch out there if he'd been involved in the drug stash. And he wasn't even in the country when his wife was murdered."

"Yeah, I agree, and I'm sure a handful of lawyers will make that point on Di Rossi's behalf. There's one more thing, and I hate to piss in your Post Toasties so early in the morning, but it looks certain that Maria Di Rossi was strangled in or near that old cottage. There was a piece of cord found in her shallow grave that we overlooked at first... but it matches... well we went back out to the shack and it seems we overlooked that a piece of drapery or curtain cord had been cut off... and it matched... So, the County is gonna formally request that Ricardo Avila be transferred to our custody too. We've got questions..."

"Okay, Ike, I've got no problem with that. He's lawyered up over here, and it'll be interesting to hear what your guys can get out of him. We've only got circumstantial evidence on the hobo's murder in our case, so unless something else turns up, we're gonna suck hind tit on prosecuting him anyway. Sticking with the restaurant murder scene angle as an excuse to keep him here for a couple of days served our purpose, but I think we both knew this was a more likely outcome."

"Okay, well, I'll keep you in the loop... meanwhile, I've gotta deal with a tangle of lawyers and bail hearings and a meeting with my major... and, well, you know the drill. I'll check in with you later in the day."

"Thanks, Ike." Stevenson clicked off his phone and eased his car back out into the flow of morning traffic on A1A. He began erasing items from his mental agenda, called Gino Macina, and then moved His Honor, the Mayor to the top of his list.

Simms had no problem getting in to see His Honor, and they were joined by the City Attorney within minutes. He was surprised at how easily both men had acquiesced to moving Ricardo Avila to the Sheriff's custody. In fact, Simms came away with the distinct impression that His Honor was relieved to not have a high profile case in his lap, given the fallout over his disgraced police chief. Perhaps it was a credit to the City Attorney's admonition that they only had a circumstantial case against Ricardo Avila in the matter of the homicide of Rodney the Tibetan Monk. The headline in the local paper had already generated bad publicity,

Did Chef Really Kill Homeless Tibetan Monk?

The disinformation swirling about town was approaching EF warning levels, and the City's prosecutor saw no upside to the publicity storm. As soon as he left City Hall, Simms called Ike Harris and told him to send a prisoner van for Avila.

Suddenly, Simms had nothing to do—except paperwork, the bane of his existence, a weight that would anchor him to his desk for the rest of the day.

Detective Macina, on the other hand, felt free as a bird as he drove over to the Third United Baptist Church Wayfarer Shelter to pick up Davo for lunch. He knew Simms would handle all the paperwork and then tell him what to say and when to say it. He chuckled at his fortunes, so good so early in the day. Breakfast at Emilia's, a liberating call from Simms, and now, lunch with a twelve-year old. *"Just another day in the life on the Treasure Coast,"* he told himself.

Davo turned out to be a dark cloud, however. The boy moped out of the dank hallways of the residence, and not even the prospect of a cheeseburger and root beer cheered him noticeably. He was more disheveled than usual, and his new shoes were missing. Once Macina had him away from the squinting eyes of the matron and buckled into the rattling Dodge, he asked, "What's up with Davo today? There's no sparkle in his eyes this morning. And where are your shoes?"

"Stoled."

"Somebody stole your new shoes?"

"'At's what we said," he grumbled.

"Well, I'm a good cop, I can look into that crime. What else?"

"Davo seen the T-V about the Monk. Dey says da cook might not be da one who kilt ol' Rodney. Dey say..."

"Davo, listen to me. That chef almost certainly killed Rodney, and he for sure killed the owner's wife. The Sheriff took that chef over to his jail, and that man is never getting out. And, as a bonus, remember the White Witch and the fat man?"

"Yeah," said Davo, his spirits improving, "what about dem?"

"They're both in jail too. And at least the fat man isn't ever getting out, and the White Witch isn't gonna be flyin' around or casting spells anywhere, anytime soon. She's just a broken old lady now. And you know what? You were a big help in getting these people caught."

Davo's spirits were gaining, but he had questions, "What about ol' Rodney, though?"

"Well, you were a witness to Chef Ricardo and Rodney making their little plot... but that was for a fake murder scene... maybe not enough to convict the chef of a real murder... see the problem?"

Davo nodded, "But what if there was more, Detetive?"

"Like what? Did you see something more? Or were there others?"

"Yes, Suhr. Der's ol' Shiny, and Bill... and Noreen... dey say dey seen the murder... dey say da chef brained ol' Rodney wit a stone."

Macina tried to keep his car in the correct lane and avoid oncoming traffic. "Uuhh, maybe tell me more, Davo... like why didn't you tell me this last time?"

"Davo was scared. But now all dem killers is locked up."

"Okay, who...? Shiny? What's his name?"

"Davo don't know... just Shiny. He a black man wit no hair at all. And Bill... Noreen say she Bill's woman, but Bill say not. Still, they always togetha."

"Where? Can we find them... maybe after lunch?"

"Yes, Suhr... dey nevah go far... dey gotta walk wherever dey go... so, two, maybe three places to look..."

"Okay, my friend... first, we're going to stop at this Sears store and get Davo some more shoes... and a new shirt and new jeans... we have to make a good impression on Shiny and Bill and Noreen—they have to see that cooperating with the cops can pay off. Then, we're going for your burger."

Trinity called Simms before lunch. Normally, he might have been irritated by the interruption, but even a car wreck or a lost puppy that took him away from paperwork would have been welcomed at that point. Her message, though, made him second guess his decision to answer. "Simms, they locked up Joey! Valeria is trying to get a call in to his lawyer... he called Val first, and that's all they'd let him do. Can you help? Please?"

"Like what? I told you it'd be out of my control once the Sheriff got involved. Listen, for the record, it's the County Prosecutor who is the problem. The Deputy I work with doesn't think it'll take much to get Joe out, so let Joe's lawyer handle it."

"Well, that's not what Val said... the State Attorney something or other wants him held for something else..."

"Trini, let the lawyers handle it. Joe's made a mess of something with that casino business, and it looks like the State isn't happy about it. They're gonna be a big hassle to him... let his lawyers sort it. It's way, way out of my jurisdiction."

"Well, what the hell, Simms? How...? Okay then, can you help with something else? Joey wants Val and me to keep the restaurant open and running. Can you get me over there this afternoon? Val says Joe had already given instructions to his lawyer to make sure it was all legal and stuff... but somehow, the staff needs to be told that we're in charge, and Joe can't do it from jail."

"Trini, I can take you over there... but it's way out of my league to interfere with Joe's business..."

"Yeah, yeah, I know, Simms, but you can verify the story, right? I mean, you said they've been serving you lunch for weeks, so they know you."

"Listen, if that's all it takes to bluff your way into the kitchen at Giuseppe's, then sure. We can... I can also advise the assistant chef that he can go over to the Sheriff's jail and speak with Joe... I'm sure I can get him in..."

"Well, if that doesn't work, and they don't accept that we're in charge for a while, then the restaurant will have to close..."

"So, that's Val's best angle, right... they all know her, and none of them want the place to shut down... I'm sure they need their jobs... and I can verify that Ricardo is almost certainly never getting out of prison, so there's that."

"See, I knew you'd figure it out Simms... I'll let you know when to come home to get me... I need to talk to Val again in a few minutes."

"Hey, Ike, it's me, Simms... I've got a favor... the assistant chef at Giuseppe's needs to speak to his boss... seems Joe wants his girlfriend to run the restaurant, and...."

"Sure, no problem... what's his name?"

"Silvio something..."

"Just have him ask for me when he gets over here. Listen, did you speak to Macina earlier this afternoon?"

"No, I missed his call..."

"Well, he's all excited... seems he located three eye witnesses that saw Ricardo crack your hobo's head open with a rock..."

"No shit? Macina did that? Well, now you guys can really twist the screws on Ricardo... our City Attorney would love to get his hooks back into Avila's hide, given this turn of events."

"No doubt... we're gonna have another session with him and his lawyer first thing in the morning. Hey... wanna meet me at Dilly's tonight?"

"Sure thing... how about... well, are the steaks still tough as rawhide?"

Ike laughed, "Yeah..."

"Sounds great, but I gotta split by about nine or so... gonna pick my lady up from work."

"Cool, I'll call Gino..."

Stevenson was waiting for Trinity and Valeria when the restaurant closed, and got out of his car to greet them when the lights went out. Val lagged behind her sister when she spotted Simms, but he put his arms around them both, then stepped back. "Do you two want a late supper—on me—no pizza, though... or maybe just go somewhere for a drink."

Val shook her head, "No, not really," she said in a frosty tone. "You two go ahead... I'm gonna go to my place. I already called Scarlett, and she's home alone with just her kid. I need to catch up with her."

Simms nodded, and Trinity gave her a hug, "See you at eleven tomorrow, then, Val. I've got a lot to figure out still—it's way different than 'The Drunken Chicken.'"

Valeria gave a weak smile, turned and walked to Joe's car, then drove away into the night. Simms said, "She's pretty down... probably pissed at me, too."

"A little... I can't lie. But she's mostly just disappointed... she pretty much had Joe convinced that he wouldn't be in any trouble..."

"Yeah, I get it. But my best guess is that the County Prosecutor is holding onto Joe as a favor for the State. And, you know, they're pretty pissed about the shit he and his people pulled out at that old graveyard. Other than that, though, there isn't much substance to this murder conspiracy bullshit... they're just gonna let him stew for a few days."

"Are you sure?"

"Yeah, look... the fraud charge with the State over the shark factory property is a waffler... it could be criminal or civil... but I don't think they can convince a judge that he's a flight risk, 'cuz he basically came in on his own..."

"Right, but he didn't expect..."

"Oh, we both know that, but his lawyer will argue otherwise... see... upstanding businessman, and all. Besides, he might not have been at the heart of the fraud in the first place... maybe he'll throw Zev Harmon under the bus."

"Okay, Simms, take me home and get me drunk... but not too drunk."

"Hey, Ike, what's up. Thanks for the steak last night."

"Stevenson, it was my pleasure. You and Gino have really helped me thread the needle on this case. So, the reason I called is that we just had a session with Ricardo Avila and his lawyer, and I figured you'd be interested in a turn of events."

"Sure, I mean... did he confess, or something?"

Harris laughed, "Not exactly. He's put all the blame on Valeria LaCroix... Avila says she's the one who dreamed up the plot— the entire scheme."

"Say what? You have to be shittin' me... which scheme, exactly?"

"According to his new story, she's the one who planned to frame Maria Di Rossi for killing her..."

"Wait, it was all a plot to fake Valeria's murder, and pin it on Maria?"

"That's the crux of it..."

"That makes no fuckin' sense."

"So, he says that he then scared Maria so she'd go into hiding out in the woods, and hoped people would just think she was on the lam after murdering Valeria in a fit of rage."

"So, why'd he kill her, then?"

"Oh, his lawyer postulates that it was the drug ring that killed Maria when she stumbled onto the drug stash..."

"Does he know that you have evidence that she was killed in the cottage? And the drug ring was actually her cousins and in-laws.?"

Harris laughed, "Not yet. We just let the two of them dig themselves in deeper and deeper."

"Well, in this fairy tale, what role does Joe Di Rossi play?"

"Well, Avila didn't say, and we haven't asked him yet... for now, he's letting us think that Di Rossi was just Valeria's dupe in all of this..."

"You know this is the complete opposite of what he told me when we arrested him? He blamed it all on Joe..."

"Yeah, I'm aware. I played that tape for our prosecutor too, so he knows that at least one of those stories is a lie."

"I'd bet next month's paycheck that they're both bullshit stories."

"I agree, and I think the evidence puts it all squarely on Avila."

"What does that mean for Di Rossi's incarceration?"

"Well, the State still wants to play hardball, but everybody is kinda laughing about that, because, if it weren't for Jaega-boy planting all that fake Indian crap, the State would have never found all the gold coins and... hell, they're still finding cool pirate shit, and they haven't even started on the Indian midden..."

"Not to mention bustin' up a drug ring and putting a crooked cop in jail for drugs and murder..."

"Exactly... so, you figure bail... or?"

"Yeah, probably, no medal though. Oh, when Macina was over here, he asked one of the State bureaucrats to look in to some malfeasance at some community shelter down your way... the Third United Baptist something or other... seems they're probably taking State funds under false pretenses and violating all kinds of rules about child labor and schools, and... I don't know what all."

"Gino did that? Good for him! Yeah, he's befriended... well, hell, you know, he talked about it last night at dinner."

"Yeah, hey Simms, I gotta run now. We'll keep you posted... Chief."

Epilogue

Giuseppe's Holding Cell—A Week Later

Stevenson Simms negotiated the long hallway, halting only to allow security doors to be methodically opened by his Deputy Sheriff escort. He'd beaten Joe Di Rossi's lawyer to the station as intended, hoping to have a word or two with the soon-to-be-released prisoner. Joe would be out on bail as soon as the paperwork was completed, and Simms felt compelled to speak to him one more time before the air of freedom changed his willingness to talk. Simms knew the State and local prosecutors weren't entirely convinced that their case had evaporated once the pirate treasure and native midden had been discovered, and the district attorney, for one, wasn't sure that Joe was innocent in the murder of his wife. But bail had been set by a judge. Simms wanted the one-on-one facetime with Joe without the noisy Valeria or the obnoxious attorney that Zev Harmon had provided.

"Good Morning, Joe... I guess you've gotten the good word already, bail has been arranged..."

"Hey, Detective, yeah... earlier this morning... about damn time. Are you here to spring me?"

"Nah, that's a job for your mouthpiece. He's already in the facility, and Valeria said she'll be waiting with a ride."

"Okay," he sighed. "This has been a long stint... you didn't let on that there was more than an investigation into Maria's death going on back here."

"Well, it wasn't in my realm, Joe, and there were ongoing issues with the Sheriff and the State boys. You're lucky that the Feds bowed out and went home. And if you hadn't returned, it might all have gone in another direction."

"I guess... that's what everybody has been telling me. What about Minerva? Is she going to get out? This has to be hard on an old woman."

"I dunno, that's for the prosecutor and a judge to decide... she helped herself a lot by turning state's on Albie Whitehead. It seems clear that he took it upon himself to murder her two cousins, but there's the drug distribution issue hanging over her head. However, there could be enough of a public relations factor... you know, over the chief of police being dirty— and coupled with her assertion that he conned an old lady, well, she might get off easy. She's a sly old vixen."

Joe laughed, "That's for sure. Well, she's gonna have to move out of my house as soon as possible. There's no way we can be under the same roof after all of this, and I won't subject Val to her abuse either. But she'll be okay— we have plenty of family properties for her to haunt."

"So, Trini told me that you and Val are gonna go down to Key West if your bail provisions permit..."

"Yeah, well, I need to meet her Aunt Sonia..."

Simms smirked, "Just a word of warning on that front, Joe... Val's Aunt Sonia doesn't care much for Italians, so when you meet her, don't be surprised."

Joe looked at Simms quizzically, "Really? Val has said nothing like that... and you know this how?"

"Well, maybe she just doesn't like white folk much, or maybe it springs from her disdain of old-world witchery. She has a real thing about old country witches giving her spiritualism a bad rep, and she's convinced that it all started in Italy..."

Joe shrugged, "What does that have to do with me?"

"Nothing, directly. But when has that ever stopped this sort of thing..."

"Well then, what does she think of you, Detective?"

Simms chuckled, "She calls me a 'black rooster—very virile.'"

Joe shook his head in disbelief and grumbled, "Fine... any suggestions, then?"

"Yeah, first off, try to forget about ethnic divides as much as you possibly can if you're gonna be serious in that family. Embrace the differences instead. Second, take Madame a box of Cuban cigars—only Cubanos. Nothing else."

"You can't be serious... the old aunt smokes cigars?"

"Yeah... don't you and Val talk about stuff? I mean, this is critical."

"Well, Val smokes a little cigar once in a while, but where the hell am I going to find a whole box of Cuban cigars, for cryin' out loud?"

"Call my friend Baxter... he goes to Cuba quite often. Here's his card... he runs a fishing guide operation just up from Key West."

Joe looks at the card, "Baxter Silverman? Is he Je..."

"Irish, Joe." Said Simms holding up his hand to stop Joe from saying what he was about to say. "Half Irish, anyway—hates 'em all, too. In fact he doesn't like anybody from the 'I' countries... Ireland, Italy, Israel, India, Illinois. He's odd that way. But I'll tell him to make an exception for you... hell, he might even take you to Havana with him next time he goes.

"He goes to Havana...? How? I mean, why.. well, it's closed to gringos, right?"

"Yeah, well, he has a fast boat, and he married a Cuban girl..."

"So... a... guy named Silverman married a..."

"Yeah, but like I said, you gotta let go of these ideas you've got... You are getting involved with the entire clan, not just one dame. Now don't waste time... call Baxter, and get those cigars before you visit Madame LaCroix. It's gonna be time for you to let go of your old roots once-and-for-all. Seriously. And by all means, get on island time if you're gonna have a chance with the LaCroix family. I oughta know."

Capt. Tony's Saloon, Key West—Six Weeks Later

Stevenson, expecting Baxter to show at any minute, picked a small round table at the far end of the saloon and ordered two beers from the barman. While he waited, he studied the enormous tree trunk sprouting through the floor of the joint and stared at the woman's tombstone at its base, wondering why he'd never gotten to the bottom of that oddity. Then he remembered that Baxter had derailed his train of thought every two minutes during their last visit to Captain Tony's. "*Well, Baxter has always created chaos around me, so why should it have been any different on that day?*" he muttered under his breath.

There were two old drunks hunched silently like vultures at the bar, gripping beer mugs possessively, and they looked like they'd been sitting on their stools all night. Other than that pair and the barman, the place was oddly deserted. Well, there were several characters peering out in terror from an old movie poster, where they still hyped a film about a Cuban invasion in the 60s. But they too were silent now. Simms imagined himself in a scene from another time, and wondered if he and the bartender and the two drunks, amongst all the rest of humanity, might have somehow slipped quietly into the past, unnoticed by the gatekeepers of time. Such a thing certainly would explain why the place was deserted. But then he realized that it was hot and humid and raining outside, and the tourists were likely still nursing hangovers from the street scene the night before. Once Baxter finally darted in out of the dog breath weather, Simms put his imagination on hold, abating his fears of time travel. Right then, he knew it was going to be a good day.

"Hey, Bax," Simms hailed, "Over here, have a seat."

"Right—it was hard picking you out of this crowd... how's it goin', Brother?"

Simms laughed at Baxter's well-worn jab, "Well, you know... some good and some questionable, and the rest... well, anyways, thanks for coming into town to get me..."

"Yeah, no worries... but I was surprised to hear from you... and why aren't you gonna stay with your girlfriend?"

"Well, Trini has to explain me to her auntie a little at a time... she's gonna stay with Madame LaCroix for a few more days... she gave up her apartment a month or so ago when she moved up..."

"Well, right, I get it. And You *are* quite a lot to explain—but you already met the old lady, right?"

Simms laughed at his friend's insults, and said, "Yeah, a couple of times, but that was all about business back then... this is gonna be a different kind of interview... Trini says *I'm* on the grill this time. So, are you sure it's okay with your bride if I hang around for a few days?"

"Yeah, well, right... about that... she's gone to Cuba again..."

"Really? Sick mama again, or has she got a sugar daddy over there?"

Baxter flipped him the bird, then laughed and said, "Maybe both. Anyway, what else is happening? On the phone, you sounded like you were off that murder case..."

"Well, yes and no. The Feds have Whitehead locked away somewhere—pending the drug trial... they unlocked an entire international distribution ring. Meantime, the County Sheriff is waiting to get his hands on him for the murders of Minerva's cousins. And that entire mess over at the shark factory in Manatee Wells is now officially a pissing contest between the Feds, the State, and the local Sheriff's office for control of that case—well, now it's as much about the land and the gold as it is about the murders, but all of that is out of my jurisdiction anyway."

"But they promoted you, right?"

"Again, yes and no. After nearly two months, the city fathers finally decided that I should be named the interim police chief while they look for a fulltime replacement for Whitehead."

"Really? I mean, congrats and all, but *interim*? And what took 'em so long?"

"Well, what do you think?" Simms answered, trying not to grumble.

"Same old shit, eh? You know, my offer still stands... come down here and be my partner... fuck those hypocritical bureaucrats up north. We'll get semi-rich together and have a blast doing it. I mean, we'll be multi-thousannaires in no time."

Simms chuckled and took a couple of gulps of his beer, letting the cold harshness slide down his throat. Then he laughed out loud, "I'm not sure I'd be an asset... I'm a lousy fisherman... besides, I still have the fallout from the Giuseppe's Restaurant case to process... "

"Right, well, has anything changed? You couldn't talk about it before."

"Yeah, I can now... Ricardo is locked up... I think there was already a pretty strong circumstantial case that he killed the old hobo, Rodney, but then three eye witnesses came forward, so that iced him on that count. And then he murdered Maria too, and the Sheriff has him by the balls on that rap."

Baxter leaned back and folded his arms, "What's the motive? I mean, why would he kill the wife? He was boinkin' her, right?"

"Yeah, forensic evidence showed he'd been sleepin' in her bed and all, so that corroborated witness testimony. So I think his motive was to get sole control of the restaurant—see, by double-crossing Joe and framing him for Maria's murder, Giuseppe's Restaurant would have been his—or so he imagined. The hobo was part of the ruse—Ricardo knew Rodney from his panhandling at the back door of the restaurant, and it got the hobo killed, we think, because Ricardo didn't trust the old guy to keep his trap shut about staging the fake murder scene in the first place. The D-A's gotta prove it, of course."

Simms took another swallow of his beer, then continued, "Joe has been singing like a bird—he says he only promised Ricardo part of the business so he could focus on the casino deal. The way I see it, when Ricardo seduced Maria, it gave Joe grounds for divorce or an annulment or some such decree, something he could get his Priest to wave his wand over... and so he'd be free to be with Valeria. That's why Joe didn't raise hell over that affair." Simms stopped for another swallow, and Baxter waited for him to continue.

"Now, when we first arrested Ricardo, he started off claiming that Joe propositioned him to strike up the affair in exchange for the share of the restaurant... and Ricardo himself is the one who suggested the divorce angle of the plot. He said that there was never any plot to kill Maria or anybody else... murder was never part of the deal. But when being interrogated by the Sheriff later, Ricardo blew up that whole story by claiming that it was all Valeria's idea in the first place... seduce Joe, fake Maria's death, and the rest of it. He told the

Sheriff that he lied initially to protect Valeria, but now he claims she was the mastermind behind it all and double-crossed him."

"So, wait! He's saying that Valeria planned the whole thing and killed the wife...what's her name... Maria?" Baxter thrust his face out across the table as if challenging some heretic.

"No, no! He's not that stupid... well, he's pretty stupid... but his lawyer is asserting that it was the drug dealers—Minerva's dead cousins—who killed Maria when she stumbled onto the drug cache while she was living in the old shack. And so he's trying to tie Joe to Whitehead and Minerva and her cousins on that front. The D-A isn't buying it... he says the defense lawyer is just throwing shit on the wall to see if anything sticks. See, Joe lucked out that Whitehead and Minerva were storing drugs out there at the same time that he was trying to defraud the state... he wouldn't have been involved in both endeavors, right? I mean, he invited the State and Fed guys onto the property, and they discovered the drugs, which put Whitehead and Minerva in the spotlight once Whitehead was caught with the cocaine. Not to mention the two killings... And now, after seeing all the evidence that blows up his stories, Ricardo isn't saying much. It seems he forgot how to speak English, so everything has to be translated through an interpreter and his lawyer."

Baxter shook his head, and laughed, "Sounds like something right out of a bad movie plot..."

"Well, yeah? I mean, who can make up shit like this? Anyway, Joe is cooperating in the case against Ricardo— and he's out on bail. As for the State and Federal charges surrounding the burial grounds and the casino scam, the State might come back at Joe down the road. But once the treasure and native midden were discovered, it really did become a potential historical site under the antiquities act... so the fraud charge is kinda murky. He obviously hopes that his penalties for tampering with the graveyard and planting Indian artifacts will be tossed—or prosecuted as misdemeanors at worst... but that's gonna be up to the State prosecutors."

Baxter sat silently processing the information while Simms picked up his second beer and swigged down a couple of gulps. Simms went on, "According to the D-A, there *is* a certain added piss-off factor attached to what he was doing with the antiquities and graves—the fraud case—even though it's a separate one from the murders— the State seems aggravated enough to keep throwing charges his way. Trying to get the old shark factory property declared Indian land so he could build his casino was—is—pretty outrageous... but the weight of most of that plot might fall on that South African operator, Zev Harmon, and the Indian fraudster he hired. Funny thing... that guy turned out to be a Seminole—and trying to declare that he was a direct descendant of some obscure extinct tribe has the Seminoles just as pissed off as the Feds. Oh, and Joe has offered to donate the entire spit of land and the old shark factory to the State of Florida in lieu of the maximum fines. So if they take control... well, the irony is, it could all wind up in the hands of the Seminoles anyway."

"So, he might get his casino after all?"

Simms laughed, "I doubt it... no way the state of Florida lets him operate a gambling enterprise."

After absorbing Simms' explanation, Baxter asked, "And Valeria? When we spoke on the phone, you said she and Trinity were working at Giuseppe's?"

"They're running the goddamn place... Valeria is sticking by Joe through all of this. I suspect that he cut her in on ownership just to preserve her loyalty while he was in a cell, but what do I know? Trini's not divulging anything either, and I'm not going to press my luck on that front. I'm pretty sure that Joe arranged his deal cutting Ricardo in on the restaurant without filling Val in on the whole plan, contrary to what Ricardo asserted. But if I were to be found wrong, my relationship with Trinity would taint any action the D-A might try to take against her sister anyway. But none of this is out in the press yet, so who knows what might surface?"

"Sounds to me like you cracked a pretty complicated case... or did you?" Baxter stuck his chin out and waited for the challenge to sink in. "I mean, it could have been the woman all along, just like the stupid chef said... can't trust 'em... you know that."

Simms quit laughing for a moment, scratched at his ear, then said, "The thought has crossed my mind... Valeria *is* pretty shrewd, and she's way too cool when the pressure is on. But hey, all the evidence adds up to that agreement between Joe and Ricardo—it set the stage for Ricardo's plot and, like I said, there's not much I can do because of Trini. If the D-A sees something on his own, he's got investigators to pursue it."

Baxter chided him for being crooked and sloppy, then, once he had Stevenson on the defensive, he ventured into the plot, "Look, an alternate hypothesis is that Valeria and Ricardo *did* plan this... they're both Cubano, yeah? That seems suspicious to me, and I'm married to a sneaky one, so I oughta know. So, what if they cooked up a scheme to get the restaurant for themselves... Don't you think Ricardo could have rigged the kitchen scene to look like Maria killed Valeria out of jealousy... see, because Joe rehired her, so the wife would have been pissed about the mistress? Get it? Not the other way around, like you say. See, the fake voodoo shit fits either plan, and the women disappeared at the same time."

Simms chuckled, "Right... but the tongue is the giveaway... everybody said Maria had a sharp tongue, and leaving the tongue to be found was a way to get people to believe that it was Maria who was dead."

"Or," Baxter challenged, "the tongue was a plant to make you think that it was an Italian hit-—you know, mafia style..."

Simms hesitated, remembering Madame LaCroix's disgust at the tongue question, but regained his ground quickly, "So what about the fact that Valeria's house was smeared with fake voodoo shit too, just like the restaurant?"

"Oh, easy, my man—The chef did that too, just like you surmised... right after you told him Valeria was back in town... Look, you bumbled along and showed up in the islands, and their plans had to change. Val already had the perfect alibi, 'cuz she's far away in the islands, and *you* knew it first-hand. So you weren't ever gonna suspect her of vandalizing her own place. You suspected Ricardo right then, right after you returned home— you scared him and so he panicked and tore up Valeria's house to make sure you didn't suspect her— it was probably Valeria's idea. See? So then, all she had to do was get somebody to whack Maria and get it pinned on the dupe Ricardo. And then she and Joe could live happily ever-after. Or, Joe falls out of a hotel window in the Bahamas... Or, even better, he's framed for Maria's murder, and she gets it all by pretending to stand by him."

"Nah, Bax.. Ricardo and Valeria hated each other... they wouldn't have worked together on such a complicated scheme. Besides, the casino deal was worth far more than the restaurant."

"Who said that? Who said they hated each other? Valeria? Ricardo?"

"Well, no, but I read between the lines..."

"So, bupkis. You got nothin' but a quick impression, and maybe she didn't know anything about the casino until she got down to the Bahamas with Joe... if she played her cards right at that point, she gets Joe, the restaurant, *and* the casino! Ricardo would be quite expendable then."

"Well, why wouldn't Ricardo have told Joe that his wife was missing when he called him down in Nassau? I mean, if the plan was supposed to look like Valeria was dead and all— instead of Maria?"

"Well, in my theory, Ricardo wouldn't know that Valeria was gonna double cross him right then, and he wouldn't have given any thought to a casino deal... he wanted the restaurant—a bird in hand, see? So he would stick to the original plan up there, and that would be screwed up if Val and Joe returned early, because then..."

"....Everybody would know that Val was still alive-—ergo, Maria couldn't have killed her," said Simms, completing Baxter's sentence. Simms was squirming now. "And... no crime... everybody's still alive. Well, there is the hobo, Ricardo did kill him."

"Right, my friend, but stay on point—the longer Val and Joe stay away, the worse it looks for Ricardo when Maria turns up dead. Then it doesn't take much to frame Joe... the cops know he's been off with his mistress—Valeria—and you all assume that he divorced his wife, Italian style."

"But in your scenario, Ricardo still killed the wife. Besides, Val is the one who encouraged Joe to come back.. it was Zev Harmon who tried to keep Joe in the Bahamas..."

"Who said that?"

"Valeria..."

"Exactly. And who's to say that Valeria didn't sneak back to town at some point?"

"Well... why? How could we know it?"

Baxter chuckled as if he'd just hooked a prize fish, then he asked, "Did you ever figure out who painted the big ol' evil eye on your porch?"

"Well, I suspect that it was Joe's Aunt Minerva..."

"Wait... you think an eighty-year old woman went out in the middle of the night to paint a voodoo masterpiece on your house, then scurried back home before the milkman saw her? Really?"

"Well, Bax, you've got a point... but maybe she commissioned it..."

"Why? To scare you off?"

"Probably to protect herself... she was scared of me, hated the sight of me... she had some real old deep-seated prejudices..."

"Maybe, but what if Valeria did it?

"Why? Why would she come back from the islands to do that?"

"Well, you said your voodoo experts have told you that the painting of the evil eye could have been to ward evil *from* your doorway... or to scare you off—either one. What if Valeria did it to protect you—did it for her sister—or because maybe you were more valuable alive than if Zev Harmon put a hit on you? I mean, they needed you alive, 'cuz you were their alibi. Or... better yet, what if your girlfriend did it to protect you from harm? I mean, you're messing around with business for that South African character... if these sisters knew more about the business than they let on, maybe you were in danger. That guy is almost certainly connected to resources that could take you out."

"Nah, that's too far-fetched. Besides, the sisters didn't know that much about voodoo and such..."

"Who said that?"

"Trinity—and her Aunt Sonia, the priestess."

"So, these three women are all related... and..." Baxter left the challenge hanging.

Simms filled the silence, "Wait...back up to your plot line for a second... Joe's Aunt Minerva knew that he was with Valeria far away somewhere... so the plan to have people think Val was murdered wouldn't have ever worked."

"She told you that? The aunt told you about Valeria?"

"She told Macina..."

"Oh. By name?"

"No, Minerva didn't know the name of Joe's mistress... just said she was a Haitian whore."

"That doesn't describe Valeria, does it? So, did anybody else know Valeria was alive? I mean, those would be loose ends and..."

"Yeah, her roommate Scarlett... but she's a close friend. But that would take three women to keep a secret... or four. Not likely. So you think I fucked up this case..."

"No, dummy," Baxter laughed, slapping the table. "I'm screwin' with your head. You got the suspects all in a row, and it's up to the D-A to figure it all out. Ricardo killed somebody... Still..." Baxter paused for effect, just to be Baxter.

But Simms just sighed, "Well, Bax, if you're right, then she's pulled off the perfect crime..."

"Maybe, but then, what was her crime? Conspiracy? Maybe. But even if she did mastermind it all, there's nothing solid to corroborate the chef's story, which is the second story he's offered up, so he's a liar on at least one of those points. And the evidence points to him killing the hobo and the wife. So, it goes down as a case cracked by the brilliant new police chief..."

Stevenson laughed nervously, "Not by a long shot... Macina turned out to be a pretty good detective in this one... he's the one that put Whitehead and Joe's old Aunt Minerva behind bars. Of course, he had help from a twelve-year old homeless kid..."

Baxter shook his head in disbelief, "I never would've dreamed that would happen... Macina, I mean. And you told me a while back that he was helping look for a foster home for the kid?"

"Yup... in fact, if he can negotiate it with his fiancé, he might try to adopt the boy..."

"He's proposed to that girl? Has she even finished night school yet? No? Yes? Good for him! What's the sticking point on the negotiations then?"

"Well, Emilia—she's not sure that her parents down in San Juan are gonna be too happy about having a Haitian kid for a grandson..."

Baxter started to laugh. "Really? That's what they're worried about? They live in poverty in Puerto Rico, their nearly illiterate daughter is marrying an Italian American cop with a good job and good shoes, and they're worried about having an adopted Haitian kid as a grandson? Buy me another beer, Stevenson. We've got all afternoon to hash out the rest of the world's problems."

Punch Line

Who puts gravy on a hamburger, for crying out loud? Apparently, it's a 'thing' at a burger stand in the Atlanta airport. To my mind, it was grossly inedible and an affront to hamburgers everywhere. Besides, it nearly made me miss my connecting flight to south Florida, where I was bound to meet up with friends for a long-planned fishing expedition to the Bahamas.

Imagine two years of virtual pandemic lockdown, cancelled plans, lost friends and family, and then emerging from isolation for a cross-country jet plane ride in the early throes of winter. And imagine, surprisingly, that it all went quite smoothly. Except that the airplane kibble in coach was still as unpalatable as Korean War K-rations. So the disgusting gravy-smothered burger in Atlanta was exceptionally disappointing.

Arguably, I carry enough excess weight that I'm in no danger of succumbing to malnutrition during a 12-hour journey, but at the time, it seemed like it was a choice between starvation and gravy-triggered aortic stenosis in Atlanta. Fortunately, once off the plane in Florida, I was sufficiently distracted from this preoccupation with food until we got settled on the boat, and then conversation turned to dinner plans. The consensus was that we'd journey a few miles from the marina to a restaurant called, as the reader might anticipate, 'Giuseppe's', where I would be able to sample—no, the 'active voice' is important here—they promised me— the best pizza in the world. The car ride was no more than 20 minutes, during which time, my stomach began preparing itself for work.

We pulled into the little strip mall, eased past the old church, and parked right in front of Giuseppe's. It was closed. It was dark. And it was deserted, all of these adding up to my second food letdown of the day. The sign indicated that the restaurant was normally open seven days a week, and we were there well within the dinner hours. Nope. Closed. Disappointment and discussion ensued, focusing on the question of why it was closed. I suggested, "Maybe there was a murder inside, and it's closed until they finish the investigation."

It might be supposed that lack of food had driven me a little mad. Unanimously, and in the spirit of giving me the benefit of the doubt, my companions decided that that this was the stupidest thing anybody had heard all day. "Well, it does sound like a good book title," I offered, to another round of chuckles. "But, what's the back story? I need to find out if there have been any good murders around here lately." More scoffing, and the topic was dismissed while we sought another place to dine.

I had a gourmet burger that night, no gravy, and it was quite passable.

Our next stop on the trip was Nassau, The Bahamas, where we did eat pizza, but it certainly drew no favorable comparisons with Giuseppe's pizza by those in the know. The night after that, we were in a harbor on San Salvador Island, and found ourselves far too busy and tired to eat a regulation meal. Instead, we ate leftover Nassau pizza, met our local fishing guide, and invited him aboard to get acquainted. After being coaxed to have a rum, he bragged that he himself knew of Giuseppe's, and name dropped many other places in Florida where a person could get a great meal.

Now, by way of defense for what happened next, I *was* two rum drinks into my dinnertime. With no real context, I wondered aloud if our new guide had heard of any good murders lately. Well, there on that boat in that darkened marina, for this startled, lone local man amongst three white strangers, my question proved to be a momentary conversation killer. After many reassurances, apologies, and explanations to put the query in the context of our aborted visit to Giuseppe's, our evening continued. However, it is fair to say it may have taken another 24 hours for our guide to completely feel at ease, and another day or so for us to be able to kid around about it. Only later, did it occur to me that perhaps our new friend's shock at being asked about any good murders was the fear that we were on to him.

In the end, the fishing was successful (and exhausting), as hoped. We imbibed, laughed, and ate well on the rest of trip, and I minded my manners and tried to pay attention to local customs. We also made new friends, including the crew of the *Moza Woya,* a couple from South Africa cruising the Bahamas.

After we returned to Florida, conversation returned to the matter of supper. We picked up another friend and finally made it to Giuseppe's, where, not only was the pizza fabulous, everything we sampled on the menu was worthy of a glutton's holiday. The stories and suds and laughter flowed, too. And, no, there were no 'good' murders in the area (recently, anyway), and certainly, there was never a murder at Giuseppe's.

RBB

January 2023

Also by Rodger B. Baird

The Rebeca Hoffmann Files

The Vicar and I - Interviews with a Spy

Last Friday in Belfast

Africa Swindle

The Devil's Trade

The Demons of El Búfalo

Standalone

Fool's Beach

Spell of the Lotus

Murder at Giuseppe's

About the Author

The author is a chemist with a career in the environmental sciences that spans more than fifty years, and he has co-authored dozens of research papers and book chapters. He is a lifelong boater, fisherman, diver and avid explorer of Baja. *"Murder at Giuseppe's"* is his eighth novel.